Totally Bound Publishing books by Sira Banks

Criminal Desires
Breached

I0598558

Criminal Desires

BREACHED

SIRA BANKS

Breached
ISBN # 978-1-80250-957-1
©Copyright Sira Banks 2022
Cover Art by Kelly Martin ©Copyright June 2022
Interior text design by Claire Siemaszkiewicz
Totally Bound Publishing

Published in 2022 by Totally Bound Publishing, United Kingdom.

Totally Bound Publishing is an imprint of Totally Entwined Group Limited.

BREACHED

Dedication

To Becca – The light of my life!

Chapter One

Suppressing a sigh, Sharon Richards wondered why she hadn't decided on a different job.

Murder was always a grisly affair, but some days it was harder to deal with than others. This time the location, more than the crime itself, had her on edge.

Surrounded by the sights and scents of death, she scanned the place where a young woman had lost her life only a couple of hours earlier.

The room was decorated in deep shades of red and black, advertising the fact that it wasn't a common bedroom, but a place meant for seduction. Although she wasn't sure that seduction had played a large role in the murder.

If it weren't for the two spotlights brought in by crime scene technicians, the lighting would be dim, with only a small chandelier on the ceiling and a lamp on a bedside table. There was no daylight, the window hidden behind heavy burgundy drapes. She suppressed a snort. Of course there wasn't. She couldn't imagine the people coming here wanting any spectators. Although who knew, really?

Scanning the room's contents, she tried not to let her uneasiness show. The last thing she needed was her colleagues thinking she was squeamish. Anders and Jones, the two crime scene technicians, were nice guys. She had worked well with them on previous occasions. Still, if she showed too much of a reaction, word would spread throughout the precinct at the speed of light.

Turning her back to them, she focused on the rest of the location instead of the people crowding it right now. Even though the space was bigger than her living room, there was scant furniture. Well, cabinets for the fine china and a coffee table with a vase of fresh flowers weren't needed in a room like this. Not when its sole purpose was to help people find release. Release of a special kind.

Why? Why do it this way? She twisted a lock of her hair around a finger before she realized what she was doing. She crossed her arms over her chest and hoped Anders and Jones hadn't seen her.

She couldn't let her feelings get in the way of what really mattered — the victim.

Looking over at the victim for a moment, Sharon tried to ignore the pang of sorrow in her gut. She pried her eyes away.

The murder itself must've happened quickly, as everything inside this place seemed to be untouched, especially the four-poster bed. That didn't show so much as a crinkle on the sheets. Sharon's hands, sweating inside the cursed latex gloves, itched to touch the sheets to find out if they were indeed satin, as she believed. *Ridiculous.*

The bed was sturdy, with an upper panel but no curtains. There was no pillow, no extra sheet for warmth, nothing to indicate any measure of comfort. It was so damned impersonal, almost a caricature of what a bed should look like, in her opinion. At least the lush carpet underneath the bed—black again—looked comfortable.

Instead of giving in to impulse, she looked at a bench on one side of the room and the pair of rings attached to the wall behind it. Rings to shackle someone. Who would want to lose their freedom to another man or woman, to be helpless in front of somebody promising not to hurt them? *Still, isn't pain the main part of the experience?* a tiny voice inside her mind piped up.

A selection of what Sharon assumed were toys was placed on a rudimentary wooden table next to the bench. She counted several paddles, a whip and some other things she couldn't place quite as easily. Well, she could always ask. *Yeah, right.*

As she took a deep breath, the coppery smell of blood permeated the air so strongly that she fought the need to retch. The first and last time she'd thrown up had been when she and her partner had investigated the death of a prostitute, Cindy. The woman had been stabbed to death and left to bleed out beside a dumpster. The mixture of scents had been too much, and she'd only been able to take a few steps to the side before she'd thrown up.

Reining in her wayward thoughts, Sharon walked over to the victim, kneeling down in front of the body. So young, so beautiful and so untimely deceased.

Making sure she didn't touch the corpse, she focused on the gaping wound caused by a bullet, tearing skin and ending a life within seconds.

The shot which had taken Marlene Davis' life had left a barely discernible pattern of blood on the dark red wall. If it weren't for the fetid air, the woman lying like a broken doll on the floor and her glassy eyes, nothing would've said this was a crime scene.

Sharon crouched down in front of the wall next, trying to see the crime, to understand what had happened. She looked closely at the blood spatter. It wasn't hard to interpret. She'd seen patterns like this one often enough to know the shot had been delivered from close range. Most likely from a person Marlene had trusted.

She got up and walked a few steps around the body. It was easy to imagine how somebody had stood in the spot she was now, close to Marlene. Had Marlene and her murderer laughed, argued? One thing was clear — at some point the perpetrator had pulled the gun and fired it at the unsuspecting woman. The bullet entering Marlene's chest had gone right through her body, spraying the wall behind her with her blood. It would've been a quick death, at least. The bullet was still stuck in the wall, waiting for the crime technicians to remove it. A small caliber, most likely a semi-automatic, if Sharon had to guess.

So they knew how it had happened, but had to answer the question of why next.

They could do it, and they would do it. While a crime like this always caused drama, suffering and pain for those left behind, in a twisted way, it was routine for Sharon. Eight years of working in homicide had dulled the edge of walking into a crime scene. There would always be a moment of pity, but she'd learned to be objective, to see the crime scene first and foremost. She had to detach the emotional part of herself, or her work would consume her.

Hell, it was the job. Her job. Every murder was a puzzle she was hell-bent on solving. She would solve this one. The only question was when.

She smiled, almost calm once more. Her work had led her to a lot of places throughout the last years, but in all her years in this city, she'd never been in one of the city's BDSM clubs—not for work reasons and certainly not for private ones. There really was a first time for everything.

At the end of the day, this was just another workplace. A place where a murder had been committed. How ironic that the victim had been shot when so many weapons had been so readily available.

She walked over to the table and picked up one of the paddles. Pictures had already been taken, so she didn't have to worry about mixing up anything. The paddle was heavier than she had expected. How much pain would it cause when it touched human skin?

At that moment, Sharon sensed him behind her again, and the fine hairs on her neck stood up.

He was watching her—she didn't need to turn around to confirm it. She couldn't remember the last time she'd felt such an instant disquiet in the presence of someone else.

There was only one thing for certain. When a main suspect was such a distraction, it was a sure sign of trouble. Putting the paddle down, she turned.

As she'd known, Simon Carter, the subject of her musings, was watching her process the scene, his dark eyes following her every movement. As the owner of this club, he had a vested interest in her investigation, yet she'd have preferred it if he had let her work in peace.

She couldn't afford to let herself be perturbed. Trying to focus on the crime scene instead of the man, she hoped the effort wouldn't prove futile.

Carter radiated charm and danger in equal measures. One look and she had understood he wasn't someone to mess with. She shouldn't find him attractive either, but she couldn't ignore the way his deep blue shirt didn't quite hide his muscles, how the dark pair of jeans fit his otherwise lean frame.

Carter's eyes twinkled. Hell, he didn't even try to hide his amusement. From the very first moment of meeting him, his knowing smirk had told her he knew about her discomfort.

In his business, Carter needed to know how to work people, how to charm or placate them. He wouldn't charm her. She wouldn't let him.

In contrast to her, he stood there calmly, as relaxed as anybody could be in the face of such a tragedy.

No, she didn't like him, if only for the fact there had been a spark of interest the moment they had shaken hands. Not that she had to like him. She was here to investigate a murder, and he could be the killer. As the owner of this establishment, he was at least a main suspect.

Ignoring him for the moment, she concentrated on the medical examiner who'd entered the room and had just called out to her.

"Hey, Richards. I'd like to bag her now. If that's okay with you."

She returned his smile. He looked tired, and she wouldn't be surprised if he'd had to pull a double shift again.

"Sure. When do you think you'll have first results?"

"Whenever I'll have them." He raised a hand to forestall the complaint he knew would come. "I know you need answers and need them quickly, but there are two autopsies before this one. I'll call you, okay?"

"Yeah. Thanks, Amaro."

She stepped aside so he could do his work. She'd seen enough. Looking at the body for the last time,

Sharon silently promised Marlene she'd find the one who had killed her.

She turned around again and faced the man still watching her. "Mr. Carter, I need to ask you some questions. Standard procedure. Do you have an office where we could talk?"

Sure, they could talk here, or she could let him come to her office for a formal interview, but truth be told, neither place held any appeal to her. She didn't have time to waste.

"I do."

He gave her a look that was longer than necessary, sending a shiver down her back for no good reason. As he passed her, his arm brushed against hers, and she bit down on her bottom lip. Damn, had it really been that long since she'd gotten laid?

It was either that or the man itself, a notion she didn't like to entertain.

He led her to a different part of the house. Hearing someone scream—a man—she stopped, but Carter didn't break his stride. Another scream—it lay on the tip of her tongue to speak out.

"No one's getting hurt. Not in this club. Not in a way that's unwanted. What you're hearing is a vid someone forgot to turn off. We're closed for today, after all."

She hurried to keep up with him.

"Do you think Marlene Davis was of the same opinion? That no one gets hurt here unless they want it?"

"Marlene Davis is dead."

"And there you've just made my point."

"Whatever happens here is consensual."

People meeting to inflict and enjoy pain. She shook her head, put her hands in the pockets of her blazer. It took all kinds. They reached the end of a long hallway and

13

opened the last door on the right. He gestured for her to enter.

Again, Sharon was surprised. In contrast to what she'd seen of the rest of the house, this room was all about business. It wasn't sumptuous. It didn't scream sex. Dark, sleek furniture ruled its center. There was a desk sporting a phone, a laptop and other accessories to run a business. Along the wall were filing cabinets and a print of a city alleyway. It was a spartan room, one that echoed her own basic tastes.

Carter rounded the table and sat down, gesturing to the seat on the other side of the desk.

"Can I offer you something to drink? Water? Coffee? Something stronger?"

The smell of fresh coffee tempted her to accept his offer.

"This is not a social call, Mr. Carter."

"Call me Simon."

It was unsettling how his eyes rested on her. His gaze was piercing, focusing on her in a way that made her think he could see right through her.

"I don't think so, Mr. Carter. And the sooner we start, the sooner we'll be finished, and I'll be out of your hair for the time being."

"Interesting. You really don't feel comfortable here."

She took a deep breath to steady herself and made a point of holding his gaze. She'd been a cop for too many years to be easily intimidated, even if her poker face needed some work.

"Did I say that? And what I feel or don't feel is not the point. Marlene Davis is. Was she a regular customer?"

"What unsettles you about this business?"

She didn't snarl, but she came close to it. This man had missed his calling. He should've become a cop.

14

They always needed more detectives with good intuition who knew how to corner someone in interview. Only this wasn't his interview, and she didn't like being cornered.

"Just answer the question, Mr. Carter."

"Yes, she was what we call a regular customer. She didn't *visit* on a regular basis, but she was here about a dozen times. I'd have to check our appointment book to be sure. We're not the kind of club that you can just walk into."

Appointment book? It made sense, but the thought of people scheduling sexual activities of this kind as they would a dinner date was hard to grasp. She'd been aware that there were people with rather specialized tastes. It didn't mean she'd taken the time to think through the details.

Carter's eyes still rested on her. Although she was proud to keep his gaze, it was as if he could still read her. It was disconcerting, to say the least.

"If you could check the dates and get them to me, it might help. Did she always prefer the same company?"

"You mean, did she have her own personal Dom?"

"Dom?"

"A Dominant. The male equivalent of a Dominatrix. Davis was masochistic. To answer your question, no, she didn't meet with one of our employees. She only used our premises and scheduled her own appointments. At least for the last few times."

At her questioning look, he elaborated. "Her first few times here, she had appointments with Marco. That's why I know she was a sub."

"Sub as in submissive?"

He nodded, a slight smile grazing his lips that was gone as quickly as it had appeared.

"But even so, you must've seen who she was with. Her...Dom. I saw the security camera at the entrance."

"It doesn't work that way. We have another door at the back of the house. Only someone already in the house can let you in through the second entrance. This door only works one way. It's not covered by a security cam. Our clients value their privacy. Everything happening in the back of this house is private."

He was one of those who had an answer to everything, wasn't he? She held his gaze for a long time, remaining silent. It didn't faze him. He didn't so much as twitch. Nobody was that calm. They all had cracks in their armor. The only question was, what was his weakness?

"Doesn't mean you can't have a hidden security cam, or cams for that matter," she finally spoke.

"If anyone gets wind of a secret cam, our credibility will suffer."

"Having someone murdered on your premises won't help business either."

His lips curled upward in a slow smile. "Touché."

"So do you have any kind of security cam covering this area?"

"No, we don't. When I started the business, I didn't plan on anybody being murdered here."

"All right, let me get this straight. Davis booked a room and met with someone she let in herself."

"Yes."

"Did she come in through the front entrance or did she have someone let her in?"

"I already checked our cam. Yes, she came in through the front. You'll get a copy of the data."

"Thank you. But tell me, aren't you worried that your customers could let in more than just their personal guests?"

"Are you asking if I'm worried our clients have big orgies or let in thieves?"

"Thieves, murderers, yes. If it were my property, I'd make sure I was protected. It's one thing to ensure people's privacy, but I'd also make sure it's not my butt in the sling if things go south. I'd be the one in control."

Another smile and her pulse sped up.

"Control can be a burden. One reason for places like this one. But this will only be a sanctuary if people can trust us. If they can't, they won't be able to let go."

"They need a safe environment, knowing there'll be no pictures of their naked glory in the paper next morning," she mused. She had to admit it made sense.

"Yes. It doesn't mean there aren't safety measures. Each room has a panic button. If something's happening that the client isn't comfortable with, or if there's an intruder, the client can summon help."

"I didn't see one in the room we found Davis in."

"Under the bed. Davis knew that, and one of the crime scene techs dusted it for prints when I checked earlier."

Sharon was annoyed she hadn't spotted this herself. A slip like that was unacceptable. She ignored the thought. She could beat herself up over it later.

"Davis knew how to call for help," Carter repeated.

It was a nice concept, in theory. But help was not in the cards for *guests* that found themselves literally tied up. She focused on Carter again and relayed the thought to him.

"Everyone tied up is in control of his Dom at all times. And if a Dom breaks the rules and actually hurts his sub, they'll be banned for life and, depending on what happened, we'd file a report with the police."

"Has that happened before?" She would check, and he had to know it.

"No, it hasn't. But I wouldn't hesitate a second." His face got hard. "Safe and sane are the key words here. And if I find out who did this—"

He left the thought unfinished. So he didn't like when something, someone, slipped by his control. His chink in the armor.

"Someone got around your security measures." She shrugged. "There was a hole and he or she used it."

"Only known guests, or guests cleared by them, are permitted outside the private rooms. We have bouncers to ensure no one wanders the premises."

"You still trust your system?"

A smile made his lips curl. It was as enticing as it was dangerous. "Our business is all about trust."

She shouldn't take the bait. Although when had she ever done what she should do? "Trust? Didn't Marlene trust your system too much? Someone used her, killed her."

"No offense, Sharon. You don't know what you're talking about."

He shouldn't use her first name, and it shouldn't affect her that it had.

"It's Detective, and I think I know enough. I know a woman got killed here, and it's my job to find out who. You don't have to like this investigation. Just know, I won't rest until I have answers to my questions. Speaking of which—where were you for the last five hours?"

She hadn't shaken him or his composure. If anything, his smile had become a bit more taunting. For a second, she contemplated how his lips would feel pressed against hers, then she snapped out of it. She hoped her face hadn't shown her struggle. It was bad enough the thought had been there in the first place.

"I was right here. Before you ask, during that time I spoke to various employees, wrote emails, took calls and made some calls myself. In short, I worked. I suggest you check for yourself. But you're smart enough to have figured it out on your own. I could have snuck out to meet Marlene. It wouldn't have taken long to kill her, but I didn't. Sorry to disappoint."

"You sound pretty relaxed, Mr. Carter."

He leaned back in his seat. "Well, that's because I am. Don't get me wrong, I'm sorry about Marlene, and I'm pissed that someone killed her. This shouldn't have happened. I'd do anything to undo it, but I can't."

His eyes had narrowed, but then he took a deep breath, his smile back in place. "I might not be able to prove I didn't kill Marlene, but you won't be able to prove I did it, either. I'm innocent, at least when it comes to that." His dark eyes sparkled with challenge. "It's your task to find out who murdered her. I can only offer you my help. If you want it, that is."

Something told Sharon they weren't only talking about the case. She didn't like it. Not one bit.

Chapter Two

"Shar, stop pacing. You know it always makes me seasick to watch when you're doing that."

Stepping into their office, Jenn Reynolds got out of her jacket, putting it over the chair before she took a seat at her desk and made herself comfortable, looking right at home. She ran a hand through her short blonde hair, tousling it in the process. Not that it bothered her. Jenn was a lot of things but vain wasn't one of them.

"What's up?" Rolling back with her chair, Jenn put up her feet on her table.

"Nothing."

Her partner and friend of six years chuckled. "Try again."

"It's just—"

"Just?"

"Long day. I'm trying to think something through here." Sharon didn't stop pacing. She couldn't. She did her best thinking while moving around, always had. It was hard enough to appear calm and collected at crime scenes. Here in the sanctity of their office, there was no need for pretense. Sharon paced. Jenn picked her cuticles. Whatever worked and got them the results needed.

"Geez, Shar. How about you offer me some of this deliciously burned coffee? For starters. Then, for the love of Pete, sit down. I love you, but it's too early for, well, that."

Sharon rolled her eyes, but stopped in front of their coffee maker anyway, pouring Jenn a cup of the acid brew.

"Next time you'll get *me* a coffee." She smirked. "And a muffin. Chocolate."

She put the cup in front of Jenn and poured one for herself. Boy, this stuff smelled nasty. They should really chip in for better coffee. Although the one time they had, their coffee powder had disappeared within a couple of days. Sharon sat down on the edge of her desk, looking at the comings and goings outside. She still hadn't gotten used to the new office. It was bigger—which wasn't hard, seeing as the old one hadn't been more than a card box—had a glass wall and faced the hallway leading to the interview rooms.

"New case has your panties in a knot?"

Jenn had spent all of yesterday in court, giving testimony, while Sharon had been at the Davis crime scene, had talked to Davis' parents and conducted a few interviews with Marlene's friends. They hadn't seen each other all day. How Jenn had gotten wind of the new case was anyone's guess. Although, it wasn't all that surprising. One could count on the fact there were no nosier people than cops. Rumors in this department, in every department, really, traveled at the speed of light.

"Yeah, it's...let's say unusual."

"Because the murder happened in a sex club?"

"For one."

"For one? So once more, what is it, Shar?"

Jenn leaned back in her chair. Sharon was still waiting for the day she'd fall from her seat. Hell, there even was a betting pool waiting for that occasion.

She shrugged. "It's hard to describe."

It wasn't like her to be lost for words, but it wasn't like her to contemplate the suspects — one suspect — more than the case, either.

"How about you start with giving me the basics?" Jenn suggested. Folding her hands behind her neck, Sharon's partner waited.

Outside, a man in handcuffs was being led to interview. His head was bent but the briskness of his movements showed his frustration. How long until Marlene's murderer would walk the same way? That he or she would, Sharon didn't doubt.

"Vic's name was Marlene Davis. Twenty-eight years old, parents still alive, one sister. Worked as a broker. Made quite a buck in the last few years. Marlene wasn't married, wasn't in a steady relationship. Her colleagues hated her because she was too good at her job. Her friends at least pretended to like her. Make it pretend with a capital P. Once in a while she got an itch she couldn't scratch herself. Made appointments at the club where she eventually died. She booked a room there for the day she died."

She gave Jenn the basics about how appointments were made and executed.

"If everything had gone as planned, she'd have gotten herself beaten up, maybe banged, would've gone home all sore and happy. Only this time someone saw to it she didn't. I'm still waiting for confirmation from the ME, but it looks like she was shot with a semi-automatic. I'm sure a suppressor was used, or somebody would've noticed the shot, even in there. Anyway, it was one shot to her chest delivered from close range."

She made a face. "There were no signs of restraints or any other bodily harm. She was still fully clothed. Seems she hadn't gotten down to business yet." She snorted. "And of course, nobody saw anything, nobody heard anything."

Jenn raised an eyebrow. "Okay, sounds like a pretty straightforward, old-fashioned murder if you ask me. What's there to be riled up over? Again, was it the location?"

Sharon took a sip of her coffee. "One of the main suspects turned out to be...different, that's all."

Jenn straightened and took her legs from the desk, her arms coming to rest on her desk, her hands cradling her cup of coffee. "Who? Different? Why?"

Jenn's eyes had hardened, her focus completely on Sharon now.

"Geez, Jenn. No reason to interview me."

Her partner's sudden grin was fully unrepentant. "Spill it, Sharon."

She gave Jenn a long look, and the blonde woman bore her scrutiny without batting an eyelid.

"Simon Carter. Club's owner. He's slick, although that's maybe not quite the word I'd like to use. How about, he's self-assured to the 'nth degree? Nothing I said seemed to faze him. Quite the contrary. He was nicely amused by everything I said or did."

"And you find him hot." Jenn waggled an eyebrow.

"Not at all." Was it hot in here or was it the fact her friend was nailing her feelings way too well?

"Uh-huh, and I'm Santa's elf. You've got a weakness for the arrogant kind. Sharon Richards' got a kink for bad guys. Nothing new here. So he irritated you as much as you wanted him to screw you senseless."

Sharon would've liked to wipe the grin off Jenn's face. "No need to be rude."

"Truth tends to be rude."

"Who says it's the truth?" She sounded desperate, but damned if she could change a thing about it.

"I do. I know you. And I'm one of the two top investigators of this boy's club. Guess what? You're the second one."

"No trouble with ego, I see."

"Nope, none at all." Jenn shifted and took up her cup, draining nearly half of its contents in one go.

"Coffee whore," Sharon said, hoping to change the topic.

"Among other things. So you don't like that you like him? Or is it the fact he's a suspect?"

Moving around her desk, Sharon sat down in her chair, telling herself for the umpteenth time to replace this all-but-broken piece of furniture. She raked her hand through the tangles of thick red hair. She should've taken the time to straighten it out. She hadn't. But damn it, she was a cop, not a beauty queen. After a nearly sleepless night, taking care of her hair hadn't been on top of her list of things to do. "A bit of both, I guess. But screw it, I don't have time for stuff like this."

"Hey, *stuff* like this happens. You know it, I know it. Guys happen. We may not want them but sometimes we still go back, begging for more. Why don't you gimme the rundown on him."

Sharon sighed. Should it scare her that she knew all the pertinent data without having to glance at her notes?

"Carter, Simon. Forty years old. Grew up in New Jersey. His parents died a few years ago. He's got a sister and a brother. After high school he went to college, got a full scholarship and finished his business studies at Harvard. No, I'm not kidding. He worked for an oil mining company for a few years, made quite some money. And by some I mean a shitload of it. Used it to open his *business*. Runs same business since then. Nine years and counting. For all I could see his income is duly reported, taxes paid on time."

"Good-looking bastard?"

She didn't even try to lie. "Good enough to eat." The thought of his lean yet strong body, his dark eyes and three days' stubble made her grit her teeth. "And damn his charisma. But honestly, what kind of guy runs an establishment like that? I'm not a prude. Never have been. But really, what kind of living does it make? And pain? Why do people choose pain over pleasure?"

"Endorphins. And for some pain *is* pleasure." Jenn spoke as matter of fact as if she were discussing the latest weather report. Sometimes Sharon would've liked to borrow some of her calm.

Jenn opened the drawer of her desk and got out some chocolate, offering it to Sharon who declined.

"Don't tell me you're into this kind of stuff," she said, studying Jenn as if she were seeing her for the first time.

"Define *stuff*. But hey, it's a business like any other. There are people with needs, others who fulfill them for a price. As long as you've got two consenting adults, there's no harm done."

"True."

"But you don't get it?"

"I'm not sure I want to get it," said Sharon.

Jenn broke off a piece of chocolate. Then she drained her cup and put it on the table with a clank. "Want my advice?"

"No, though I doubt it'll stop you from giving it to me."

"Damn straight. And here it comes—let's split the list of suspects, we both interview our half of them. And you go and ask Carter."

"What on earth should I ask him?"

"Why? Why pain? What's the allure? If anyone will be able to tell ya, it's him, no? You should have a follow-up interview with him anyway. Maybe you can get your attraction for him out of the way at the same time."

Sharon shook her head. "No way. I won't sleep with a suspect. I can't."

"Easy, girl. Didn't say you should. But you can't ignore him either. You have to make sure you can think straight. Most often a closer look at a guy is all that's needed to see why he's not so appealing after all."

She hated when Jenn was right. After she assigned a couple of interviews to Jenn, Sharon got the pad where she had scribbled down Carter's cell number.

She called him before she could think twice. He took the call after just a few rings and readily agreed to another interview. Instead of making him come in, she scheduled it for the end of her day, at his apartment. She was curious to see how a man like him lived. Did he enjoy the same living style he'd chosen for his business, or did his living space resemble the sleek, impersonal style of his office? And why did she care?

Once she'd wrapped up her tasks at the office for the day, she walked toward the next subway station, glad the worst of winter was finally over. The wind was still cold, but spring was finally in the air. Times like these she missed Vermont, where she could literally smell the beginning of a new cycle, the clean air carrying the scents of plants and flowers leaning towards the sky, waiting for the warming rays of sunshine to help them grow.

Ignoring the people around her, she mulled over the case's facts, trying to make sense out of what didn't make sense yet. There were two possibilities. Either Marlene's date was the one who'd shot her, or it had been someone already in the club. If it was the first option, and no one had indeed seen him, their chances of finding him were limited. Although they would concentrate on her background, her acquaintances. Maybe something would pop up. Whoever Marlene had intended to meet was someone she had to have met somewhere, face to face or online. Sharon preferred online as it would increase the chances of finding out who he was. It would take some days for the computer experts to look over Marlene's data, but they might find something on her laptop. And if she'd met him somewhere else, one of her friends might know. She'd interview them all again. She still had to talk to Marlene's sister. Marlene's cell phone records showed they had spoken the morning of her death.

Still, if it hadn't been someone Marlene knew, if had been someone from the club, the question was whether it had been another guest or one of the club's personnel. She'd have to ask Carter for his employees' data as well as the guest list for the day. He wouldn't like it, especially the latter.

Tough luck. Not that she cared. Maybe he was the killer, although that was a possibility she'd rather not contemplate for too long. She could do without the irony of being intrigued by a killer.

Her traitorous mind went back to yesterday when Carter had walked her out of the club. He'd given her his card and told her he'd be available whenever more questions arose. So far so good. Everything would've been in perfect order, would've been innocent, if it hadn't been for the hand at the small of her back. Usually, she'd have protested such a move, but yesterday she hadn't. The shiver running down her back had made her thoughts spin, yet she hadn't said a word, and neither had he. This man was playing her, but she couldn't figure out why. If she went by instinct, and hers was a pretty good one, she'd say it wasn't related to the case. But if it was related to her, where did it leave her? Did he want her? Was it that easy? Was it simple physical attraction? It happened, and under different circumstances she wouldn't have minded getting it out of her system. Not with a suspect though.

At this time of the evening, the subway was crammed, making her curse New York once again. She loved working and living here, but some things she'd never get used to — crowded trains and the smell of wet dog combined with something deep-fried hanging over them all. Thankfully, she didn't have to go far, only a few stations.

When she got out, she looked up at the Upper West Side apartment building Carter had named. She shook her head. *Those who said sex sells were right.* If she had to place a bet, she'd say Carter's apartment looked nothing like her three-room place in Queens. Although she'd also bet she wouldn't be envious. Her place was well lived in, had personality and, best of all, it was hers. It was all she needed, and all she could ask for.

Inside the building, the doorman cleared her without any problems, telling her she was expected.

She wasn't quite sure what to think about that. Carter planned ahead, not unlike herself.

What an absurd thought. We're nothing alike.

He lived on the second to last floor, not penthouse level—something she hadn't expected. She'd figured he'd be one to go for the best, and wouldn't rest until he had it. Was it a lack of money, or didn't his ego reach that far? Closing her eyes, leaning back against the wall of the elevator, Sharon cursed quietly. She had to stop thinking about him like that. The elevator stopped too soon for her liking.

There were only two apartments on this particular level. She didn't have to guess which one would be his, as the door was already open, and he was standing in the doorway, hands in the pockets of his pants. Tonight he wore jeans and a casual dark sweater. It made him even more appealing. Another curse died, unvoiced, on her lips. She shouldn't have come, should've conducted this interview in her own office. *Should have, could have.* Hindsight was always twenty-twenty.

In all her years with the force, she hadn't tangled with a suspect, and she'd met more than one who was attractive. She wouldn't start venturing off the path now.

"Detective," he greeted her.

She nodded and passed him when he simply gestured for her to proceed into his apartment. The door shut a moment later. He was right behind her, the proximity making her uneasy. Years on the job had made sure she didn't react, but it didn't mean she didn't feel it. Her breathing had sped up and her pulse beat faster than it should. *Damn this man.*

"Can I take your coat?" he asked, and she shrugged out of it quickly, only half turning to hand it to him.

The apartment, big as it was, was a surprise, at least the part she could see. There were two doors to the right, which she suspected were the bedroom and the bathroom. They were closed, as was one door further to the left. An office, maybe.

It was the living room that had her break her stride. It was bigger than she'd anticipated, and it was furnished in a way that was stylish but comfortable at the same time. What got her attention was that Carter had several bookshelves adorning the walls with books that actually looked read. She'd have liked more time to peruse the titles.

Carter entered the living room behind her. Knowing his eyes were on her, she just moved on, noting the big leather couch and the two armchairs. The couch was in the center of the room. It was facing the windows, the city. Did he like to sit here in the evenings, watching over the city that had made him rich? Did he like living in New York, or did he miss his home, just like she did from time to time? Who cared? God, she had to stop this. Although, wasn't it part of being a cop, that need to always unearth the truth?

The dark-blue rug underneath her feet was thick and would surely feel heavenly under naked feet. The kitchen adjoining the living room was an open construction that would allow him to keep in touch with his guests, and a big table with eight chairs occupied some of the space between the actual living room and the kitchen. All in all, it was a place that looked comfortable, a place that invited people to live in it, yet there were no frills.

Carter was silent while she perused his surroundings. She took another look. Something was missing. She turned to him.

"You don't watch TV?"

Of course he smiled a half-smile that drove her crazy.

"You don't miss much, do you?" His voice was deep, smooth. One of those voices she liked to listen to, no matter what was said.

"And you answer questions with questions."

"Guilty as charged. I have a TV in my office and one built in a closet in my bedroom. I don't want to spoil the view in here. Society relies too much on distractions."

It was true. Especially in the city. So often people were in too much of a hurry to actually stop and see the beautiful sunset, the children laughing in the parks, or the way raindrops made the city sparkle when the light was reflected in the puddles created by a downpour. Who had the time when they had to be somewhere, or when the latest text on their phone took up their full concentration?

"You don't like distractions?"

"Not of this kind, no. But please take a seat. Do you want something to drink?"

She was too restless to sit, but pacing his apartment wouldn't do. "A glass of water would be nice. Thanks."

She chose an armchair, which was more comfortable than she'd have thought. Carter walked over to his kitchen, and she wished she didn't follow his every movement, or notice the way his jeans nicely accentuated his ass. Obviously, she liked distractions more than he did.

He turned to her in front of his fridge. "Are you still on the clock?"

"No, I'm not."

"Then we'll have a glass of wine. Do you like white or red?"

Arrogance. In shovels and spades.

"Water. Thank you."

"You don't drink?"

"I drink *if* and *when* I want to." She spoke quietly, making sure none of her anger at his presumptions showed.

He nodded and opened the fridge. "What is it about me that makes you uneasy?" he asked, his voice carrying easily.

Another question hitting the mark. He managed it without even trying. Hopefully she wouldn't find out how it would feel if he put his mind to it.

"Why do you think you make me uneasy?" Two could play this game, and in the end, she didn't owe him any kind of explanation.

She watched him pour a glass of water and a glass of wine, red, for himself. He still had his back to her, his movements efficient yet unhurried.

"It's palpable. Your business is people, Detective. It's mine as well."

Walking back into the room, he handed her the water and sat down on the couch opposite her.

"Frankly, I'm not here to discuss my feelings." She kept eye contact with him.

"You're evading me. Your prerogative, though. So what are you here for?"

"Some follow-up questions. Simple procedure."

"Then shoot."

The flash of unexpected humor delivered without as much as batting an eyelid nearly had her laugh out, but she bit it back. Her reaction didn't go unnoticed by him, and there was a flash of amusement in his eyes as well. Their gaze held longer than it should.

Next time she'd send Jenn to interview him. She should have ignored her partner and sent her in the first place, a realization that had come too late.

Concentrating on her main purpose for being here, she checked his alibi once again. She let him give her the movements of his employees as best as he remembered, telling him to send her the information via email as well. That covered, she asked him if he carried weapons.

"As you have undoubtedly checked my records, you know I don't own a weapon's license." He smiled. "I own what you could consider weapons, but I never saw the appeal of guns and the like."

Her gut said he was telling her the truth. Although he might have had the opportunity for the kill, she didn't think it was his doing. She didn't think he'd arranged for it either. There was no hint he'd ever met with Marlene outside the club. He owned stock, but Marlene hadn't been his broker. There was no record linking Carter's stock to the firm Marlene worked for. The answer to the question of who killed Marlene Davis and why would lie somewhere else. She would bet that the person they really needed to find was the person Davis had had an appointment with.

"You've got more questions?"

She had, yet she hesitated. Curiosity killed the cat. But it was the one vice she couldn't swear off. She wasn't a nosy person by default, didn't care for her neighbor's or other people's antics, but she had questions, many of them, and wanted answers. Would her curiosity be her undoing in the end? Still, to learn and understand, she'd have to ask.

"Why pain?"

A smirk danced over Carter's face, and he took a sip of his wine. He took his time to study her. She didn't give him the gratification of reacting.

"You mean what drives people into my club?"

"Yes. There must be quite a number of people wanting your services to afford an apartment like this one," she said, looking around the room.

"By now you should know, I made most of my money in my prior job. But yes, my business grants me a sufficient income. To answer your question, though, I think the answer's a different one for everyone. Although the endorphins released in the process of enduring pain are a thrill that many seek again and again."

She shook her head, not quite happy with the answer. "There are easier ways to get an endorphin kick. Marathons, other sports, chocolate — plain old sex can do the trick."

He was unfazed. "True, but I think you asked the wrong question in the first place."

Was he toying with her? If yes, why was she letting him? Or was he simply trying to be helpful?

"What would be the right question?"

"You're the cop, you're smart. Figure it out."

Definitely toying. She looked at him, considered him and what she had asked for a moment and tried to get to the core of the matter.

"All right, if it's not just the pain, what makes people frequent your club?"

"Better." He nodded. "Again, the answers may vary, but there's one thing most have in common. They want to forget, want to lessen a burden."

By being whipped? Or being the one doing the whipping? She began to wish she'd accepted his offer of a glass of wine.

"Forget what?" she asked after too many seconds had passed. Usually silence didn't bother Sharon. Tonight it made her restless.

Carter took another sip, put his glass on the table and leaned forward, his elbows on his knees.

"Have you ever engaged in sex that wasn't plain vanilla?"

She should have expected it. He didn't seem to have any qualms about going straight for the jugular. She felt cornered, put on the spot. But she'd started it. It was only fair to answer his questions when he answered hers, although her questions pertained to her investigation, mostly, and his were simply personal.

"I don't see how this could be any of your business."

They were both aware she was evading him.

"It isn't, but as we're discussing the nature of sex, lifestyle, of choices people make, I'd like to know your take on things."

"Well, have you?" she shot back.

"Certainly." His answer came easily.

Time for quid pro quo.

"I haven't engaged in any sexual acts like those that are offered in your club."

"I thought so. But to come back to your previous question, asking me if I have done it or not isn't quite the right question when it comes to my life either, is it?"

"And this time the right question would be?" She was getting pissed. Maybe it was time to leave.

"I might tell you later on."

She was short of cursing him out loud. His arrogance and that slight, almost ever-present smile irritated her more than she could or would let on.

"Carter—"

"Call me Simon."

"No. We've been over this before, haven't we?" She wished she had sat on the couch instead of the armchair so she could let the view of the city soothe her when the intensity of this man became too much. She balled her left hand into a fist before she could reach for one of the locks of her hair.

"Yes, we have," Carter finally answered her. "Anyway, what you're trying to understand is the nature of people trying to relieve pressure." His eyes were burning into hers now. "Most of the people using the club's services, whether they be on the one side or the other—meaning Dominant or submissive—are individuals who are successful in most areas of their lives. But sometimes you have to step outside the box that is your life. Dominants want complete control over at least one area of their life, but submissives want to forget about any kind of control for a short while."

"And controlling and beating people, or being controlled and beaten by them, helps?" That was not how life worked, was it? If it was, everybody would be into S&M. Not everyone was, not even every successful person. And what would life be without a modicum of control? People either controlled their lives or life would control them.

"It's only one small part of the whole experience, but yes, it can work. Focusing on a scene out of time, you can either control a bit of your life in a fashion you choose, or you can decide to leave the thinking, the decisions, to someone else for a while. Of course, it's only an inadequate description for something you might never understand if you didn't try it for yourself."

A picture formed in her mind. Putting her own misgivings away for the moment, she focused on Davis, who had worked successfully on Wall Street and had been known to be neat and reliable. Was it all too much to handle for her sometimes? Did the pressure get to Davis so that she needed an outlet?

Unrelieved pressure, building up until a person was ready to explode. Didn't she know something about it as well? Sharon didn't want to think about that, especially not now.

"Thank you," she said, meaning it. She allowed herself a slight smile. "Did I earn the right to know the correct question now?"

Carter nodded slightly.

"You did. I think the question should be, is dominance or submission my preferred way to engage in sexual relations or just a diversion I choose to enjoy from time to time?"

A smile curved his lips upward, and she was trapped by his gaze. "In the same vein, the other question for you should be, even if you haven't experienced the pleasure of pain yet, aren't you thinking about how it would feel?"

He waited a beat. "And the last question is, will you answer me this time?"

Chapter Three

Seconds ticked by while Sharon debated whether to brush him off while trying to find the right answer at the same time. Carter's gaze held her captivated, making it impossible to retreat into herself, to find the reply that would be the suitable one to give.

"Don't think. Answer." There was a note of command in his voice she didn't care for.

"I could tell you it's none of your business."

"As you did before."

"It was true then, is still true now."

He shook his head. "Sharon" — he lifted his hand to stop the protest he knew would come — "it won't work this way. If you want honest answers, you have to be open with me. Or at least be honest with yourself."

His gaze, piercing as it was, made her body flush. The space between them wasn't enough to shield her from the intensity of this man, her own feelings. Her body, reacting to his proximity, was several steps ahead of her mind, which was still refusing the very possibility anything could happen between them. She was a cop. He was a suspect. It should be easy.

"Well, to answer the first question, it is not hard to see that you prefer dominance over submission. If I had to guess, I'd say it's more than a temporary diversion. And the second question, no. I don't want to experience pain." Was it the truth? At least her voice had been strong, unwavering.

He tilted his head, finally looking away, taking up his glass. "You're missing out."

"I've never missed a thing." For the first time since she'd come here, she was at least partly in control. That was until he looked at her again, making her the focus of his attention once more.

"You never wanted to try something new?" He took a small swig, and her gaze got caught on his sensual mouth. *Dear sweet lord.* Could her body please get the message she wasn't a horny teenager any longer?

"You don't have to go to extremes to try out new things. People are wired differently."

"Which is part of the answer you're looking for. Marlene was wired a certain way. She had needs we tried to fulfill." He let the liquid in his glass swirl and for a moment it looked more like blood than wine to her. She looked up at him.

"I don't associate pleasure with pain."

"Too bad, don't you think?"

Why did she have the feeling she'd just declined an offer? It was past time for her to leave. She had conducted the interview she'd come for, and gotten some of the answers she'd hoped to find. That she might leave with even more questions, most centering around Carter, was nothing she needed or wanted to contemplate with him right there.

"No, I don't. Anyway, thank you for your time."

She got up, looking at the glass of water, still untouched on the table. She turned slightly and granted herself a moment to take in the view of the city. Sometimes, especially at night, New York was beautiful, all the lights accentuating a hive buzzing with energy. Up here, she could almost detach herself from the hectic pace of life, the stress that people radiated like an illness.

"You want to leave?" Carter asked, getting up too.

"Yes." She didn't exactly want to leave, but she needed to, something he didn't have to know.

He didn't question her, but simply nodded. "I'll see you out." He gestured for her to go ahead, and her gaze caught on his hands. Elegant hands, smooth, with long fingers. She'd always had a thing for them.

"Tell me, why does it feel like you're running away?" he asked.

She didn't turn. "Does it? I'm not." She'd nearly reached the door—safety. From what? She was sure Carter wouldn't do her any harm, at least not if she didn't want him to. Her own thoughts had her recoiling. This wasn't about her. A woman had been murdered, and it was her task to stand for her. It wasn't more, and it wasn't less than that.

"There's no reason to be afraid of me."

She whirled around to find him standing closer than she'd expected. "I'm not."

"Aren't you?" he asked, reaching out to brush a strand of hair back from her face. She shivered, unable to hide her reaction.

"Don't."

"Don't what?"

His hand lingered, his fingers warm against her cheek. She took a ragged breath. *Why*—she groused—

does he have to ask questions I don't have answers for? All the fucking time.

Jenn's words came back to her. Her partner was right. She had always had a thing for *bad boys*, for men who exuded arrogance. But this wasn't just some top-notch lawyer, some business executive, one of the men she'd met at her gym or somewhere else.

This was a man who could be a murderer, no matter what her instincts might say. How could she even trust her judgement when her own body conspired against her?

And Carter was more than arrogant. There was a dangerous edge about him. Although, was she afraid of him or of herself, of what she could learn about herself?

"What's your game?" she asked, not able — or rather not willing — to hide her thoughts any longer. "What do you want? What is in this for you?"

"I find you attractive, fascinating. Not a crime, is it?"

"And is this a reason to needle me with questions? To try prying into my private life? To step into my private space without invitation?"

From one moment to the next it had become personal. She had made it so. Or had it been him from the very beginning?

"No."

"But?"

He made a small step forward so their bodies were almost touching. "I see it brooding under the surface."

Frustration began to rise inside her. "What's that supposed to mean?"

He ran a finger over her slightly parted lips, his eyes following the movement. She trembled and knew he'd noticed.

"You wonder. This is more than just theory for you. You wonder what it would be like. What the thrill is.

But you don't want to feel this way, and you're too scared to try."

"You're not my fucking shrink."

She hadn't intended to unleash such rough language at him and noted it came out weaker than she'd have liked. A smile appeared on his face, slow and seductive. Her body, so far ahead of her mind, longed for his touch, and was disappointed when he pulled his hand away.

"How lucky I'm not."

He leaned in, slowly but without hesitation. If she had any intention of leaving, it would be now or never. He was giving her a choice.

She didn't move, damning her heart for beating faster, her body for reacting with ferocious want. His lips touched hers, and she balled her hands while she let her eyes fall closed.

His mouth on hers was hot. *Damn him for having lips so soft, so inviting.* He pulled away, only to take her mouth again a second later, this time running his tongue over her lower lip. Her lips parted for him, her body's final betrayal over her mind.

Before she knew it, he had his hand on the back of her head, sliding his tongue into her mouth. She let him, gave him free rein, lost in a sea of unexpected sensations. He mapped out the cavern of her mouth with his tongue, sliding over hers, and the jolt of arousal, sharp and urgent, woke her out of her passivity.

She meant to shove him away, to flee the scene, but all she did was fist his shirt, pulling him even closer. The kiss soon morphed into a duel, both of them wanting to be the one to dominate this encounter. As he moved them forward step by step, her back collided with the wall. This was spinning out of control fast. A last shred of sanity told her she needed to leave right fucking now. She had her career to think about. An encounter like this to silence her raging hormones wasn't something she could allow. It didn't make her stop holding on to him, giving as good as she got.

The need for air made them part, and, as if knowing her mind still hadn't quit thinking, he didn't give her the time to contemplate leaving, kissing a hot trail along her neck, biting the part of shoulder bared to his sight. A moan escaped her lips while ripples of pleasure coursed through her whole body, pooling at the juncture of her thighs. Her body wanted him, and her mind was rapidly giving up the fight.

She didn't protest when he unbuttoned her shirt and cupped a bra-clad breast. At this moment, she wanted what he was willing to give. Just this one time, to get it out of her system. It didn't have to mean a thing. Who would know about it anyway?

Carter shoved his free hand up her skirt, making her tremble with want when his fingers grazed along the naked skin of her thigh. She wasn't sure whether to be thankful for the fact she'd not opted for pantyhose today or to curse it. She'd been freezing all day. Now she wasn't.

Carter's mouth found hers again, dominating the kiss now, sucking on her tongue. She couldn't believe how wet he made her, how horny. At least this wasn't about love or any deeper feelings.

He nipped at her bottom lip, demanding her attention. He was right—she was distracting herself. Either she went in for the kill or she had to leave.

It wasn't a hard decision, even when it should have been. She gave up on even the last shred of resistance and reached out for his belt buckle. She wanted to feel him inside her—the sooner, the better. Carter opened the front clasp of her bra, tweaked her nipples between his thumbs and forefingers for a second and dragged down her panties next. Sharon tried stepping out of them when they pooled around her ankles, though she only managed to free one leg. It didn't matter. She didn't care, and neither did Carter. His kisses were still sending her mind reeling, and before she knew it, he had freed his hard cock and was ripping the wrapper of a condom. For a second she chided herself that she hadn't even thought about contraception. She hated that he was still in control when she wasn't.

"Stop thinking."

He had pulled away slightly, his gaze locked with hers. She wanted to look away but found she couldn't. He was still so damned calm while there was a storm of emotions raging inside her. He didn't break the connection when he lifted one of her legs, and she wrapped it around his waist.

A small smile played around his lips when he urged her leg a little higher, lifted her with his hands under her ass and slid inside her, filling her with one long thrust.

A moan was ripped from her throat while her body adjusted to the presence of him inside her. It had been too long since she'd been with a man, the last time just a casual fling with a guy her friend Erin had thought would make a good date for her.

It didn't matter — that had happened months ago. She took a deep breath and her body relaxed. Carter wasn't moving. He waited for a sign from her. *What a gentleman*, a snarky voice inside her piped up. *No — he might be a lot of things, but clearly not a gentleman.*

She put her hand on the back of his neck and pulled him closer for a kiss. He obliged, easily gaining control of the kiss once more. It was too easy to let herself be swept away by this man. She moaned when he finally began to move. He pulled away, only to thrust into her again and again in a steady, hard rhythm. The more he gave, the more her body craved. He was kneading one of her breasts again, his caress rough yet sending sparks of pleasure through her body.

Time lost its meaning as she gave herself over to the demands of her body.

Each time her conscience wanted to raise its head, he pinched her nipple, bit her lip, her shoulder, and thrust just that much harder so she would stop thinking once more. Her hips began to undulate in a primal way, the tension in her body rising until she thought she couldn't take it any longer. His lips folded around her earlobe, tugging lightly. The slight pain it caused helped her stay focused and enhanced the pleasure.

"Let go."

It was a command, no question about it. While it would've been in her nature to bristle at such a comment, all she could do right now was obey.

She moaned loudly, her body shaking from the force of her orgasm. Her hands had found purchase in Carter's shirt and she fisted the fabric while she clenched around his cock, unable to breathe, to think, to do anything but hold on. She was only dimly aware when she heard him groan while he followed her over the edge.

It took her a minute to come back down from her high, for her breathing to regulate. Carter had both of his hands on the wall next to her head, supporting himself, his breath coming fast but regular.

Her back, still pressed against the wall, began to hurt, and reality set in. If she could have erased the last ten or fifteen minutes, she would have. What had she been thinking?

Her flight instinct kicked in. All she wanted was to leave. Now. She needed to get away.

Either Carter had read her body language or he had good timing. In any case, he extricated himself from her and gently lowered her to the ground. Her legs were hardly able to support her weight.

He dressed quickly but without hurry before he left for a minute to dispose of the condom. He didn't speak or offer to help her with righting her own clothes. It seemed to take forever, and Sharon's thoughts were racing a mile a minute.

For a second she closed her eyes and bit her lip. She wouldn't have a nervous breakdown here. The deed was done and no outcry of indignation would change a thing. She forced herself to look up, meeting Carter's gaze. Either he was a better actor than she was, or he really wasn't as affected. He appeared calm, that slightly arrogant smile playing around his lips again. She wished she could wipe it from his face right fucking now.

"I'd better…" She trailed off.

"Why are you questioning yourself now?"

He reached out and stroked her cheek with a thumb. She fought the urge to lean in. Instead she laughed.

"Please tell me that was a rhetorical question."

"It's not. Are you doubting yourself because I'm a suspect? Because we haven't known each other for long? Or do you think I do this on a regular basis and this is a problem for you?"

"Take your pick. Anyway, I've got to leave now."

She met his gaze and held it. He pulled his arm away, taking a step back. *Will he leave me now?* He turned but only to fetch her coat. She would've forgotten about it. Quickly putting it on, she expected him to stop her when she crossed the short distance to the door and opened it, but he only spoke when she'd already stepped outside.

"I know you've got no reason to believe me, but I didn't kill Marlene, and seducing women I've barely met isn't my habit."

She looked over her shoulder. "Why did you do it then?" She hadn't meant to ask him, had spoken before she was even aware of the question forming in her mind.

"As I said before, you're a fascinating woman. Beautiful, intelligent, stubborn. You're rather wound up, afraid to admit you're curious how it would feel to cede control for a small measure of time. I like interesting women."

"Of course you do." She kept his gaze, wanting him to know she wasn't afraid of him analyzing her. "You're wrong, though. I'm not curious."

She left without another glance back.

Chapter Four

The door of her apartment fell shut behind her with a loud bang. She wished she could shut out her feelings just as easily as she'd just shut out the world. Unfortunately, life wasn't that easy. She kicked off of her shoes, letting them lie in the middle of the corridor, before she made her way into her living room where she collapsed on her couch. She buried her face in her hands, allowing herself to sigh once.

This was a mistake she'd never made before. She knew other officers who had slept with a suspect. Her male colleagues were not always shy when it came to bragging about their sexual adventures. It was something she would have never seen herself do. She had been attracted to suspects, yes, but never slept with one.

Until tonight.

Sharon leaned back, her head now resting against the headrest. She closed her eyes, her mind going back to this evening, to what had transpired only a short time ago. She drummed her right foot in a nervous rhythm against her carpet, not at all as lush as the one in Carter's apartment.

Carter. Again.

By all means, their encounter should've been awkward as hell, but it hadn't been. Strangers didn't have close-to-perfect sex. Yet that was what had happened. Although who knew how many women he had entertained this way?

The thought didn't sit well with her. She wasn't jealous, didn't know him or even like him well enough for such feelings, yet the idea of being just another notch on his belt was irking her. He had said it wasn't a habit of his, but did she trust him? No.

He had said other things as well.

She wasn't curious, was she? She hit the pillow to her right in anger. It should tell her something that she was afraid of the answer to such a simple question. She shoved the thought aside, focusing on the real problem at hand. If someone learned she'd slept with Carter, she'd be in deep trouble. *The understatement of the year.*

No one knew yet. No one had to know. Especially not that she had enjoyed it, that her body was already craving Carter's touch again.

Her phone rang, interrupting her reverie. Seeing the name on the display, she considered not taking the call. Knowing Jenn, though, her friend would just try again. And again.

Sharon finally answered the call. "Don't tell me a new case came up."

"No, I'm just curious. I tried calling you twice before, by the way." There was a noise in the background, surely Jenn closing the fridge after getting herself a snack.

"I only just came home." *After having sex with a suspect. Yay.*

"Did you go and see Carter?" Some liquid was poured. Most likely milk. Sharon smiled. Jenn kept Sharon's secrets, as Sharon did hers — one of them being that the hard-ass cop liked milk and cookies after dinner.

"Yes, I did."

"You don't sound as if you got the answers you were looking for."

She had, partly. "I still don't rule him out."

Jenn remained silent, waiting for her to continue. She didn't. When it came down to it, Sharon had won each and every battle of wills between them.

"Come on, Shar. If at all, you sound even more frustrated than you did before."

"We didn't quite get around to talking about his...business."

They had, and it had led straight to the opening of Pandora's box. God, she hated lying to Jenn.

"I saw some pictures of him, you know." Jenn changed the topic.

Feeling too restless to remain sitting, Sharon got up, pacing the narrow confines of her living room. How different her place was from Carter's. Her apartment wasn't a quarter as big as his was. A bedroom, a living room with a tiny kitchenette and a small office. Oh, she had a window, but hers looked out into the alley behind the house, the dumpster not far, the smell bad enough in summer she had to keep her window closed. The only thing they had in common was that there weren't many frills inside her apartment either. She had put up a few pictures of friends and relatives, had books occupying nearly every free surface, but that was it.

"Pictures of whom?" she finally asked.

"Carter. He made the news a few years ago. Some deal he made for this company he worked for. It was a couple of years before he started his new venture." Jenn snorted. "I guess being stinking rich helps with living out your fantasies. Anyway, this is some good-looking man, and if he really makes you feel uncomfortable, I could take over the case for you."

"Forget it." This had come out a little harsher than expected.

Jenn laughed out. "Someone has the hots for suspect. All right."

Her first impulse was to rip Jenn a new one. She wouldn't, even if she'd like to. They were friends, and Jenn meant well. If she could trust anyone, it was this woman. Whatever she chose to trust her with, Jenn wouldn't spill.

"I think it's a mixture of being fascinated by the man and what he does," Sharon admitted, walking over to her own kitchen and contemplating getting herself a snack. Burning calories through sex made her hungry. She suppressed a sigh.

"No harm in that," Jenn said.

Not if one kept it at that. "You remember Michael?" she asked, apropos of nothing.

It took Jenn a few moments to answer, and Sharon heard some rustling in the background. Jenn liked to be comfortable, to lie down on her couch when they were up for some serious girl talk. It made Sharon smile, and she realized how tense she'd been all day. She decided against a snack for the moment and went back to her own couch, sitting down. She put her feet onto her coffee table, resting on the last two books she'd read, and grabbed a pillow and hugged it.

"You mean Michael the ax murderer, the guy selling hot dogs on Fifth Avenue or the asshole DA who played your boyfriend for a couple of months?"

"The last one." Jenn had nailed that *relationship* with one simple sentence.

"Yeah, unfortunately I do. You shouldn't think about him, really. He treated you like dirt."

Jenn was right. He had been an arrogant jerk, one who had cheated on her with two women — at the same time — as it turned out. While Sharon had kicked him out of her life the moment she learned about his infidelity, the harm had been done. She'd doubted her instincts when it came to men for months afterwards.

"It's not about him. Not really anyway. But, and I have no idea why I'm telling you about this, one time we had sex, he was rougher than I was used to. He held me down, his fingers digging into my shoulders, and then he turned us so I was on top and when I lifted myself, he…slapped my ass."

Jenn whistled and in spite of herself, Sharon laughed. "That's not funny, you know."

"It so is. Because I thought you'd deck anyone daring to do that to you."

"Don't think I didn't think about it. Later. I didn't because…oh shit, because I liked it. I came hard like I hadn't in ages. Afterwards, I tried not to think about it, told Michael to never do it again, yet, it had happened, you know? For some time I wondered if I was a freaking pervert. And today, I began to wonder again."

"If you're a pervert?" Jenn laughed again. It almost made Sharon laugh, too. Voiced like that, it sounded a little silly.

"No. I wondered if there's something about pain. If I'd like it. And Carter, he looked at me as if it had been spelled out on my forehead."

It was good to admit to being curious, to speak out about what had been nagging at her all day. She didn't trust easily. It had taken her years until she could trust Jenn.

"And here I thought you'd reveal some true showstopper."

Sharon snorted. "Thanks for appreciating my dilemma."

"From where I stand, there is no dilemma. Most of us like it a little rough from time to time."

Jenn was right, yet she wasn't. It wasn't about liking it a little rough. Sharon had no problem admitting to herself she liked it. It was the question of how far she was willing to go, how much pain she would enjoy if she allowed herself to feel it.

"I guess you're right. It just was a long day."

"It was. Cut yourself some slack, darling."

Easier said than done.

"I will. Thanks for calling, Jenn."

"Hey, I called you to still my own curiosity. Nothing to thank me for. See ya tomorrow, okay?"

"Yeah. Bye, Jenn."

The call disconnected. Sharon was aware she should get up, get herself ready for bed, yet she was too drained, too confused to move. There was a murder to be solved, two other investigations were still ongoing, and on top of it all, she was attracted to a man she shouldn't feel anything for. A man who had made her question who she was, and right now, she cared for neither the question nor the answer.

After a while, she couldn't bear her own thoughts any longer, how they would go back to Carter, to the pain of bites only serving to heighten her need, her lust. She turned on the TV and settled for the next best movie. It was always better to pretend everything was all right, wasn't it?

* * * *

Jenn was already at her desk when Sharon came in the next morning. There was what passed for fresh coffee and bagels waiting for her.

"Morning," Sharon greeted her, beginning to unfasten her coat.

Jenn looked up from a file and frowned. "How much sleep did you get last night? Did you get any?" They were used to long days and short nights, so she had to look shitty if Jenn saw any need to comment on her appearance.

"I did, no worries. I was just contemplating the Davis case. You don't go into a house full of people, walk into the next room, shoot a woman and leave without anyone being the wiser." Sharon put her coat over her chair.

Jenn narrowed her eyes and gave her a long hard look. "I don't have to mention that I don't believe you, right? Anyway, talking about the Davis case, I bet you won't like what I got to tell you."

"Which is?" Sharon stretched, swallowing a yawn before taking a seat.

"We got a call an hour ago."

"From whom?" There was a new file on her desk, and pouring herself a cup of coffee, she waited for Jenn to go on.

"Davis' appointment. That's your copy of the whole conversation by the way. The man, Mark Raddart, claims he went to the club for his appointment with Davis but she wouldn't open the door for him. He got in thanks to another customer who had seen him at the club before. He went to the suite, found Davis dead, got scared and ran off."

Sharon frowned. "Sounds fishy if you ask me."

"It does. But he gave me the description of the other customer in question and well, it rang true. Call it instinct. Raddart will come in for a formal interview later on. I said you'd call him regarding a time." Jenn's mouth curled into a smile. "I think it should be rather easy to verify his story and Carter should be able to help with identifying the other customer. Do you want to talk to him, or would you rather have me do it?"

Sharon ignored the flutter in the pit of her stomach and kept her focus on the case. "You know Raddart could have gotten in, shot her, then walked outside and waited for someone to let him in again, right?"

"Yes, I do. I tell ya, it's instinct. But you didn't answer my question." Jenn smirked.

"I'll talk to Carter. No problem. I'll call him in a little while."

"Okay then. I should head out now anyway. I got a tip regarding the Smith case." Jenn got up, shrugging into her jacket. "Will be back later. And, Shar?"

"Yes?"

"Whatever is bothering you, you should know you can talk to me."

Jenn didn't wait for an answer and left the office. Sharon looked after her for a long minute before reaching for a bagel. She could talk to Jenn, trusted her, but for as long as she didn't even like to think about her confused feelings, she doubted she would. Even a laid-back person like Jenn would raise an eyebrow if she learned Sharon had slept with a suspect.

As no one paid her for being confused, Sharon took up the Davis file, looked for the telephone number of Carrie Davis, Marlene's sister, and scheduled an interview with her at eleven.

* * * *

Meeting Carrie gave Sharon a slight jolt. While she'd known Carrie and Marlene had been identical twins, the sight gave her pause. Only two days ago she had stood over Marlene's body, looking into her dead eyes. Now she looked at the same face, so very alive, pain clouding her expression while tears streamed down her face.

"Why? Why did Marlene have to die? Who could have done something so horrible?"

"I don't know, but I intend to find out."

Throughout her career, she'd been faced with this very question more often than she could count, yet it never got easier to answer. She waited for the other woman to calm down a little.

From the sparse info Sharon had been able to gather so far, Carrie Davis had decided on quite a different career than her sister. She was an artist. There were paintings almost everywhere around the woman's small apartment, city impressions in bold colors. While they weren't quite Sharon's taste, they showed talent.

"Ms. Davis, you spoke to your sister the morning of her death. What did the two of you talk about?"

"Dying in a club. A sex club. Marlene never told me she was...well, that she did things like this."

Did she even hear me? "Ms. Davis?"

"Yes, I know, I'm sorry. We didn't talk about anything in particular. We played catch-up. I asked her how she was doing, she wanted to know how I was doing. Damn, she didn't mention that bloody club. We wanted to meet tomorrow, have dinner. And now…now…"

Sharon wouldn't get much more out of this woman, not in the state she was in. So she kept the interview short, asking what Davis knew about her sister's friends, her habits. None the wiser, she was about to leave, her hands burrowed in the pockets of her coat.

"Ms. Richards?"

She turned to the other woman once more and waited for her to speak.

"Please find the perverted bastard who killed my sister."

"I'll try my best."

At the beginning of her career, Sharon had made the mistake of promising a family to find the killer of their only daughter. She hadn't been able to, the calls getting more and more desperate still too vivid in her memory. She tried to shove those memories away once more, but didn't quite succeed.

Sometimes it could all become a bit too much, the pressure inside her building while thoughts whirled around in her mind. She bit back a laugh. Was that what had driven Davis into the club? The need to forget, to shut off the mind for a few precious hours?

Sharon went on to talk to a few more of the people who had been named as Davis' friends by Marlene's colleagues and her sister, but she learned nothing new. No one knew if Marlene had been dating someone, no one thought she had felt threatened by anyone or anything, she didn't have any enemies…

The only interesting thing was that a few of them had described Davis as driven when it came to her career. An ex-lover even went so far to say she loved money more than she could have ever loved any person. It was likely there was a grain of truth in his statement, but most likely not more than that.

Back at the office, she penned down her notes, never taking a break as she wanted to be done before she called it quits for the day. She was also avoiding calling Carter. Hell, she only needed him to verify the information, nothing more.

Only he wasn't just another suspect any longer. She'd slept with him, and even though it had been casual, there was nothing casual about the situation. Too bad it wouldn't help her at all not to call him, not if she wanted to solve this case.

Stretching, she took a look at her clock. It was almost seven. Most of her colleagues were already home. Jenn's computer was still on, meaning the other woman planned to come back to the office eventually. She should talk to Jenn about working so much overtime. It wasn't healthy, although it would be a case of the pot calling the kettle black.

She sighed. It was better to take care of calling Carter now. The thought that Jenn could be overhearing the conversation, a knowing smirk on her face… The idea made her shudder. She quickly picked up the phone. He should be at the club, as it had reopened this morning.

"Carter."

Sharon briefly wondered what protocol said about addressing a one-night stand one had to interview in the course of an investigation. She mentally shook herself out of it.

"Mr. Carter. It's…"

"Sharon, what can I do for you?" *Leave it to him to breach any professional barrier.*

"I need you to verify some information. I hope it's not too late to call."

"Not at all. As you might be able to imagine, this time of the day, things just start to get busy here."

She rolled her eyes.

"Yesterday you were at home at this time of the day." She'd no idea what made her say that, and told herself to get a grip on herself and this interview.

"You're correct. I'm sure you understand there are no fixed hours to a business like mine. But I usually don't leave the office before ten or eleven at night, sometimes later. Yesterday the untimely demise of Ms. Davis made me crave some privacy. The club was closed as well, as you might remember. Never mind, I think work hours are kinda similar for cops, aren't they?"

Sharon wished she'd feel a tenth as calm as he sounded and chided herself for her stupid remark. She *had* known better. Well, he had asked a question, rhetorical as it had been. "True, only we don't get to decide when we have to be at work and when not." Damn, she shouldn't be so harsh with him. This man definitely rubbed her the wrong way — or was it the right?

"You feel uncomfortable about last night," he stated.

She did. On so many levels. Although the thing annoying her most was that there was a part of her that was not regretting what she had done.

"This is not about last night, Mr. Carter. Let's get back to the reason I called." She heard a voice in the background but couldn't understand what was being said.

"I'm sorry, Sharon. There's something I have to take care of now. If this is really urgent, I could call you later. Or how about you stop by on your way home? It should be more or less on your way."

She raised an eyebrow.

"Why do you know where I live?"

"Relax. I'm not a stalker. You remember that you mentioned getting take-out at a place near your apartment yesterday? You spoke to one of the crime scene technicians, and I looked up the restaurant. Like you, I like to know who I'm dealing with."

"It's my job to know the people I'm dealing with. It's the law allowing me to get my hands on any information pertaining to an ongoing investigation." How could one individual annoy her so much?

"True. I'm sorry for making you uncomfortable. Anyway, I've got to leave now. Come by tonight or call me again tomorrow."

He hung up without so much as a goodbye.

Chapter Five

Sharon was staring into space, debating her options, when the door to the office opened. It had to be Jenn, but Sharon didn't turn around to confirm. It was one of the good things about knowing her partner for years. She didn't need to make polite conversation if she wasn't up for it.

Carter didn't seem to feel the need to be polite either. Was he the same when he had to deal with his customers? Surely not.

"Sharon, did you hear me?"

Surprised, she whipped her head around. She faced her boss, who was leaning against her desk, his face concerned.

"I'm sorry, sir. I didn't hear you." With Hastings in the room, the office was instantly crowded, a fact she attributed as much to his over-six-foot frame as to his personality.

"It's after hours. Call me Luke."

"Not doing it, sir," she said, wishing he'd used a tad bit less of his otherwise nice cologne.

He smiled. "How often do we have to have this conversation?"

"For as long it takes until you realize I won't call you by your first name." Now she smiled, too. She liked her superior, both on a professional and a private level. He was a good cop with sharp instincts and wasn't fazed too much by the politics of his job. To him it would always be the investigation first, in contrast to other captains who were too busy kissing their superiors' and the mayor's ass. Hastings always had his people's back, although he wouldn't shy away from letting them know when they messed up.

Jenn had no problem addressing Hastings by his first name, but Sharon wanted the professional distance. If she was honest, it had something to do with the fact that Hastings had asked her out to dinner once. It had been over two years ago, and he had made it sound like he wanted to offer her an ear as she'd been dealing with a complicated case, but she hadn't quite bought it. Yeah, he'd have listened to her, would have given her good advice, but it still hadn't been all. The way he'd looked at her made it clear he was interested in her as a woman, and back then she wouldn't have compromised her career for any man. Heck, two days ago she wouldn't have thought she would do anything to jeopardize what she'd built here.

"So what's the matter? Is it your latest case?" he asked her now, his stance relaxed while he waited for her to speak.

For a moment she just looked at him. She had to admit he was an attractive man. Tall and solidly built, he was strong, his blue eyes kind when he wanted them to be, colder than ice when he was annoyed. As far as Sharon knew, he had been married once and was single now. She could be wrong, but didn't care anyway.

"It's an...unusual one," she finally said.

"I read yesterday's preliminary report. So it happened in a sex club. Unusual, yes, although I've seen murders happen in stranger locations."

She had, too, but these other locations hadn't stoked her curiosity, hadn't had her step out of line. Breaking eye contact, Sharon looked down at her report. Hastings could never know, or she would be toast.

"Sharon, what is it?"

Her first name again. Anger welled up in her. Was nobody respecting her boundaries lately?

"Sir, I'd really prefer if you didn't call me by my first name."

There was a brief flash of hurt in his eyes, and she regretted her words the very same moment.

"So noted, Richards."

His voice had gotten colder and was all professional now. Maybe it was better this way. Or she was kidding herself and she'd managed to piss off her superior for good?

Silence spread between them, and instead of waiting him out, she met him halfway.

"It's the fact that Davis was murdered in a house full of people and no one seems to have seen a thing. No one seems to know a thing."

He accepted her peace offering and sat down in Jenn's chair.

"Why don't you give me the rundown? Sometimes a fresh pair of eyes helps."

She quickly briefed him about all that had happened since her original report, and he didn't interrupt her once, sitting back with his hands behind his head.

"I don't buy that this was a spontaneous kill. There's too much of a risk that you run into someone in an establishment like this one. The fact that there are no witnesses with something useful to add speaks for premeditation."

Sharon agreed, wishing she had a window to open. It was too warm in here and the stale air made her tired. "I will interview Davis' date, see if he sticks with his story. Furthermore, I'll talk to the club owner to confirm the story."

"Do that. And I think you should take another look at Davis' life. There has to be something leading to this. A jealous ex we don't know about yet, a man who never got a chance with her, an envious colleague…"

"Or it could be the money. So far I only heard good things about Davis' work but we all make mistakes. Maybe one of her mistakes cost someone a good buck, leading to the wish for exact revenge."

"Killing Davis wouldn't get them their money back."

Hastings had a point.

"I don't buy it either. Still, I'll have another look at her business dealings."

"Do that. You never know. Sometimes the least probable option will lead you to the truth of the matter." He got up. "You should go home. It's late, and no matter how long you'll stay, Davis will still be dead."

"True. But on the slim chance it was a serial…" She wished she'd remained silent. It wasn't as if she believed in this option. Well, she could hardly tell her boss that she'd rather stay here than face her own thoughts, or that she'd been that close to calling it a day anyway. She had to decide whether to head for home or Carter's club next.

"Does it read to you as if it could be one?" Hastings asked. His eyes had softened slightly, making her hope she'd be forgiven.

"No, but..."

"Forget the *buts*. If you start to live for the job alone, you'll burn out before you know what has happened to you and your life."

"You're right." She got up and stretched, a yawn escaping her. Hastings smiled.

"I don't know about you, but I'll head over to Sammy's for a drink and a burger."

Even if it wasn't phrased as one, it was still an invitation. Yeah, she was forgiven, and Hastings would never learn.

"I'll go home now. I'm beat." Her head had begun to hurt over an hour ago, and she could do with a long soak in the tub and bed. She would see about both, once she had talked to Carter, that was. It was better to get it done today. Anything to close this case a little bit faster so she could forget about it

Hastings nodded, his hands clasped in front of him. Hadn't he been in the army for some years? "See you tomorrow, Richards." He left and didn't look back, although she looked after him until after he was out of sight.

Why couldn't she fall for a nice man like him for a change? Because she wasn't attracted to Hastings. It was sadly as simple as that. Furthermore, he was her boss and an affair would mess up her life even more

badly than a one-night-stand with a suspect would —
that was why.

Waiting for a few minutes so she wouldn't run into
him, she shut down her computer and grabbed her coat
and purse. One last stop, then she could run a bath, take
up her book and have a quiet evening. It would be nice,
wouldn't it?

* * * *

She hadn't counted on the noise, muted cries
distracting her the moment she entered Carter's club.
The last time she'd been there, it had been the middle
of the day, with not many people around and the club
being closed thanks to the crime scene technicians
processing the scene.

Tonight it was business as usual as far as she was
able to guess. A murder had happened here only a
couple of days ago, but either people didn't know or
didn't care. To Sharon, it was a vivid reminder that life
went on.

It was the police's job to make sure the victims
weren't forgotten, that there was a chance of justice for
them. What happened in the courts later wasn't
something she could influence, which had been a tough
lesson to learn.

Although one of the security guards she'd already
met and interviewed yesterday had greeted her when
she rang the bell, he made her wait for Carter in the
hallway. While she could have insisted the man let her
pass, she didn't. In a way this was still a crime scene,
but as the crime, as far as they could tell, only
concerned one room and all evidence had been bagged,

it had been agreed that the rest of the house could open for business again. What sense was there in arguing?

She didn't have to wait long as Carter appeared in fast order, leading her to his office. For no good reason, Sharon realized that he wasn't wearing any cologne. *He smells delectable anyway*, her traitorous mind piped up, reminding her of how close they'd been only last night.

"Are you okay?" Carter asked, looking at her over his shoulder.

"Yes, I am. Why do you ask?" She heard a sharp cry, then a brief moment of silence before there was another scream. She had flinched, but dammit, she had sworn to protect people and listening to this went against her every instinct.

"You seem to be ill at ease." Carter stopped, and she did the same, waiting for him to go on. Instead he looked at her and stepped closer, cupping her jaw, turning her face to the dim lighting spent by one of two lamps in this corridor. "You've got dark circles under your eyes. You look tired."

Sharon stepped back. She didn't like to be handled that way. "Don't touch me like that."

She wished she could slap herself when his mouth curled into a smile.

"How would you like me to touch you then?"

"Okay, this has to stop here and now. What happened yesterday was a mistake. It shouldn't have happened. I apologize. But whatever has happened, it doesn't give you the right to treat me like that. We don't know each other."

He inclined his head before he walked on. "I'd like to change that."

Sharon wasn't sure she'd heard him correctly. "Pardon me?"

He met her gaze. "I'd like to get to know you better."

Too many thoughts entered her mind at once, but thankfully someone left a room right then, passing them without even looking in their direction. It was a man in his fifties, a little overweight, bald. To her surprise he didn't look ashamed or unhappy but oddly tranquil.

They reached Carter's office, and he opened the door for her. This time she didn't wait for his invitation to sit down.

"He's a submissive."

"Huh?" Not the smartest reply she'd ever given.

"The man passing us, he likes to submit to a Dominant."

"He looked peaceful." It had quickly become a habit that she spoke her mind in front of Carter even though she didn't mean to. There was something about his blunt honesty making her reply in the same fashion. People wore masks all the time, here it wasn't necessary.

"There's a certain freedom in letting go of everything, to submit to the moment."

She shook her head. "We had the same discussion before. I still think it's hard to believe."

"You'd have to try it yourself to understand. Some water?"

The change of topic was so abrupt it made her snap out of her reverie.

"Yes, thank you." He poured her a glass and one for himself, too.

"You're still on duty?" she teased, mentally kicking herself the next moment.

"If you believe it or not, I don't make drinking a regular habit. Yesterday was just a trying day for all of us. I'm glad things are under control again for the moment."

"Do you like to control everything in your life?"

"Yes, I do."

A simple statement, no explanation offered. It irked her. What had made him this way? Why did he see a need to be in control?

Geez, it was none of her business. She cleared her throat, reached for the water in front of her. "We found Davis' date," she began after she'd taken a sip, giving him the gist Jenn had given her. "We have to confirm Raddart's alibi. Does the description of the man he described ring any bells for you?"

"We've got a lot of customers," Carter said, looking thoughtful.

"And you said so yourself that you make it a habit of knowing them."

"I did. And I didn't say I don't know him. I can't be certain, but it sounds like Ernesto Rodriguez to me."

"I guess you're not willing to give me an address. You'd rather protect his privacy?"

"And prolong this whole investigation? No. I trust you to handle this as discreetly as possible." He'd surprised her again. Every time she thought she understood him a bit better, he threw her a curveball.

"So you'll give it to me?"

"No, but I'll arrange for a meeting within the next two days. If that's not good enough, you'll have to get a warrant or interview all Ernesto Rodriguezes in the city."

It was a generous offer, yet it annoyed her. Carter gave a little but never all, as if holding back part of the information, part of himself, were just another game for him, another way to stay in control.

Suddenly she was dead tired, the last two days catching up with her. She couldn't live on the edge forever, even if it was only the edge of her own emotions.

Although sitting completely relaxed, Carter was watching her — missing nothing, she was sure.

"Okay," she said. "But if you don't contact me by then, I'll have a warrant the next day." She met his gaze, not breaking eye contact. As much as she wanted to, she couldn't read him, not in the way he could read her. Why was that? She was good at reading suspects. Usually she wasn't attracted to them — that was why. Her judgement was clouded in this case.

Carter, he was...attractive, intelligent, dangerous. Her rational self told her to get out of here, but the primal part of her wanted to stay, to see where it would lead her. The chemistry between them was fascinating, tantalizing. It shouldn't be. Not for her anyway. In this game she was the moth circling the flame, always in danger of being burned if she got too close.

"I didn't think you'd come here tonight," he finally said.

"Why? You offered to give me the information I needed."

He reached for his water, taking his time to answer. "It could have waited until tomorrow. You're uncomfortable here."

She was, yet she was not. Being here made her more aware of her surroundings, of herself. Fear, curiosity, want, anger — it all coursed through her veins, the mixture had her feeling a little lightheaded, making it harder to focus.

"Is everything in life just a game to you?"

"No. Not everything."

Curling a hand into a fist, she considered growling at him. Would he ever do more than just answer her questions with the most basic of replies? Would he ever offer information voluntarily?

"Well, thank you for your time. I'll leave you to your *business* now." She got up, wanting nothing more than to be out of here before her tiredness, which quickly morphing into anger, could get the better of her.

"I can't help but try pushing your boundaries."

She stopped in her tracks and waited.

"I already told you. You fascinate me."

"I've got to go." If she didn't, it would all be a repeat of last night, wouldn't it?

"I fascinate you, too," Carter continued as if he hadn't heard her. "My world fascinates you. I can see how badly you want to know, how afraid you are of yourself."

She held her breath for a second and released it too fast. She could lie to him, tell him he was wrong, but they both would know it wasn't the truth.

"Let me tell you what I know," she said, her voice firm. "I'm a police officer and you're a suspect in my ongoing investigation. This is the beginning and the end of it. What I did yesterday was a mistake, one I can't excuse, but can't undo either."

He got up and rounded his desk. He leaned against it. They were less than a foot apart, and she damned her body for failing her once again as her heart began beating faster in her chest, her breathing speeding up.

"You're a smart woman, Sharon. I trust you to solve this crime, and when you do, you'll learn it wasn't me who killed Marlene."

"Which will be the point when we'll both move on."

"Move on together or separately?"

His smile all but killed her resolve. She wanted to reach out, trace a finger along his sensual lips, have him suck at her digit, bite down on it.

"I don't want to play this game any longer." She hadn't intended to speak out, but she didn't regret that she had.

"You do. Come on, let me give you the tour." He straightened, then passed her, waiting at the door to his office.

"The tour?"

"Of the club. If you want to understand things, you have to study them. I'll offer you this chance once. Take it or leave it." He left the room, not waiting for her to make up her mind. Either she'd follow him or not. It was up to her. By all means, she should go home and prove him wrong, but she wasn't a coward either. Walking after him, she closed the office door, muted noises reaching her ears once more.

Chapter Six

Sharon heard a woman's suppressed moaning, then a moment later, a tiny cry.

"Why didn't you soundproof the rooms?" she asked, hurrying after Carter.

"Why would I have? There's nothing unnatural to the sounds you hear. In other societies, it's common to be vocal about one's feelings, to let out the emotional and physical pain. Don't you think it's better that way?"

"Do you make it a habit to cry your eyes out in public?"

He didn't bat as much as an eyelid. "No, I don't, but I'm not afraid of my tears either. Yes, I do cry, yes, I do feel pain, and I don't think I'm weaker for it. You know, it's people who refuse to acknowledge their feelings, who internalize their stress, who come here most often."

"And I thought people enjoyed themselves here," she said.

"Once they let go of their bottled-up feelings they do. Although I'd say most of them aren't looking for enjoyment in particular but for release." He opened a door, leading her down a staircase.

"Where are we going?"

"I want to show you our dungeons."

"Why have a dungeon when there are outfitted rooms all over the house?"

"There are more opportunities to live out your fantasies down there. Come on, I'll show you."

Did she really want to see this? Slight nausea battled with her determination not to show any sign of weakness. He led the way, and she was thankful he wasn't looking at her right now, afraid her face would give too much away.

At the end of the staircase there was a corridor, and she was sure she heard someone yelling, but the sound was muted as the doors down here looked to be made of steel. There were six of them, three to either side. It was noticeably colder, too, and a shiver ran down her back.

Four of the doors were closed, two partly open. Carter fully opened the first of those two, gesturing for her to proceed inside. She hesitated for barely a second, knowing he had noticed.

Inside, the room was dark, but Carter passed her then switched on some dim lights.

Another room in mostly red and black, just like the one where they had found Davis. Although that was the only thing the rooms had in common. This place was even barer than Davis' had been. The walls were made of brick, painted black. The floor was concrete painted in red. It wasn't exactly cold inside but warm would've been something different. She suspected people were supposed to feel a little uncomfortable in here, that it was part of a deliberate set-up.

She tried taking in the whole setting, to identify what she saw. Carter didn't give her much time to make herself familiar with her surroundings. He pointed at a bench more or less in the middle of the room.

"It's a spanking bench. Some people call it a whipping bench or bondage bench. I guess it's rather self-explanatory."

Unbidden, the thought of Michael came back to her, the way she had felt when his hand had made contact with her skin, how it had made her skin prickle, warmed it, before pleasure had begun flooding her veins.

"You can use it with or without restraints. Have you been spanked before, Sharon?"

She chose not to answer. Couldn't. "A cross, really?" she asked instead, referring to the large wooden construction forming an X at one side of the room. It was bolted to the wall, surely to keep the construction stable when in use.

Carter looked at her for a long moment, then he spoke again. "A St. Andrew's cross. It provides restraining points for wrists, ankles and waist. Again, it's for spanking purposes. The submissive will be attached with their back or front facing the cross."

Sharon was unable to look away. How would it feel if it was her attached to this cross, being helpless, having to trust another human being not to go too far? How could anyone stand such a total loss of control? Although, wasn't that the point?

"Speaking about spanking," Carter said, pointing to some toys hanging from the wall, "these are the most common toys used for this kind of scene." He explained them all but at some point she stopped listening. Why? What made people interested in all these things? A little spanking, maybe. This, though…paddles, floggers, ropes, nipple clamps…

They moved on, and Carter pointed to shackles used to chain someone to the wall. Geez, she was a cop—she was the one putting people in chains, not the other way around.

Her eyes fell on a couple of blindfolds on a rough, wooden table, right beside a bed that was simple but sturdy. It wouldn't take much to fasten someone's extremities to the bed posts. She focused on the blindfolds again. This was actually something she'd like to try. Forgetting about Carter, she walked over, reaching out, her fingers gliding over the soft satin. It was said to lose one sense meant to enhance all others.

"Would you like to try?" Was it her imagination or did Carter's voice hold a playful note? She whirled around to him, letting go of the blindfolds.

"I thank you for this tour."

"This is the second time you haven't answered me."

"Maybe I finally learned that answering your questions just won't lead to anything good."

He stepped closer, well into her personal space, so they almost touched.

"You didn't ask me, but I don't think last night was a mistake." He reached up and palmed her chin, lifting it a fraction. This time the gesture was gentle, but he still had a firm hold on her. "You don't have to worry. I won't run to your boss, make your life more complicated. I don't have a hidden agenda."

She wanted to believe him. Badly. A part of her told her to tone down her attitude, yet another part urged her to caution. At the end of the day, she knew next to nothing about this man.

Well, he knows how to kiss me so my better sense flies right out of the window. Her mind betrayed her once more. The wish to reach out and touch him became almost unbearable. She blinked, once then twice, willing her mind not to go down this road.

"I don't sleep with every woman I meet, either. There's just something between us, and I know you feel it too." Abruptly, he let go of her, making her miss his touch when she should have been relieved. He hadn't stepped back, though. She could feel the heat of his body, and would only have to move her hand to touch him.

"I need to leave."

"If you think that's what you have to do, I won't keep you."

"Good." She took a step back. He just looked at her, his stance relaxed.

"You are beautiful." It was a compliment she'd been paid before. When she was a teenager, she'd been flattered. Later, though, it had made her wary. Too often it was just a line being used as a means to an end. With Carter, she didn't think it was a line. So far he'd been serious with everything he'd said, and she'd like to believe he meant his words, that he truly found her beautiful.

"Thank you."

"What for? Let's be candid. I want you, Sharon. I want to have sex with you again."

She laughed, not having expected him to be *this* candid. "We shouldn't."

Not *we can't* or *we won't.* *"We shouldn't."* Sharon wanted to kick herself hard. She had enjoyed herself, his mere presence making her crave more of him, but giving in once more couldn't be an option.

"I won't tell if you won't tell," he said with a small smile not quite reaching his eyes. "But as I said before, it's your choice. Everything's your choice."

She frowned. "What are you talking about?"

He stepped in again, following the contours of her lips with his forefinger, doing to her what she'd thought about doing to him earlier. "You want to know. About this world. I can show you, satisfy your curiosity." He trailed his finger along her neck, the touch light. Her nerves fluttered, desire flaring up inside of her. "I would only ever take you as far as you want me to take you."

Yesterday she'd have said no without thinking twice. At least to this. Tonight, she wasn't so sure. Too many thoughts flickered through her mind at the same time. Should she trust him with her body again, trust him to… no, she didn't want to *play* with nipple clamps, ball gags, whips…

Without warning, he stepped back, then walked to the room's door. "I won't impose myself on you, and it's your decision. You know where to find me."

Her breath caught in her lungs as hot anger flooded her, making her want to release it all in a loud scream. Who did he think he was to begin seducing her only to leave her a minute later, in some torture chamber?

Temper, one of her worst enemies. It had ended with her in trouble quite a few times, especially when she was younger. Whenever she acted on instinct, instead of thinking her actions through first, there had been a price to pay.

She remembered the time her parents had told her she couldn't go to her best friend's party since no adults would be around. Of course, she'd gone anyway, ending up drunk and passed out in the backyard. Her parents never told her what had made them appear at said friend's house around three a.m. to pick her up in silence. It hadn't mattered. To this day she was thankful they had. Thinking about what could have happened chilled her to this day. She'd been sick for days afterwards, then she had to deal with being grounded for a month and her parents only speaking to her when it was absolutely necessary.

There had been a few other mistakes like that one, and the worst one had almost ended in a car accident when she had argued with her then-boyfriend. The argument had begun when he'd informed her he thought that seeing other people was a smart idea. She hadn't paid attention to the road, hadn't seen the truck braking before them. If Sean hadn't screamed out, making her break instinctively, it could have ended badly.

She'd been a normal teenager, or so her parents said, but the almost-accident had changed her. Since then, she'd learned to deal with her anger and frustration internally, and went to the gym to beat the pulp out of a sandbag when it all became too much. Jenn said keeping it all in wasn't healthy, and she was most likely right. Still, it was a habit deeply ingrained into her very being by now.

Now her anger rendered her speechless as conflicting urges tore at her. There was a world of difference between what she wanted to do and what she should do. Was there a part of her that wanted to *play* in a room like this? No. But she wanted Carter. Her whole body was hypersensitive, aware of the man who was walking away without granting her another glance.

Another scream made her aware she didn't want to be left behind here. She wasn't afraid, she knew how to defend herself, but she was out of her comfort zone. Switching out the light, she left the door partly open then climbed up the staircase.

When she'd reached the top of the stairs, there was no sight of Carter.

To leave or to stay? If she stayed, there was no doubt of the outcome of this night, and she couldn't claim it was a spur-of-the-moment decision. She'd have to claim full responsibility. Last night had put her job in danger, but she would be fired for a repeat performance without a doubt. She could call yesterday a mistake. This would make it an affair.

She turned, then walked toward the exit of the house. If she only got out and caught some fresh air, it might clear her head. At home she could call Jenn, her friend Erin or her mother, run a bath, just do something ordinary. This was Carter's world, not hers. It never would be. Once the investigation was over, she wouldn't see him again.

Still, it was far from over. She didn't have the slightest idea who could be responsible for Davis' death. That she had an inkling there was more to the story than met the eye wasn't evidence, wouldn't impress any court, especially without a suspect in custody.

She would meet Carter again. She'd feel the temptation again. He'd told her it was her decision, that he wouldn't try to force himself on her. But being himself was enough to tempt her.

He was a damned good-looking bad-boy with manners and a definite edge who was promising her a glimpse into the abyss of her own desires if she only dared to look.

She turned, short of reaching her goal, her mind a mess, chiding herself as every step took her closer to Carter's office.

Was this worth risking her job for?

He'd said he wouldn't make their dealings with each other public, but could she trust him? Her instinct said yes. Should she trust her instinct? So far it had always been right. With each of her ex-boyfriends, it had screamed at her to keep her hands off them. The fact she hadn't listened was nobody's fault but her own.

This time it told her to trust Carter, if not the situation itself. *If I'm wrong...*

The door to Carter's office wasn't quite closed. Stopping, her hands trembling slightly, she reached out and opened it. Quickly letting herself in, she closed the door behind herself.

Chapter Seven

Carter was at his desk, bent over some papers. He looked up when the door shut. When his eyes met hers, Sharon didn't see any sign of surprise. He was as calm as ever, his gaze serious, not at all like a man about to devour a woman. Had he wanted her to leave? "I didn't think you'd be back so soon," he said, closing a folder and getting up.

"Me neither. You left your door open…" Was this a mistake? Had she'd misread him? Although he had said it was her choice.

"Hope dies last," he said.

"You hoped I would be back?" This time their bodies were touching when he stopped in front of her, and she had to look up to see his face.

"Yes. I told you I want you." He fell silent, as did she. Seconds ticked by. *Is he waiting for a sign from me, any initiative?* So far he had always taken the first step. Finally, he lifted a hand, then put it on her shoulder, squeezing lightly in a gesture she could interpret as comfort. Or it was simply the dominant part of his nature he couldn't shake.

"Relax."

"I can't. I... Listen, Carter. No one, and I mean absolutely no one can know about this. I'm risking everything here." Her career would be over if he let her down.

"I promise. And don't you think you should call me Simon now?"

She laughed, nervous energy flooding her system. "And here I thought you'd insist I'd call you *sir* or *master*." She had no idea where that came from, and wished she could take the words back as soon as they'd left her mouth.

"That might come later, if you want it," he said with a twinkle in his eyes. "So tell me, what *do* you want?" he continued.

"I want to stop thinking," she said.

Yesterday, while being with him, the chaos in her mind had quieted for once. She wanted that again, just as much as she wanted to feel him inside her. He didn't reply, only tilted his head, his lips meeting hers in a kiss that was neither tender nor bruising. It was so good to have his lips against hers again, his slight stubble scratching her skin in the most arousing way possible.

She parted her lips for him without any prompting. He slid his tongue inside her mouth, tangling it with hers, urging her not to hold back. One of his hands tangled in her hair, pulling her head back so he had even better access. The other was on the small of her back, keeping her in place. He was a strong man, a fact she liked about him.

Dizzy from the lack of oxygen, she whimpered, and he released her.

"Come," he said, taking her hand when she didn't move.

"Where do you want to go?"

"I don't want to have sex with you against a wall again." Have sex, not make love — somehow she was grateful for the distinction. While she didn't harbor any romantic feelings for this man, it was good to hear he shared the sentiment, and wasn't trying to make more out of this than it was — an itch they both wanted to scratch.

Wouldn't it be even better if she found a man with whom she could have both? Well, if such a man existed somewhere. Maybe one day.

She followed Carter out of the office and up to the second floor, where he led her to a room at the end of the corridor. Once inside, she turned away from him to look around. The room was almost a replica of the one Davis had been found in, apart from a mirror right over the bed.

She crossed her arms over her chest, not sure about all of this once again. As if sensing her doubt, he stepped in, his front against her back. He had to be aware she could feel his erection, that her breath caught.

"This is my room."

She didn't understand, so turned around. "So this is where you bring the women you want to *play* with."

"Yes," he said. He didn't make any excuses, and why should he? New questions formed in her mind, but he shook his head, placing a finger over her lips.

"This will only go as far as you want it to, Sharon. Now do you want to be here?"

"Yes." She couldn't shake off a certain trepidation, but she wanted *this*, wanted *him* anyway.

"Then stop thinking. Nothing will happen if you don't want it, too. You can put a stop to anything at any given point. Consent is the key to everything here. You have my word. Understood?"

"Yes." She couldn't say why, but she was sure he would do as he said.

"Then stop thinking." His sharp tone finally registered with Sharon. It made her angry, yet she didn't move. Hadn't she asked him to make her churning thoughts stop?

Carter moved around her to a table at the side of the room. There were various toys and she began shaking her head, but he reached for a blindfold, then came back to her.

"We take the blindfold off whenever you want me to."

If she said *no* to it now, he would comply — he had said so himself. She debated trying him, but she was too curious, the idea of a blindfold too intriguing to resist.

"Okay." She was still nervous, but it was as much fear as it was arousal. What was she getting herself into? It was all happening so fast, yet with time to think about what she was doing, she wouldn't be here.

"Trust me."

"It's hard to," she admitted, hating the fact her voice was shaking a little. "Why should I trust you? Is sexual desire enough to leap off a cliff, to…" She stopped her rambling. Sometimes too much talk only made things worse.

"More often than not, the people who come here meet with complete strangers, trusting them with their bodies, their safety. No one was ever made a victim here. Well, apart from Davis." Again he looked angry, though then he schooled his features and she couldn't read him any longer. "We had someone trying to overstep the boundaries of another customer once. He was banned, and the only reason we didn't file a report was because the victim asked us not to. She was, or rather is, a high-ranking politician, and didn't want the scandal. But I can give you the name so you can look it up. If you're unsure about any of this here, you better leave now. It's still your choice."

She wouldn't leave. She wanted him too much.

"No," she said, when he waited for her cue.

He finally kissed her again, the touch of his mouth soft, alluring and oh so tempting. This was more than simple foreplay for casual sex. She wasn't sure she liked it, although maybe she just liked it too much. A moan escaped her.

"You're safe with me, Sharon," he said as he stepped back.

Reaching for her coat, she began to unbutton it. It earned her a smile, and out of the blue she was hit with the thought that they hadn't bothered with removing many clothes last night. Today, she would fully undress, the idea causing her fingers to linger over the last button of her coat. While she was in reasonably good shape, this was different from her usual sexual encounters. It was neither happening in the haze of sexual passion nor with a long-time lover with whom she wanted to enjoy some prolonged sexual play. It was something in between, and with a man who was used to being in control, whose scrutiny wouldn't miss a single thing about her or her body. She didn't believe he'd judge her by what he saw, but the feeling of uneasiness remained. Finishing with her coat, she let it glide to the floor.

"Now the shoes, the shirt," he ordered her, standing completely still and watching her. This was different from all the other times clothes had been discarded in a hurry or when undressing had been part of the encounter. She would do well to remember that Carter himself was different.

After slipping out of her shoes first, Sharon didn't take her time unbuttoning her shirt, but didn't hurry either. Once the two halves of fabric were parted, she shrugged out of it. Only in her bra and pants now, she felt the slight chill of the room, her nipples hardening. The tiniest smile flickered around his lips, but it was his only reaction. Well, apart from his obvious erection. She shouldn't want any man that much, but damn it, if the sight didn't send a shiver right down her back.

"Pants next."

"You don't have to order me around, you know."

"It's part of what I do," he said. "If you wanted to make sweet love, you wouldn't be here." Harsh words, but it was true in a way, although when she'd turned around and gone back to his office, she'd expected a repeat of last night, not this, whatever it would turn out to be.

Soon she was standing there in only her underwear. Ridiculous as it was, she was glad she'd opted for black lace in the morning instead of her regular cotton panties.

"Good. Now what's your safe word?" Carter asked. He spoke with a patience that she wished she could feel herself. Where was the limit of his control? Every person had a limit. What made him crave complete control anyway? There had to be a story behind it. Or was he simply wired this way?

"Your safe word, Sharon," he repeated.

"Pardon me?"

"I want to know your safe word. It will tell me when to stop." It finally hit her. This was real. She wasn't only about to repeat a delicious mistake but dip her toe into waters unknown to her. In a mere two days, her world had tilted on its axis.

"Sharon?"

"Phoenix."

He raised an eyebrow and inclined his head. "Interesting choice."

Somehow Sharon thought it was apt. Some wall inside her was crumbling, and she was trying to rise from the ashes of her preconceptions.

"May I touch you further?" he asked, putting his hands on her shoulders. The slight contact of skin on skin raised goosebumps all over her upper body. Would she even be able to stand this torture of a slow seduction or whatever she should call it?

Without meaning to, her eyes scanned the room again—the various toys, or would it be tools, for that matter? She almost sighed at her mind that just wouldn't rest.

"Yes," she finally answered him. "But your politeness drives me mad."

"Does it?" He chuckled, which only annoyed her more. Leaning in, he closed his lips around her earlobe, his teeth nibbling, his tongue dipping into the shell of her ear. His breath was hot, and her skin flushed as sudden heat flooded her.

"You're aroused," he whispered, tugging at the sensitive flesh of her earlobe again.

She gritted her teeth to keep in the moan that wanted to escape. Right now she didn't want to give him the gratification of knowing how right he was. He was a smug bastard, but one she wanted to be close to, one who made her feel alive like she hadn't in years. When was the last time she had been the sole focus of a man's interest? Although wasn't it the sad truth that she hadn't even wanted to be?

"So are you," she said, pressing against his hard flesh, furthering her own desire.

Without warning, he pulled away so his gaze could meet hers.

"When I came up here, I only planned on having sex with you, but I hope you can forgive me that I'd rather play with you. Anyway, here are the rules for this game. You only speak when I ask you to speak. You do as I say. And if at any time you're uncomfortable with anything I do, you use your safe word."

It was fair yet unfair at the same time. Who had made him God and let him and him alone decide what he would do and when he would do it? She was as confused as she was dizzy with want, but she had agreed to this game. She wanted to play, and at the end of the day, if she gave her safe word, it all would be over. She'd give him the power to control her but still have the ultimate say. It was comforting knowledge.

Didn't she want to know, to lose control? This was her chance to find out how far she was willing to go, why people went to these clubs to find release.

"Do you understand and agree?"

A voice inside her popped up, telling her it was not too late to leave. There was still time to salvage her job and mental sanity. As if she would...

"Sharon? Do you understand and agree?" Carter asked again. Close as they were, she couldn't see his eyes without leaning her head back, but she didn't move. She took a deep breath instead, enjoying the male scent she couldn't define. It was dark, spicy...but it was him, not some cologne.

"Yes, I do."

"Good, then we'll begin now."

"But..." He took a step back, put a finger over her lips, his eyes stern, reminding her she'd agreed to only talk when he allowed her to. She locked her arms in front of her chest. She couldn't stop herself. She was glad when he didn't comment on it.

"I'll put the blindfold on you now."

Without meaning to, Sharon held her breath when he stopped behind her to place the soft black cloth over her eyes. She had thought she'd still be able to see, if a lot less, but Carter knew what he was doing. Her world went from colorful to utter darkness in a heartbeat. After a second, she closed her eyes, took a deep breath and tried to relax. It was in her power to stop this at any time — she only had to say the word.

"Tell me how you feel?" Carter's voice interrupted her musings.

She focused on herself, fishing for a way to answer his question honestly.

"I'm nervous. I'm getting cold again." Not her back where he stood close enough she could feel the warmth radiating off his body, but her nipples were almost painfully hard from the slight breeze of air inside the room.

"You won't be cold for long." She considered it a promise, hugging herself tighter to provide some warmth for the moment, to calm herself. He walked away, and was at her front suddenly, unlocking her arms and putting them at her sides.

She heard the slight rustle of fabric when he moved, his even breathing, muted noises from elsewhere in the house. Distracted by focusing on her hearing, she stiffened when he was at her back again. He reached for the clasp of her bra, deftly unhooking it.

Instead of pulling the straps over her arms, he lifted her hair and brushed it over her shoulder before he ran a single finger from the base of her neck, all the way down her back to her ass, where he stopped with the tip of it dipping into the crack of her ass cheeks. If he ventured a bit lower... He wouldn't, would he?

Her whole body tensed.

"I won't. No worries. Not tonight, anyway."

He implied it would be a continued affair. He sounded as sure about it as he did about everything else. How could he be so sure she wouldn't kick his sorry ass after the night was over?

Both of his hands went for the straps of her bra now, carefully removing the item of clothing.

"Beautiful," he murmured, his lips closer to her ear than she'd reckoned. A shiver of pleasure ran down her back.

"Step out of your panties now. I'll hold you."

So he didn't like to get on his knees? Sharon almost snorted. Reaching for her panties, she didn't make a show of divesting herself of them. She just kicked them to the side. As he had promised, he held her steady, standing behind her with his hands on her shoulders.

"I'll lead you to the bed now," he said.

At least there was a real bed. Thinking of the dungeons downstairs, she was glad he had taken her here. The dungeons would've been too much too soon. They might always be too much, and nobody was talking about a repeat performance here.

It was five steps to the bed, and once her knees bumped against the mattress, Carter told her to get up on the bed, to lie down on her back. She did, with her arms at her sides, her legs closed. Expecting the mattress to dip as he joined her on the bed, she was surprised when nothing happened. All she heard were some noises she couldn't quite identify. Was he stripping out of his clothes, too?

Carter didn't speak, and seconds began to stretch far beyond their means. If he meant to take her mind off things like this, he was doing a poor ass job of it. Finally, he got up.

"Prop up your legs. Spread them."

While everything inside her screamed not to do it, not to give in to the command so carelessly thrown at her, she still complied without a second thought. She had decided to stay, so she wouldn't give him the gratification of seeing her hesitation, knowing he made her feel vulnerable. He was not her enemy. Hadn't she said so herself? They were not playing for different teams.

She more felt than heard him move. He still wore his pants, and the fabric of his jeans brushed against her naked legs as he settled in between them. She moved her hands, wanting to know if he still wore his turtleneck. He didn't, but he was wearing a shirt.

Her exploration lasted all of a few seconds before he removed her hands from his body.

"No touching unless I tell you to." She almost voiced a complaint, but thought twice about it. Although what could he do if she didn't play along? A lot of things, going by the possibilities provided in this room. She could voice her safe word, true, but it would mean the game was over before she could find any release. God, why could she never stop thinking?

His lips on her skin were a surprise. Her neck tingled where he touched it. Lingering over her pulse point, he kissed it again before he sucked at the spot. She twitched a little as the pressure of his lips began to sting, then his lips wandered on, over her collarbone, her chest, stopping between her breasts.

She was already wet for him, and he would know it, too. What would she see if she looked at him right now? Was he looking at her with interest or did he wear the stoic, slightly amused expression she'd gotten used to? She moved a little, unnerved by the silence, realizing out of nowhere that these were indeed satin sheets. The urge to giggle almost became unbearable, and she wished he would speed things up. It had been bliss when he had been inside her last night, when he took her hard and fast, filling her body and her mind with his presence. This slow pace left her wanting, frustrated.

It was for her sake. If he had put her on the bed, grabbed a paddle, bruised her skin, it would've scared her away and ended the game for good. It would've been too soon. Unbidden images of the rough sex with Michael came back to her and she thought about Carter. How would it feel if he treated her the same way, if he led her even further tonight?

"Damn," she mumbled, the single word out before she could stop herself.

"I didn't allow you to talk."

He enclosed her nipples between his thumbs and forefingers at once, tweaking the tender buds. The sensation was uncomfortable, bordering on pain. He increased the pressure before he let go, then leaned in to brush over one of her taut buds with his tongue, slowly dragging over it a few times.

Sharon moaned, her back arching, the pleasure exquisite after being toyed with for an interminable time. Hadn't the game really started as soon as she'd set foot inside here tonight?

Chapter Eight

Carter stopped, waited a moment, then switched to her other breast, subjecting it to the same treatment. It was good. So good. She wanted more of it, of him. He sat up way too soon, but she didn't want him to, tried finding him by touch. He easily evaded her.

"I think I'd like to secure you to the bed, but only if you're okay with the idea."

A wave of unease rolled over her. While she had never been a prude in bed, no one had ever taken away her mobility before. She didn't like feeling helpless. Anger and fear battled excitement, arousal even. *What should I do?*

"Sharon?"

It was her decision. "Yes, do it." She hoped it was the right decision, but if not, she could still give him her safe word. He would stop if she wanted him to. She had trusted him this far.

He moved again, taking both of her arms and lifting them over her head. The next thing she felt was a soft kind of cloth binding her wrists together before she was chained to the wall. She'd seen the rings, but hadn't thought he'd use them to secure her to his bed.

If anyone had told her last week she'd find herself bound to a bed a few days later, she would've deemed them crazy, but now she was, her whole body pulsing with nervous energy, raw need.

Carter put a hand on her stomach. His skin was warm, and the gesture calmed her, even though she didn't understand why.

"The goal is for the mind to quiet down. Do you know that peaceful state when you're simply existing, no worries or thoughts bothering you?"

This time she didn't repeat her mistake and remained silent.

"You're allowed to speak."

"No." She had felt a measure of it last night. Still, to be at complete ease for more than a few seconds — no, she hadn't experienced it. Her mind was her worst enemy at times, making it hard for her to fall asleep at night.

"I will lead you there tonight."

A threat? A promise? Both his hands were back on her body now, stroking, caressing, inflaming her nerve endings, although he avoided all erogenous zones. A kiss to her neck, a hand gliding over her arm, the inside of her thigh. It was good, but just wasn't enough. She wished he'd stroke her breasts, dip a finger between her folds, that he'd finally caress the swollen bundle of nerves that throbbed almost painfully.

He did neither. He just continued to drive her crazy until her back arched once again, her arms beginning to hurt as she couldn't stop the impulse to try breaking them free. As it was, she could hardly move, couldn't see, and if he left the room now, she'd have no means to free herself. The thought chilled her, yet couldn't take root as Carter never slowed down his sensual assault on her nerves.

Would he keep her hanging like this forever, providing stimulation but not even a hint of relief? Sharon wanted to cry out, curse him, yet she didn't want to risk finding out what he'd do if she did. Never before had arousal been so painful, the emotional torture as bad as the physical one.

Without her meaning to, some tears escaped her eyes, a testament to her utter frustration, her helplessness. She was angry with him for not giving her even a hint of relief, for not stopping his motions for a single moment so she could get a grip, and was angry with herself for not calling a halt to it. She should end this, walk away. How could she, if no man had ever managed to drive her to these heights of desire before?

His thumbs trailed over her cheeks, smearing the trail her tears had left. He neither spoke to her nor offered any other kind of comfort, but finally he gave in, his lips closing around one of her nipples. Sucking, licking, nipping, he took his time with one breast, then the other. She was writhing on the bed, her body too restless to remain still.

"You'd look good with nipple clamps."

The mental image had her tense. *No. Just no.*

Without forewarning, Carter cupped her sex. Another set of tears flowed down her cheeks, this time of pure relief. He rested his hand for a minute, then slid one of his digits between her folds, trailing up and down the length of them, brushing her clit once. A moan ripped from her throat. More—she wanted and needed more.

The same digit stopped at her entrance, dipping in a little.

What kind of picture am I presenting to him now, naked, spread open? Wanton and writhing?

When she pushed her hips up a little, his finger slid in more deeply, but was gone the very next second, the smack of a hand against her outer thigh unexpected. Shock turned into pain, then numbness, ending in a tickling feeling that wasn't uncomfortable. Pain and pleasure, one morphing into the other. It was surely a matter of degree, of how much pain was administered, how much of it a person could stand, yet this little taste of it didn't leave her recoiling, a lesson she had learned with Michael before. Quite the contrary, she wanted more, to try it again, even though she didn't know how to ask. *Could you slap me again?* It wasn't pillow talk as she knew it, and she wasn't allowed to speak anyway.

He slapped her other thigh, this time taking her as much by surprise as the first time had.

"Don't think, just take it." As if to make sure she couldn't do anything else but comply, he ran his fingers lightly over the parts of her body he'd just hit, the extra-sensitive skin reacting more fiercely than usual, her nerve endings firing as pleasure uncoiled deep in her belly. She was more aroused than she had been in ages. It should have been embarrassing, but it wasn't.

He moved, then his hands were on the inside of her thighs, spreading them even further. Before she had time to fully register what was happening, his tongue was parting her labia, his slight stubble scratching against the tender skin on the inside of her thighs. She should have dated more men with stubble or beards. The idea made her giggle, an atypical reaction for her, but nothing about this night was anything like the life she knew.

She stopped giggling when he slid two fingers inside her, curving them so they'd stroke her inner walls, his tongue flicking her clit hard. With no idea of what to expect from this, from him, she'd have thought he'd prolong the teasing. It was time to learn not to expect anything when it came to this man.

Her climax took her hard, without warning, her body going rigid as the wave of pleasure crested and was replaced with shudders that were hardly any less intense. For a second she saw stars. Weakness wanted to grip her body, take her under. She would not faint. She just wouldn't. To simply breathe was almost impossible and a moan caught in her throat. Seconds ticked into minutes, or did they really?

She thought Carter would leave her be now, give her the time to recuperate. He didn't, just fingerfucked her harder, his lips closing around her pleasure point and sucking. She couldn't take it. It hurt as much as it felt good, but she didn't have the breath to tell him to stop.

No, no, no... She shook her head, wanting this to stop, wanting it to last, to go on forever, as the feeling of too much transformed into one of want once more. He just kept at it, steadily leading her to the edge of the sensual abyss again.

What about him? Didn't it cost him to give and take nothing? What was there in this for him?

Her next orgasm was gentler, though it lasted even longer than her first one. As if reading her correctly, knowing this was truly all she could take for now, he let go, his strong hands stroking her stomach, her thighs, the caresses soothing.

After an eternity, she was able to breathe properly again, her pulse having calmed down.

"How are you?" Carter's voice, although not particularly compassionate, was gentler than she'd have expected.

"I'm good. You?" She rolled her eyes at the polite reply that fell from her lips without any second thoughts.

He chuckled. "I'm good, thanks for asking."

She didn't think she could or wanted to move within the next hour, though her arms really hurt from the strain she'd put onto them. There was a question nagging at her, and she spoke out, consequence be damned. Maybe this part of the game was over.

"Aren't you going to fuck me?"

Sated as she was, the mere thought had her shuddering in anticipation. It was crude language but for the moment she was done with being nice.

"Do you want me to?"

"What do you think?" Did he really have to ask?

Carter didn't answer, only crept up the bed to untie her. The sudden flow of blood into her extremities was painful, but she gritted her teeth. She'd endured worse in the course of duty. Hell, with some workouts she'd endured worse. She reached for the blindfold but his voice, sharp this time, stopped her.

"Who said you could take it off? The game's not over yet."

"It isn't?"

"Turn around. On your knees. On all fours."

Though she internally bristled, she complied after hesitating for a second. Moving was harder than she'd have thought. Her orgasms had left her body comfortably weak, and her arms and legs protested the movement. If she were at home, in her bed, she'd have turned around and gone to sleep. Here, it was either leaving or continuing to play a game with rules she hadn't quite internalized yet. When she was in position, her thighs trembled and she had no idea how long she could keep herself upright.

When Carter smacked her ass, the impact was less shocking than it had been the first time. "I decide when and if you've had enough. If you think you've learned anything yet, you're wrong."

Having seen what kind of equipment this room contained, Sharon knew he was right. What was a slap, even a firm one, compared to the paddles, floggers and other things she'd seen in here? She thought her tolerance for pain was high, but she was convinced he could easily cure her of the notion.

The next thing she knew, he got off the bed. Anxiety made her want to see. Was he going for one of his *toys*? If yes, which one? What she heard instead was the definite rustle of fabric, telling her he was undressing himself. She'd love to be able to see him, to admire his body. From the glimpses she'd gotten the night before, he was strong, trained, but there hadn't been time to note any specifics.

He came back to the bed, the mattress dipping right behind her. He trailed a path from her neck to her back once more, his fingers splayed, the gesture screaming *mine*, if only for the night.

Would he tease her again or just take her? What would it be? Not knowing was an added thrill, one keeping her alert when all her body wanted to do was crumple into a helpless heap.

It turned out it was the latter, his hard cock entering her without hesitation, although he paused when barely in, giving her the time to adjust to his presence inside her.

She moaned, but so did he. It was comforting to know he was affected by this, although maybe not as badly as she was. As her body relaxed, he slid in to the hilt, filling her, arousing her. Her hips undulated, seeking friction. She couldn't stop herself. If she were allowed to speak, she'd ask him to finally move, to do something about this state she was in.

Carter chose his own pace, though, one that kept her right at the edge, but was too slow to bring any true fulfilment. It wasn't enough. She needed more. Beginning to move in rhythm with him, she all but sighed in relief when she was close again.

It was a short-lived feeling. His hand swatted first one ass cheek then the other. He slapped her harder than he had done before. She should feel the pain, shy away, try to hold still so he wouldn't do it again. Instead she kept on moving, wanting him to give her more of it as she loved the way it made her feel skin alive with sensation. She had never had any idea that such a torment could blossom into something so beautifully arousing.

This time he did exactly as she wanted him to do, administering more smacks before moving on to different spots on her thighs as her ass grew numb. He finally fucked her faster, too, making her grip the sheets underneath her hard so she wouldn't lose her equilibrium.

There were so many sensations at once she couldn't keep track of them. She didn't have the drive to actively participate in this game any longer. All she could do was absorb the feelings he created in her, cataloguing, enjoying, wishing it would never stop.

She desperately wanted to come. Her clit throbbed as it craved touch, release that was so near yet still a bit out of reach. A final smack onto her ass, then Carter stopped, one hand going for her waist, the other reaching around her, two fingers squeezing her clit with his finger pads.

There was a loud scream, but it hardly registered with her that it came from herself. He read her body as if it were his own. All she could do was let the tide sweep her away with it as another orgasm rocked her body. She was only dimly aware as he moved again, then tensed, coming with a harsh groan. Good — she wasn't sure she could stand more of it. Her body pulsed, and she gave in readily, her mind drifting as the waves of pleasure coursed through her.

Only when she was covered with a soft blanket did she fully reach consciousness again. Had she passed out, fallen asleep? The blindfold was gone, and she could see Carter beside her, propped up on an elbow, watching her. His calm gaze was soothing, as was the hand he had over her blanket-covered hip.

"How are you?"

She pondered the question and tried to formulate an answer but failed. She was physically all right, yet she wasn't sure about her emotions. She'd have to let this settle, think about it. Later though, not now.

"I'm...okay."

He smiled as if he were able to see right through her. "Let me look at your bruises."

The thought his spanking could leave a mark had never entered her mind.

"It's warm and comfortable under these covers," she said.

"You can enjoy them afterwards. Come on, turn around."

"Is this still part of your game, or do I have my own free will again?" she said, wincing at how sarcastic she sounded.

"You never lost it. That's the most overlooked part when it comes to BDSM play. People have a choice. All that happens is what people want to happen. That's why you should never agree to something like this if you don't have a safe word."

It was on the tip of her tongue that she didn't intend to engage in such kind of play again, but she wasn't so sure about it. When she turned around as he'd asked, he stroked her ass and her legs, the contact slightly uncomfortable.

"Let me get some balm onto it." She watched him open a drawer, and before long some cool balm was applied to her skin. He was exquisitely tender, taking his time. He made it hard not to sigh, curl in and just relax.

She couldn't. Not here. For all they had done, they were not lovers in the common sense. When he was done, she sat up with regret.

"Do you want to leave?"

Did he want her to leave? Did he want her to stay? It shouldn't matter what he thought at all. Panic began to spread inside her.

"I want to get back to my apartment, fit in some sleep before I'll have to go back to work again."

"Why do you still think I'll harm you or your job?" he asked. He didn't reach for his clothes as she was now doing. He was comfortable in his skin. No, she wouldn't look. More than she already had, that was. What she had seen so far had only confirmed her suspicions. His body was trained, strong, not too hairy. The thought almost had her laughing, but she only shook her head.

"As I said before, I don't know you. I have no reason to truly trust you."

"Then ask me what you want to know." Did he have an answer or fitting question for everything?

"Why would you want me to? Something tells me I'm just one of a handful of women you like to fuck for sport." For the first time since she'd met him, something like true anger appeared in his eyes. Her heart missed a beat, and she wished she was already out of here.

"You truly know nothing, but I think it would do you a world of good not to jump to conclusions before you have any solid evidence. You as a cop should know this better than anyone else."

She dressed in silence while she let his words sink in. He was right—her behavior towards him was grossly unfair, especially considering it wasn't his fault she was annoyed with herself for being attracted to him.

When she reached for her coat, she took a last look around the room. It was strange. What had looked scary and alien only an hour ago didn't shock her any longer, but only made her look at everything in here with mild curiosity.

"I'm sorry," she said when she walked over to the door.

"Sharon, I don't want you to be sorry. Just be honest with yourself. You're human. There's no shame in trying out something new. What we did tonight happened with full consent. Nothing got hurt, apart from your pride." He was right, and yet...

"How dare you?"

"Been there, done that, got the appropriate T-shirt. I didn't grow up with the fervent wish to own a S&M club. Only as a young adult did I learn to understand my unfulfilled desires, that I wasn't abnormal—just different."

It was one thing to know someone was right, quite another to apply it to one's own life. She wasn't ready to deal with the implications of tonight's encounter yet.

"Again, I'm sorry." She left quickly, and he didn't try to stop her. Relieved as she was, she was also disappointed for a moment. It only made her more angry with herself.

Chapter Nine

"You look like shit. Squared."

Leave it to Jenn not to mince words. Too tired to argue, Sharon got out of her coat, cursing when one of the buttons sprang loose. Damn it, she didn't have the time to go shopping or the inclination to bother with sewing. Grumbling, she picked up the button and sat down at her desk, reaching for her coffee cup. Jenn took it from her outstretched hand and filled it almost to the brim.

"What happened?"

Sharon would've been annoyed had Jenn not sounded so worried. "Nothing happened."

"Yeah, tell that to someone who isn't a cop. Did you sleep at all?"

She had. A little. The last time she'd looked at the clock on her nightstand it had been nearing three a.m. As calm as she'd felt with Carter, turmoil had held her in a tight grip afterwards. She had tossed and turned in bed, reliving the memories, trying to quiet the nagging voice telling her she'd started something she wouldn't know how to stop.

"I did. I appreciate your concern, but…"

Jenn shook her head. "If you want to tell me it's none of my business, try again."

"I won't, if you stop nagging me."

"Uh huh. Fat chance."

In contrast to her, Jenn looked well rested — for a cop anyway — and full of energy. While her friend had her own troubles, she had a better way of dealing with them. Contrary to Sharon, Jenn usually had energy to spare.

"Is it still the case?" Jenn asked when Sharon remained silent.

"Which case?" Sharon asked, belatedly realizing what Jenn was referring to. "No, it's not." As sorry as she was for Marlene Davis, her relatives and friends, that wasn't what was bothering her.

"Girl, talk to me. How often do I have to tell you it's not good to bottle it all up inside? You'll only end up with a shrink sooner or later." Jenn's nose crinkled as if she'd smelled something bad.

"I think you've got wonderful parents," Sharon said, smiling for the first time that day.

"I do, too. But two shrinks, really? When I was younger, Dad analyzed everything, including my choice of cereal in the morning."

"And your mom analyzed his analysis?"

Jenn laughed. "Something like that, yeah. Anyway, what I'm trying to tell you here is that you should talk to someone, and that I'm willing to listen whenever you need a shoulder to cry on. You know I never hesitate to come and find you in times of trouble either."

Indeed. Sharon doubted there was any detail of Jenn's relationships with Alec and Jorge she didn't know.

"Thank you." She smiled again and booted up her computer. It was time to look up some facts, make a few calls and talk to a few more people. Today she'd follow the money trail, and with luck it would lead her to some results. This time, even more so than others, she was wishing for a quick solution to the case. If she put the Davis murder behind her, she could try to forget about Carter and hopefully close the door she'd partly opened last night. What had she been thinking? She hadn't wanted to think — that was the problem — instead, she had wanted to fulfill her curiosity.

"You're staring into space," Jenn said.

"I'm booting my computer up."

"While staring into space. Sharon, come on. I'm starting to worry here."

"Curiosity killed the cat."

Jenn snorted. "I'd only be curious if this were all about a man."

Sharon's non-reaction was definitely the wrong one.

"It *is* about a man. I can't believe it. How did you manage to get into boy trouble within the last few days? And what's with Carter? Wait, wait. Is it about Carter?"

"No." She wasn't even lying. It was about herself, about what she should and shouldn't do, what she wanted and didn't.

"Did you talk to Carter again? About the witness?" Jenn's whole focus was on her now. She was even sitting still, something she only ever managed when interrogating a suspect.

"Yes, I did. He has an idea who this person could be and will arrange a meeting."

Jenn snorted. "How nice of him. He couldn't have given us an address or a telephone number?"

Jenn's reactions were what hers should be. When and why had the lines begun to blur? She withstood the impulse to rub her tired eyes. Jenn wouldn't let her hear the end of it if she did. "He told me to either wait a day or two or get a warrant. I figured waiting would be the faster way."

"Maybe. But getting back to men, if it's not..."

Sharon was saved by the bell as her phone began ringing. She smiled at Jenn. "Sorry, gotta take that one."

"I'll get you later. I know where you work, and I know where you live."

"Hey, Mom, what's up?" Sharon said, picking up the phone. If she knew one number by heart, it was her mother's.

"I'm good, love. How about you?"

They exchanged some niceties while Sharon took a sip of her coffee, thankful for the caffeine flooding her system, even if the taste burned her tongue. If it helped her make it through the day, she could have an early night and give her body the rest it needed. Maybe she should fit in a workout, though. Missing two days in a row was unusual for her. Although, did yesterday count as a workout? She almost choked on her next sip. She coughed, making Jenn look up and her mom ask, "Are you all right?"

"Yes, I am."

"Sharon Marie, I know you better than that." What was it with people picking up on her mood that easily? She didn't think she was an open book. Although Jenn and especially her mother were among the people who knew her best.

"I'm good. Just a new case. Little sleep."

Jenn, who was jotting down some notes, looked at her again with an 'I told you so' expression. Sharon stuck out her tongue at her.

"If there's anything, you know you can talk to me, right?"

"Yes. I do. Now tell me how it's going with Henry." When Sharon's father had died of a heart attack about five years earlier, her mother had been devastated. After being married for close to thirty years, her mother couldn't imagine life without him. For months, Sharon had been sick with worry for her mother. She had offered to move in with her, an offer her mother had declined. Last year, though, she'd gotten to know a man a few years older than her. Henry was an attorney, a quiet, gentle man who managed to make her mother smile again. Sharon liked him and was glad for his presence in her mother's life.

"He asked me to marry him."

Sharon was speechless for a few seconds, trying to absorb the news. While it made her happy for her mother, she wasn't sure how she felt about it. "That's...wonderful. Congratulations."

Marriage? It didn't mean her mother would try to replace her father, yet it didn't sit right with her. Not at the moment, anyway.

"If you don't..."

"Stop it, Mom. This is your decision and no one else's. I know Henry makes you happy, and I only wish the two of you the very best. Just give me a day or two to get used to the thought, okay?"

Her mother was silent for a few seconds. "I will. But, Sharon, I'll always love your father. I'll never be able to forget him, and Henry doesn't try to replace him. It's just nice to be happy again."

"Mom, please. I don't want you to apologize. You know how much I like Henry. When you talk to him, give him my best."

"I will. But you know, we would really like to have dinner with you again sometime soon."

Sharon liked the idea of seeing her mother again. It had been too long, almost five months since she'd last made the trip to Vermont. "I've got no idea when I'll be able to make it. We're in the middle of an investigation."

Her mother laughed, the carefree sound a balm to Sharon's nerves. "You're always in the middle of an investigation. I doubt people over there will stop murdering each other just because your mother wants to see you again."

"I know. And I'm sorry…"

"Cut it short, dear. I'll be in the city in a few weeks. Henry invited me. He thought we deserved to celebrate. If you could meet with us one of those evenings, that would be lovely."

"I'd love that. Now tell me everything about the proposal. When did he ask you? Where did he ask you?"

Jenn's eyes went wide at the mention of an engagement, and Sharon mouthed *"later"* to her.

When she ended the call, almost twenty minutes had passed. While she had more than enough work to do, she had relished the conversation. It connected her to life as she'd known it, the one that had been nicely normal. She *knew* herself when she talked to her mother. She hadn't known herself last night.

Although now she had put down the phone, Jenn wanted to know everything about the call. Jenn had met Sharon's mother a few times before, and the two of them had taken a liking to each other at once. Sharon was more than happy to provide Jenn with any information she wanted today, if it meant Jenn wasn't grilling her about her other problem. Upon finishing, she got up and grabbed her coat, frowning at the missing button.

"Hey, where are you going?"

"Out." Before Jenn could start with questions Sharon didn't want to answer again. "I'll go and interview some witnesses in the Jefferson case before I talk to Davis' boss again." She had reports to write as well, but those could wait until later. "Could you take care of the formal interview with Raddart?" She had almost forgotten about him.

"Sure, but, Sharon?"

"Yes?"

"I'm not stupid, and we'll have that talk."

"So noted." If she didn't want to, no one could force her to talk, but that fight was for later.

* * * *

It had gotten colder again, spring all but forgotten as winter tried sinking its claws into the city one last time. At least Sharon hoped it was for the last time this year. Shivering in her too-thin coat, she pondered what she'd just learned. Some people were passing her, grumbling that she wasn't moving fast enough.

At the beginning, Davis' boss had insisted Marlene had been his golden girl, that there wasn't any fault to her. Trusting her instincts, she hadn't given up asking questions, threatening to take him in for a formal interview, which was the point where he changed his story quite a bit. While he still claimed Davis had been an effective employee, he said there were plans for an external audit next month that had made Davis nervous. Lately, she'd still been bringing in big clients, but she was making less money than she should've by any reasonable estimate.

The gist of it was that Davis had possibly tweaked some numbers, with no one knowing for sure which ones or to what extent. Back at the precinct, Sharon would talk to somebody in the IT department and make sure that one of them took a look at Davis' electronic data. She was convinced they'd find something. The question was how it tied in to Davis' murder.

She was debating whether or not to have a hot dog when her cell phone rang. She answered it without looking at who it was.

"Richards."

"Hello, Sharon."

Carter. She stopped in the middle of the street at hearing his voice. She hadn't expected it, and wasn't prepared to deal with him again so soon. Although the worst was her body betraying her, humming from remembered pleasure.

"What can I do for you?"

"Will you ever stop talking to me as if we are complete strangers, or even worse, as if you can't stand the sound and sight of me?"

A good question. She never meant to go for his jugular, yet found she couldn't stop herself. "I apologize. Still, let me repeat my question. What can I do for you?"

"Nothing. I only called to let you know I'll be at the precinct in roughly half an hour. I talked to Ernesto, and he'll meet you there. He wanted me to be there as well."

"I..." Carter? At the precinct? She wouldn't manage to be back in the office in half an hour. "I won't make it. I'm at Wall Street at the moment."

"Don't worry. We'll wait for you. See you soon." He ended the call, and she cursed. The last thing she wanted to imagine was having this man at her workplace. Cops were known for their instincts, and she didn't want anyone to catch so much as a whiff of what was going on between them. It was too late now. All she could do was try to contain the damage, to make sure she didn't react inappropriately to him, no matter what.

She reached the precinct almost an hour later, thanks to subway trouble. She couldn't help but think that she might have been quicker if she had walked. Heading directly for her office, she found Carter sitting opposite of Jenn, talking to her with another man sitting in her visitor chair, looking uncomfortable.

She put a smile on her face when she opened the door. "Mr. Carter, Mr. Rodriguez, thank you for stopping by."

"I would say it's our pleasure, but..." Carter trailed off.

She walked around her desk and sat down in Jenn's visitor chair, ignoring her partner, who was grinning at her. Sharon dreaded to think what Jenn and the two men might have talked about. The only consolation was that with Rodriguez in the picture, they wouldn't have discussed her.

"How about we make it a quick and painless affair?" she finally spoke when all eyes were on her.

Carter raised an eyebrow. She hadn't meant for it to be a pun, which he should know. What was it about him making her want to strangle him after less than five minutes in his company? It was the fact he awoke desires in her that she wasn't comfortable with, as simple as that. She couldn't deny this truth any longer, but it really shouldn't have hit her right now, here in the office with several other people around.

Too bad personal epiphanies never followed any suitable timeline.

"If you all agree, we'll have the interview here. It will be faster that way," she said, pushing all private thoughts away for the moment.

She hoped Carter and Rodriguez would agree so she wouldn't have to accompany the two men through half the police station. She could too easily imagine the looks these men would get, and how some of her female colleagues would swoon over Carter. Although maybe she was a little biased.

"I would really like to leave soon," Rodriguez said, his English heavily accented.

The man looked ill at ease. He was sweating, his eyes darting from one spot to another. Sharon was always amused by how uncomfortable people were when they had to enter a police station. It was even more amusing this time, as Rodriguez didn't seem to be uncomfortable with going to an S&M club. Who would've thought the police beat that kind of establishment?

Well, he needed the one and was afraid of the other.

"Don't you worry. We only need you to verify the information we received. I'm sure Mr. Carter already informed you about our request."

Rodriguez looked at Carter.

"No," Carter answered for him. "I told him you wanted to talk to him about the day Davis died, but I didn't give any specifics as I didn't think it was my place to do so."

While he was right, it irked Sharon that he had been so thoughtful. She didn't like the feeling of being in his debt. *Damn him.* He had an annoying habit of being one step ahead of her.

"I see. Thank you for your consideration."

She focused on Rodriguez, relaying the information that he had been seen having a run-in with another customer.

"This is correct. Yes." Rodriguez nodded. "Can I leave now?"

Talk about being antsy. Too bad she didn't think this guy had a motive or the balls to kill someone else in cold blood.

"No, you can't."

Rodriguez's face fell, and Sharon clarified. "I need you to tell me exactly what happened, with as much detail as possible, then we'll need you to write it down."

"Do I need a lawyer?"

Sharon almost rolled her eyes. If she got a dollar each time this question was asked… "Did you do anything wrong, something illegal?"

To her surprise Rodriguez looked at Carter again, which made her instincts fire a warning. Carter didn't say a thing, though.

"Mr. Rodriguez, let me repeat myself. Did you do something illegal? Right now we're only talking, but if you fear something might come up that'll indicate any wrongdoings on your side, you might want me to read you your rights, so you know you can enact your right to remain silent."

"No. No. I…"

Carter interrupted him, looking first at Rodriguez, then at Sharon. "He's married. He'd like it if his family remains unaware of the fact that he spent any time in my establishment."

Of course. What was it with men? Why was it so hard for them to be faithful? It was unfair, women weren't any better than men, still...

If Rodriguez had needs his wife couldn't meet, why didn't he tell her and let her decide whether to separate, get into the game or let him find release somewhere else? It would be the adult thing to do.

"I see. We only need this information, and I doubt there'll be any need for another interview or to tell his family."

Rodriguez relaxed and began to talk without any further prompting from her. The story matched the one of Davis' date, and was quickly told. After a minute, Jenn left the office as she had her own work to take care of, but before she did, Sharon watched her whispering to Carter, her friend's flirty side coming out. It didn't sit well with Sharon, even though it shouldn't have disturbed her.

After Rodriguez had finished writing down his statement, he asked her if he could leave once again. Not seeing any reason to keep him longer, Sharon told him he was free to go. She watched how Carter was uninteresting to Rodriguez now, as the man only addressed Carter briefly before he took his leave, walking as quickly as possible, his gaze glued to the ground.

She was alone with Carter. Again. This time on her turf. It should have given her the feeling of having an advantage. It didn't.

"Why did he want you to come with him?" Sharon asked.

"He's deathly afraid of the police. He came here as an illegal immigrant. Must've been around thirty years ago. He found work, became a legal citizen after about ten years and he's made a small fortune delivering groceries to disabled people or to those who won't leave their houses or apartments for whatever reasons. Still, he never lost his fear of the police."

It was nearly understandable. Not that it made the man any more likable to her. She ran a hand through her hair, twisting a lock around a finger before letting go of it, leaning back in the chair.

"He's married. Kids too, right? You spoke of his family."

"Three." Carter's smile was tired, even though he was dressed as impeccably as ever in a dark-blue shirt and black slacks, an expensive-looking coat hanging over the chair he was occupying. Should she offer him a coffee? Nope, she wouldn't—didn't—want to prolong his stay.

Never mind. From the smell of it, the coffee had gone stale hours ago. Mingling with Rodriguez's heavy cologne it was an almost nauseating stench permeating the office, only she was used to much worse thanks to her work.

"I don't get it. Why risk his marriage for something like this? And why do you know so much about him? Do you know such stuff about all of your customers?"

"No, but some of them want to talk before they make an appointment, find out what we offer, what they might need. Ernesto was one of them. We got to talking."

Rodriguez should've talked to his wife, not Carter.

"I see," she said.

"Do you? And you shouldn't judge him too harshly."

Anger rose up inside her. She'd been on the receiving end of cheating bastards twice and didn't care to repeat the experience. "I shouldn't? Really? What about his wife? Don't you think she deserves to know the truth? If he isn't doing anything wrong, then why doesn't he tell her where he is instead of lying to her face?"

She met Carter's gaze, although she couldn't read his expression. "It's not always that simple. Some people realize too late they need more than a normal relationship can provide them with."

No, she didn't agree. "I understand that this can happen. Yes, okay. People change. But to nurture a relationship, it needs honesty. Maybe his wife is happier not knowing. Who knows? Maybe she'd even prefer it that way, but as long she hasn't told him she doesn't want to be privy to such fundamental parts of his personality, he owes her the truth."

Carter studied her, and she understood instinctively he had learned more about her than she'd wanted him to. She wouldn't back down, though. If they didn't see eye to eye, so be it. There was a certain kind of beauty in agreeing to disagree.

"I'll give you that there's some drama involved in this. Ernesto's ashamed of what he is doing. Submitting to a Dom grants him temporary relief, but soon afterwards the shame sets in again."

"Did he tell you that?"

"No, he didn't need to. You just saw him. He can barely talk about it. He's in the closet when it comes to his proclivities."

What a nice way to phrase it. She raised an eyebrow, Carter raising one in return. How could she have had sex with him twice without learning more about him than that he owned a S&M club, liked to be in control of the game?

"So what he does isn't socially acceptable behavior. It is deemed *outlandish* by most, wouldn't you say?" she spoke out.

He smiled. "Did it seem outlandish to you last night?"

Sharon wanted to growl at him, but took a deep breath instead. This man drove her up the wall. She hated him, wanted him and part of her had begun to like him, the latter being the worst part of it all. It was hard enough to step away from some ill-fated passion and would be even harder if she had to face the fact that she was becoming emotionally attached to him.

She couldn't even say what it was about him she liked. His calm presence, his way of not taking any shit from her? He might like to dominate in the bedroom, but he didn't try to dominate her outside of it or tell her what to think. She'd met many men who said they didn't have a problem with an independent woman but changed their opinion as soon as they entered a relationship with one.

"I can't believe I rendered you speechless," he said with a hint of warmth in his eyes that demonstrated the point she didn't want him to prove. She'd lost herself in her own thoughts and had trouble focusing on him. It was time to get away from him.

"Last night is over."

"So you didn't like it?"

The smirk she hated and loved in equal measures was back. "Are you so insecure you need my

121

confirmation that your performance in bed was adequate?"

He huffed out a short laugh. "Some men would deem such a comment cruel."

"Are you one of them?"

"No, and I only asked because I want to know if I went too far or maybe not far enough. I want you to enjoy yourself, and I want to know how to make future meetings good for the two of us."

He has to be kidding, right? Why is he always so impossibly candid and brazen, so annoying?

"Who says there'll be a next time?" she asked, sitting up straight again.

"Do us both a favor and don't try to deny it." He gave her a long look. "Have I mentioned you look beautiful today?"

Sharon snorted. This morning she'd been too tired to bother with making herself presentable. She'd donned a pair of jeans, a black fitted shirt, a scarf and matching boots. Her hair was pulled back in a messy ponytail.

"It's another thing we will work on. I want you to be able to accept a compliment."

The door to her office opened, and had she paid any attention, she'd have seen Hastings approaching sooner. She snapped to attention.

"Sir?"

"I just met Reynolds outside. She said you interviewed a witness in the Davis case?"

He looked at her, then at Carter, clearly waiting for introductions to be made. Not her idea of a fun time. She gestured at Carter.

"Simon Carter. He's the owner of the club Marlene Davis died in."

She turned to Carter. "Mr. Carter, this is my superior, Luke Hastings."

Carter got up from the chair slowly, like a cat uncurling after a comfortable nap. The two men shook hands, taking each other's measure. Sharon wanted them both out. She quickly explained why Carter was here, and Carter did her the favor of claiming he had to get back to his club. To her relief, his goodbye was entirely impersonal, without even the tiniest hint of any personal relationship between them. It was what she had wanted, wasn't it?

Chapter Ten

Hastings waited until Carter had closed the door behind him before he addressed her again.

"Were you able to cross Carter off your suspect list?" While he stood at ease, there was a tension in his posture that hadn't been in Carter's.

"No. Not yet. But he's way down the list." The fact she still couldn't rule it out was the least of her problems — not something she would share with him.

"Okay. Keep me updated. I wanted to talk to you about something else anyway. I got a call from Igor Jones, Davis' boss."

Sharon raised her eyebrow, waiting for Hastings to continue.

"May I?" He looked at the seat Carter had just vacated.

"Sure. Would you like some coffee?" she asked as much to be polite as to stall for time.

"No, but thanks. To make it short, Jones said he felt cornered and threatened by you, and that he doesn't appreciate such behavior. I came here because I wanted to hear your side of the story."

Jones. The little weasel. She wasn't surprised. Wall Street wasn't known for its honest approach to business. People did and said what they thought would further their careers, honesty taking a backseat when it was needed. Making sure she kept Hastings' gaze, Sharon spoke slowly, making sure to sit still, willing her body to not betray her agitation.

"While I won't say he was lying when I talked to him first, Jones was definitely holding back, and my *threat* consisted of telling him I could always bring him in for a formal interview. I guess he didn't like it. But really, just because he has a lot of money doesn't mean anybody should grant him special privileges."

"May I assume, then, it was the manner with which you approached him that wasn't quite, well, let's say polite?" Hastings allowed a small smile to flicker over his face.

"Yes, you may."

"I thought so, and before you start to worry, I told him to call whomever he thinks he has to call, but that you were within your rights telling him he'd have to come in if he didn't give you the information you knew he was holding back."

Sharon raised her eyebrow. "I didn't know a thing."

"Which he wasn't aware of." Hastings' face gave nothing away. Like Carter, he had a good poker face, though that was where the similarities ended. While she considered Hastings a more or less open book, Carter was a mystery. She didn't know where she'd have to begin to unravel it.

"Thank you, sir."

"Not for that. By now you should know I'll always have your back."

"Your" back. Not "my people's" back. She liked him, truly did, but it would be easier for everybody if he started treating her like one of the guys.

Hastings got up, walked over to the door and opened it. "If I were you, I'd take a closer look at Carter. There's something not quite right about the man."

Sharon remained calm, smiling, even though the comment made her stomach churn. Carter wanted to fuck her, the same thing Hastings wanted. It was most likely the crux of the matter regarding Hastings' bad feeling, something she couldn't very well tell her boss. Anyway, she hoped it was only that and not Hastings proving to have a good gut instinct where she hadn't.

"Yes, sir."

Thankfully, Hastings didn't linger this time and closed the door behind him, leaving without a glance back. Sharon let out a relieved sigh, sitting back with her eyes closed. It wasn't noon yet, but it was already another draining day. No matter what, tonight she'd work out, run a bath and read, and nothing would stop her from doing so.

* * * *

It was easy to ignore her landline, easy to ignore her cell, but when there was a knock on her door, Sharon began to contemplate getting up from the couch, annoyed at whoever thought it was important to talk to her at ten in the evening.

Couldn't she have one evening to herself? She wasn't even on call, dammit. So far this evening had worked out like a charm. After working out in the precinct's gym for an hour, she had picked up some take-out on her way home, run a bath and grabbed a book afterwards. Delving into the world created by the author, she hadn't thought about anything, not about the case, her mother and her engagement, Carter, herself and what she'd learned about herself those last two nights. Her plan had been to read until her eyes were all but falling shut.

Sleep. She wanted to sleep, to relax. Damn it, she'd ignore whoever this was.

Her visitor had different ideas and knocked again, even more insistently this time.

With a growl no one would be able to hear, Sharon got up and walked over to her door.

"Hey, girl." Jenn, her fist still slightly raised, smiled before she passed Sharon.

"Do you have any idea how pissed I am right now?" Sharon didn't bother to tone down her frustration.

"The way you just looked at me tells me you'd like to strangle me." Jenn took a seat on her couch, put the blanket to the side, taking a look at her book. "A romance novel, really?" She snorted.

"Yes, really." Instead of sitting down beside Jenn, she remained standing, hoping her friend would catch her drift. No, she wouldn't. In the end, it was the same every time. Whenever Jenn was convinced Sharon had boy trouble, she would pop up. Sharon should've expected her sooner.

"Hey, I don't judge. And I actually read that one a month or so ago. It's pretty good."

Sharon crossed her arms over her chest. "Funny, somehow you don't strike me as the type for romance novels."

"Hey, I'm a romantic gal at heart." If she didn't know her better, Sharon would've believed the innocent smile. Like this, with her hair tangled, wearing an old pair of jeans and green sweater, Jenn could pass for a college girl instead of a seasoned cop. Anyway, it was time to cut to the chase.

"Sure you are. And are you going to tell me why you're here? If not, I'll go to bed and you can let yourself out." She'd actually prefer the latter, as she was tired and had been close to sleepy oblivion. She really didn't want to hear what her friend thought she had to tell her.

It was petty, no question about it, but the more egotistical side of her didn't want her good evening to be spoiled. For a second, Sharon considered telling Jenn to leave for good. Her friend would forgive her sooner rather than later, but in the end, she hesitated for too long. Jenn spoke before she could.

"He's fascinating, you know."

Yes, she knew. Still, she wouldn't admit to it. Jenn would have a field day. "Who are you talking about?" Denial. It was worth a try.

"Mr. Handsome, of course."

"Okay, let's create a list of suspects. I'll assume you're talking about somebody you met today, somebody I met, too, so I'd say you're either talking about Carter or Rodriguez."

Jenn shook her head. "While you're right, of course, it doesn't suit you to play dim-witted."

Sharon tapped her foot on the floor as much from impatience as the fact the floor was cold underneath her bare feet. "Dim-witted? Here I thought I made a clever deduction."

Jenn rolled her eyes and began to play with the fringe of her blanket. "Of course it's Carter."

"There's no accounting for taste, and who knows, Rodriguez might have met yours," Sharon said, close to ripping the blanket out of Jenn's hand. Her mother had crocheted it for her, and had given it to her the day she left home for college.

"How long have we known each other?"

For years—something Sharon usually valued as it meant she didn't have to put up any pretenses around Jenn. Although sometimes, like tonight, it was more annoying than useful that Jenn knew her so well.

"So you came here to tell me you find Carter fascinating?"

"No, I actually came here to tell you I now understand why you find Carter fascinating and that the feeling's mutual."

Sharon's heart rate sped up, her emotions jumping at Jenn's words while the more rational part of her wanted to deny having heard them. "I have no idea what you're talking about. Which seems to be the theme of the evening here."

"Yeah, yeah. By the way, don't you want to offer me a beer?"

"Would you like peanuts, too?" Sharon asked, but she turned towards her kitchenette anyway. "And don't tell me you forgot the location of my fridge. It hasn't moved since last week."

"Good to know. But it's been a long day, and I've been on my feet for most of it."

"Not only you, dear." Sharon was back with two beers. She handed one to Jenn and took the other one for herself.

"Thanks. So, to KISS, Carter…" Jenn began.

"To what?"

Jenn grinned. "Hon, you've got to work on your lingo, really. Keep it short and simple, K.I.S.S. Anyway, Carter's got a thing for you. I talked to him a while we were still waiting for you to arrive. Or to start at the beginning, I found those two in front of the office, let them in and well, Rodriguez was too busy biting his nails to engage in any conversation."

Carter had a thing for her? He claimed he found her attractive, it was obvious he liked to fuck her, enjoyed breaking someone into his lifestyle, but that didn't equal having a thing for someone. For her. "I doubt it."

"That Rodriguez is as much fun to talk to as a guppy?"

"No, that Carter's got a thing for me." Would she even like it if he had?

Jenn took a swig of her beer. "I'm a cop, duh. When I let him into the office, Carter took a look around, asked for you, and when I told him you weren't in yet, he said he'd wait, that you knew he was on the way. Then he didn't talk about the case for one more second. It was just small talk about everything and nothing."

"And?" Sharon took a sip of her beer, finally sitting down beside Jenn and pulling at her blanket with her free hand. Jenn looked at her for a moment, then let go of the blanket. *Good.*

"He's good at it, actually," Jenn continued. "Talking to him, it was interesting, amusing, but it was never about the case."

"And that's evidence he's into me? How many romance novels did you read?"

"Not as many as you might think. But of course that wasn't all. It was that the guy looked over at your desk again and again and again, as if waiting for you to appear out of thin air."

Yeah, definitely too many romance novels. "For a guy like that, time is money, I'm sure he was only impatient."

"Pardon my French, but he owns a club where people will bang if he's there or not. Anyway, call it a cop's instinct if you want to."

"I'll call it a wrong instinct." Sharon put her own bottle onto the table, not wanting more of it. "Listen, if that's all…"

"Yeah, yeah, you can go to bed in a few. No, that's not all. I tried to flirt with him, you know. I mean, come on, when do gorgeous guys appear in our office just like that? But guess what, he didn't react." Jenn sighed dramatically, laughing before draining half of her beer.

"Maybe you're just not his type, and flirting with a suspect is really not something you should engage in." She should have heeded that lesson herself. Although she hadn't flirted with Carter — only slept with him. Sharon's mouth was dry, and all she wanted was a glass of water to drown the bitter taste of failure.

"Sure. Never mind, it's not even my case. Anyway, to make my point, I might not be his type, but almost all men will flirt back, even if only a little. This guy was all serious, polite, funny and so disinterested it almost hurt. And before you start it, I'll bet my apartment he's not asexual either."

He wasn't. Jenn didn't need to fear for her belongings. Too bad. Sharon had better not share this information with her friend. Jenn would never leave, and nothing the blonde could say would make her feel better.

"He definitely was interested when you finally appeared. There was a glint in his eyes, just for a moment, but it was there. Anyway, listen," Jenn continued, suddenly serious. "I really hope you don't feel I overstepped a line here."

"Jenn, as much as I want to go to bed and get rid of you, it's not the first time you barged in here, and I'll bet *my* apartment it won't be the last time."

"No, not that. With Carter. That I flirted with him. I know you're interested in him."

Sharon sat up straight, glaring at Jenn. "I never said anything like that. It's not true, either. If you want to know if you're annoying me, well, right now you're pissing me off. Stop trying to see a romance where there is none. Carter's a suspect, for fuck's sake."

Give it to Jenn to not bat an eyelash while being ripped a new one.

"Tell me what you want. There's something going on, and I know it. Yes, I get you don't want to talk about it, but to sum it all up, this guy wants you, and I'm sorry I flirted with him."

Could Jenn be right after all? Sharon mentally kicked herself. This was nothing she should consider, not for a minute, not even for a second. If her own feelings about the matter were confused, it was more than enough to drive her to distraction. It wouldn't help to wonder what Carter's feelings were.

She put her feet up on the couch table, glad it was stable, remembering the time she'd made one of her parents' coffee tables shatter when she got overly active with her boyfriend at that time.

"Listen, Jenn. Thank you for stopping by, thank you for telling me this. You're mistaken, but it doesn't make this gesture any less sweet."

Jenn chuckled. "You know how long it has been since anybody called me sweet?"

"I think it hasn't happened since the time you stopped wearing diapers."

"You got it. Anyway, I still don't believe a single word of what you're saying, but to play devil's advocate, if you spoke the truth, you wouldn't mind if I happened to flirt with Carter again, given the chance, right?"

Sharon smiled. "No problem at all. Just, I doubt you'll have any reason to see him again, and if you were right about it all, he wouldn't care anyway."

Jenn put her right hand over her heart. "Now you hurt my feelings. You couldn't have phrased it a little nicer?"

She got up, Sharon following suit to hug her. It was good to have a friend like Jenn. Suppressing a sigh, she met Jenn halfway.

"I…listen, I know I'll need your open ear sometime soon, but let me get this straight in my own mind first, okay?"

"Take whatever time you need. And you know what? I've got a date tomorrow anyway."

"You do? With whom? And why don't I know about it?" How could she have missed this?

"You were a little busy these last few days, right?"

"I was, yes. So when did you meet him?"

"A bit over two months ago."

Sharon winced, guilty at not having noticed anything. She shouldn't be so full of herself that she wasn't aware of important changes in her friends' lives.

"I'm sorry. I should've noticed. So tell me about it."

"I met him while talking to a witness. He's a friend of said witness and well, we talked, exchanged numbers and yesterday he called out of the blue, invited me for burgers tomorrow. Couldn't say no to that, right?"

Sharon smiled. She was happy for Jenn. Hopefully, this time he wasn't a class-A jerk.

"What does he do for a living?" So far she'd seen Jenn date a biker associated with the Hells Angels, a sleazy attorney making his money in traffic law and a semi-professional football player. None of them had fallen into the category of men to take home and introduce to the family.

"You won't believe me anyway."

"Try me."

"A Baptist pastor."

Silence fell between them as Sharon tried to absorb the news. "This is…"

"Unexpected?"

"Yeah."

"I can't quite believe it myself. But he's nice, interesting, and I shouldn't say no to a date only because I met a nice man for a change."

"You're right. And now go home, get some sleep. I'll do the same." If she could fall asleep now, that was. To her surprise Jenn complied, hugged her once more and was gone as quickly as she'd appeared.

Sharon brushed her teeth and headed directly for bed, but sleep was slow in coming. Jenn and a pastor? While she had engaged in light BDSM play? Add to that her mother was engaged and Sharon had to admit the pieces of the kaleidoscope of her life had shifted and were in the process of forming a new picture. How it would look in the end, she truly couldn't say.

Chapter Eleven

Sharon hadn't expected Carter to try to get in contact with her. There was no reason for being so sure, but she had been. It turned out she was right.

Over a week had passed since she'd spoken to him for the last time. So much for Jenn's theory the man was smitten with her. This shouldn't irk her. Quite the contrary — she should be relieved. Instead, she wasn't, and not only because she still wasn't any closer to solving the riddle of Marlene Davis' murder. No new leads had popped up, the evidence collected didn't help with giving them a better picture of Davis' last minutes and she was still waiting to hear back from their IT department.

In the last few days, Sharon had spoken to all of Davis' friends again and her sister, but no one had any idea about her being involved in any financial fraud. Davis' sister had thrown a fit of epic proportions at the mere suggestion that her sister might not have been the angel everyone thought she was.

While the Davis case got colder and colder, Sharon had solved another case and had gotten a new one in. The Davis case would go on for a while longer, but if there weren't any new leads...

A few times she'd tried finding a reason to call Carter, only to stop herself in time. He would see through any flimsy excuses in a heartbeat. What did she want from him anyway? At least to herself she could admit that the answer to this one question was what she was shying away from. Lying to herself, though? It had never been her habit, and it shouldn't become one now.

Bottom line was—she'd enjoyed her time with Carter and wanted more of what he'd offered. Last night she'd woken up from an erotic dream in which she relived her last time with Carter, only this time he had used nipple clamps, had smacked her harder. What the fuck was wrong with her?

Nothing. Carter had said it himself. These were simple human desires—maybe not *normal* as they weren't shared by the majority of people, but they weren't wrong or forbidden either.

She sat up straighter in her office chair, arching her back. It was time to go home. Staying way past the point she was even able to concentrate wouldn't make her sleep any better later.

While she was on her way out, Hastings called out to her. "Richards, don't tell me you're only leaving now."

She turned and tried a smile even though he was still too far away for him to see her clearly. "I am. Why?" she called back.

She waited for him to join her. They walked the rest of the way together, and he held the door open for her.

Both faced the chilly night outside. Sharon was glad she'd thought about gloves and a scarf in the morning. Wasn't Hastings freezing in just a blazer?

"You were in at barely past seven this morning." He took up their conversation from before.

"I didn't know you were keeping track."

"I'm not, but I arrived around the same time."

Should she have noticed him? Most days she would have, but thanks to a certain case and one particular suspect, she was lost in her thoughts more often than not. "And you're leaving around the same time. It sounds like a case of the pot calling the kettle black if you ask me."

"In contrast to you, the city pays me a terrific salary."

"Sorry, sir. I happen to know that's not true. You may earn more than I do, but terrific would be something else. I guess you're as obsessed as I am."

"Which doesn't make it right. And although I feel like a broken record, I'll grab a sandwich now. Want to join me?"

"Yes."

Sharon had surprised herself. Why had she agreed to this when she knew it wasn't a good idea and she didn't really want to join him anyway?

Still, anything was better than spending another night moping. These last few nights she hadn't even been able to focus on her book and had instead watched any nonsense available on TV, her favorite being crime procedurals, which were as far from reality as they could be.

Hastings looked surprised by her ready agreement, but she shrugged it off.

"I'm hungry but too tired to bother with cooking later."

He hummed in agreement and smiled. "I know the problem."

"I didn't know you cooked."

"There's a lot you don't know. Actually, I enjoy cooking. I find it relaxes me. My ex-wife used to say I cooked better than she did."

It was the first time he had mentioned his ex-wife in her presence, which she was sure had more to do with her reluctance to cross professional borders than with his reluctance to talk about it.

"Was she right?"

"My ex-wife? Yeah. She managed to burn a pot while boiling water once. I hadn't even thought it was possible."

"I guess it made for a meager dinner that night."

He chuckled, the tension between them easing. Maybe there was a chance this would be all right.

The Jewish deli he had in mind was only three blocks away. While she'd walked past it a few times, she'd never actually gone in to try it out. There were only three small tables, but one was still free when they walked in.

"We're lucky. Most of the time, I'll eat my sandwiches to go. With this kind of weather, though, I prefer sitting inside."

He pulled out a chair for her and handed her the small menu. The woman manning the counter walked over a minute later, and Sharon ordered tea and a chicken sandwich. Hastings went for roast beef and a beer. It was after hours, so why shouldn't he?

"Now tell me, do you still insist on calling me *sir*?" Hastings asked, leaning back in his booth, his hands lying on the table in front of him. At least one of them appeared to be totally at ease.

"Yes, I do."

"Can't you make an exception for the duration of this dinner? I don't want to think about the job after hours."

If it were only that, Sharon would've readily agreed. How could she refuse something he had never clearly voiced, though? Would he ever come out and be upfront with her? She took a slow breath, studying the man in front of her. There was nothing wrong with him — nothing — except he wasn't the one who wormed his way into her thoughts far too often.

"Would you rather have me leave then? I'll only be a walking and talking reminder of work anyway."

He shook his head. "Nonsense. I've got no problems with separating my professional and private life. Do you?"

She never had. Not before she had met Carter. "No," she answered belatedly.

"Good. Then don't go for my jugular when I call you Sharon tonight, okay?"

"I would never dare, si…" She trailed off, holding up her hands. "Sorry."

"No problem. But see what I mean? My name's Luke."

Thankfully, their drinks came then, distracting him. Before she left, the woman informed them their sandwiches would follow shortly after. Good. Sharon was hungry. She had skipped lunch once again.

"Lucy is a true dear," Hastings said, looking after the small woman.

"You know her well?"

"I come here often, and when they had a problem with an armed robber a few years earlier, I made it my mission to find out who did it."

"And did you?"

"Yeah. I tend to get what I want."

That remark reminded her too much of Carter. It was hard not to make a face. "That's good. Tell me about the case, or does it remind you too much of work?"

"No, it's been years."

She relaxed a bit, lean back while he told her the story. He was good at it, too, his rich voice easily carrying. This was another man with an aura of command. It was something intangible. Some people had it, and some didn't. Hastings possessed it, as did Carter.

At the core, Hastings was a good man. His kind eyes lit up with amusement when he told her about interviewing an overly nervous suspect.

After a while, in spite of her earlier misgivings, Sharon had to admit she enjoyed her time with her boss, one hour turning into two. When they finally left, the deli was closing, and Sharon knew it would be another short night. She couldn't stop herself from yawning while they walked over to the subway.

"I enjoyed this evening, Sharon," Hastings said when it was time to part as he had to take a different line.

"Me too, sir."

She ignored Hastings' disapproving look. Nice as this impromptu dinner had been, it was time to put their natural boundaries into place again.

"See you tomorrow," she said.

She turned her back to him and walked down the stairs. Why, oh why, wasn't there any spark between the two of them? It would make things so much easier. Of course, it would be another attraction she had to ignore, but right now she'd do anything to stop thinking of the one man she couldn't forget. She got out her cell phone, her fingers hovering over her contact list. If she wanted to, she could call Carter right now.

No, it was a bad idea—way too late anyway. Tomorrow would be another day, and after a while she'd stop thinking about him at all. If she could only believe it herself.

* * * *

Sharon hated the fact she was relieved when there was an actual reason to talk to Carter two days later. A woman, one of the club's employees, had come forward, claiming she'd heard two women arguing loudly in the corridor a few minutes before Davis had been shot. This came as a surprise to Sharon, even if it shouldn't. Couldn't it have been a woman who had murdered Davis? If so, what was her relationship to Davis? By all means Carter shouldn't be any wiser than she was, but it couldn't hurt to ask him.

After considering calling him, Sharon decided on a personal visit instead. She was happy to leave the office behind for a while. She was at the club a little before eleven in the morning, wondering if he was even in yet.

He was. This time the bouncers let her in without any delay. She suspected they had been briefed. It was calm inside, almost eerily so. Was it too early for this kind of activity? Almost no place in New York was ever quiet, not the streets, not the precinct, not her apartment building. It was unnatural.

Outside Carter's office, she halted for a moment while multiple thoughts ran through her head, but none of them took hold. Finally she knocked and opened the door before he could even call out for her to come in.

He smiled upon seeing her and pointed at the chair in front of his desk. There was a cup of what she figured was tea in front of him. Some papers were scattered on the desk as well as a calculator. He had the sleeves of his sweater rolled up, and she knew she was looking at his muscled arms for too long.

"Please sit down."

She'd have preferred standing, but she could hardly begin pacing his office now. The hysterical urge to laugh at herself was hard to suppress, and she took a seat, hoping she looked calmer than she was.

"What can I do for you, Sharon?"

No *how are you* or *how have you been*. Despite her better judgment, she couldn't suppress a pang of disappointment. What had she expected, really? Most likely she had read too much into Carter's words. Who knew if he had found another woman to occupy his thoughts yet?

"We had another witness, female, come forward, and I wanted your take on her report. She—"

For the first time, he interrupted her. She had caught him by surprise. "A female witness?"

"Yes, one of the women working here. I hope you won't give her any trouble because she came to talk to us."

His expression darkened, the fingers of his right hand clenching. "Who do you think I am?"

Congrats. She'd managed to piss him off. *I obviously have a knack for it, and maybe I shouldn't enjoy it.* It was only a tiny part of her, yet she was satisfied with having gotten a reaction out of him. No human being was calm and composed all the time. They all were rattled by something, even one Simon Carter. When he spoke, he still hadn't quite found his equilibrium.

"No customer and no employee have ever been mistreated here."

"It's been over two weeks since Marlene Davis died, and the woman in question came forward only now? It makes me wonder what she was afraid of."

His eyes narrowed, but she refused to look away.

It was about time she admitted she was pissed herself. Carter had made her feel discarded, like just another case of fuck 'em and forget 'em. While it was definitely better for her career if he forgot she even existed, she didn't relish the thought that she'd put everything on the line for someone who wasn't even interested in calling her.

She was being ridiculous, but emotions running high did that to her.

How could somebody who had seen every inch of her be such a stranger? What did it mean for people to remove their masks and show their true self to someone else?

She'd done it twice so far, had trusted a man with her heart and feelings, and where had it ended? Not in a happy relationship, that much was sure.

It was she who looked away first and Carter who ended the silence that began to feel strained, even more so than usual.

"Well, you can rest assured no one will face the danger of losing their job only because they told the truth. In fact, it is rather interesting to see how this murder has influenced business."

"What do you mean?" What was he going for?

His voice was hard. "The first two days, business was down to an all-time low, people being scared they could be the next one to die. As people calmed down, their fear abating, they all but streamed in here. Morbid curiosity, I guess. An extra thrill. Although by now it seems they are all tired of the talk in the corridors, the question of why Davis had to die. We're all ready to be done with it. So I'm glad new information popped up. I want this to be over as much as everybody else."

It wasn't a criticism directed at her. Still, she bristled. "We're doing what we can, but I can't pull the murderer out of a hat."

Carter sighed and closed his eyes briefly, running a hand through his short hair. The tired gesture made him seem more human, more approachable.

"This is not going to work, Sharon. We're on the same team, so let's focus. Now what did my employee tell you?"

He was right. She took a moment to compose herself, so she could be sure she had her emotions in a tight grip. "She said she heard two women argue loudly not long before Davis got shot. Working with the theory one of the women was Davis, do you have any idea who the other woman could've been?"

He took his time to think about it, finally shook his head. "No. I'm sorry."

It had been a long shot, but she'd had to ask. Now she was back to square one. They had a list of all the people who had been in the building by the time police arrived and had interviewed them. Talking to these people, they had learned about a few more who had left quickly or who had been in and left before Davis' murder. All in all, they were talking about forty-seven people, twenty-five of them women. It would be a long day trying to get in contact with all of them once again. Maybe Jenn could lend her a hand.

"I was afraid you'd say that. Thank you for your time anyway."

She didn't want to go, but with no reason to stay, it was better she left before she could say something, do something she'd regret later.

"What do you think this means?" Carter asked as she started to get up.

She shrugged, slumping back into her chair. "I've got no idea. It doesn't fit into any picture I considered so far. Davis wasn't into women as far as we know, her friends didn't know she was a customer here, at least no one admitted to it, and her customers wouldn't have known either. Why she could've gotten into an argument with some woman here…no idea."

The sympathy in Carter's eyes was unexpected. "Is it often that way?"

"What?"

"Your work. The dead ends."

"Yes. Or better said, it often happens with the more complicated cases. A lot of our investigations consist of following standard procedure. With the easier cases, I spend more time writing reports than actually investigating. This is one of the more complicated ones. There's no clear motive, or at least the only motive doesn't fit in with any of the evidence."

While she wasn't giving him any details, she shouldn't talk to him about the case at all. It was another thing they could have her head for.

"I really have to leave now. Thanks again for taking the time." She was glad she didn't hesitate this time, just stood, turned her back to him.

"Why are you angry with me?"

She should have known he wouldn't make it easy for her. Slowly, she faced him again, not sure what to say. There was too much she'd like to say, too little she should. "I'm not angry."

"You are. Tell me." No 'please'. It wasn't even a question, just another command. This was the man she'd gotten to know. Although wasn't that just one facet of his personality?

"You know, I'm tired of your games." She was. Was not.

"Which games?"

Sharon shook her head. "Listen, let's keep it professional. It's better this way."

He laughed. "We crossed that line two weeks ago."

"Yes, we did, and since then you crossed me off your mind. Which is good. I did the same with you. So let's not revert back to our very mistaken ways."

He had the audacity to smile. One of her hands curled into a fist, but she stayed calm.

"Do you remember what I told you?" he asked. He straightened as well, walking over to her until he was well into her personal space. Her shitty hormones were wreaking havoc on her mind. She wanted to step back, to step in closer so she could catch a whiff of the scent she'd learned to associate with him.

"You said a lot of things." It came out quieter and more tired than she wanted it to.

"Yes, I did. And I'm talking about telling you that I wouldn't force myself on you. I would've liked it very much if you'd called, but there was no reason for me to call you. I've already made up my mind. You have to make up your mind for yourself."

"I don't understand." She thought she had. What if she was mistaken, though?

"You do," he said, cupping her chin and making her look at him. "I want to see you again. I want to really get to know you, but only if it's what you want as well." He leaned in and kissed her with infinite tenderness that could shatter her if she allowed it. It was the last thing she'd have expected of this man.

In all his dealings with her, he had never been unkind, but this — she wasn't prepared for the soft slide of his lips against hers. The moan she couldn't control was audible proof of her body betraying her mind, of a fight lost. Carter kissed her again and again, until her lips softened against his and she kissed him back. He didn't try deepening the kiss and neither did she.

He stepped away, his hand lingering on her shoulder, the look in his eyes open. "I have no idea what this thing between us is or what it could be, but I'm interested in seeing where it goes."

He let go of her and went back to his desk, beginning to sort his papers. Now it was up to her. It was another time she really wanted him to make a decision for the both of them, yet he wouldn't. It was right that he didn't, as it would eventually destroy everything that could be between them. She had to be on board with this, had to make her own decision. How? The turmoil in her mind was the fast lane to the abyss of an emotional mess.

For a long minute, she stood there, indecision tearing at her. None of her relationships with a man had been based on so much honesty before.

Relationship? No one was talking about a relationship. She wasn't, for sure. Right?

Still, she was used to the eons' old game of courtship, of showing one's best side, of flirting to see what would happen next. Things would progress over time, the other's personality only slowly unraveling, a mystery waiting to be uncovered. If that was the right way, why hadn't it worked out in her favor, though?

There were no pretenses with Carter. He knew who he was and what he wanted, and didn't try to hide it. Not that she really knew him. Who was the man beneath it all? She was sure she hadn't seen him yet, not all of him. He didn't know everything about her, either. After all, she'd never bothered with showing him her gentler side. She almost snorted.

"How about dinner?" she heard herself ask.

He looked up, his eyes widening a fraction. It made her want to smile. "Where? And when?"

"Today. Somewhere neutral," she said, meaning neither his nor her apartment. She suggested a small Vietnamese restaurant.

"So you like it hot?" he teased.

"And spicy, yes," she said in her best deadpan voice.

Sharon smiled then, and he returned the smile. For the first time, she felt like herself in front of him. At least it was a true reaction, not one clouded by anger and trying to hide herself from the man in front of her.

"How about eight?" Carter asked.

"Yes. I'll have a lot on my plate today. Should I be delayed or not able to make it, I'll let you know."

"I'll give you my private cell phone number."

Carter walked to his desk and took a small sheet of paper, jotting down his number. He held it out to her. His thumb brushed her hand when she walked over to take it from him. The brief contact sent a shiver down her back.

"Gotta go."

"Of course. See you later," he said, walking back to his desk. A last smile, and she let herself out. Passing through the house, she heard some voices. A couple in leather walked by her in the hallway. For once there was no feeling of strangeness, not at the sight or the sounds. She was evolving...she just wasn't sure into what.

Chapter Twelve

Sharon made it home by seven, which left her with just enough time to have a quick shower and change into fresh clothes before she would have to hurry to the restaurant. After considering wearing a dress, she decided against it. Whatever she wore shouldn't scream 'date'. While she'd opened up to the possibility of seeing Carter again in the future, and not only because she wanted to have sex with him, there had been no talk about it becoming a romantic affair in any sense of the word.

Grabbing a pair of cotton panties, she snickered. The last thing she could imagine was Carter in front of her door, holding a bouquet of flowers in his hand, waiting to wine and dine her.

After another five minutes in front of her closet, Sharon had had enough of her own indecision. She went for a tight pair of jeans and a sweater that showcased her cleavage, and added some simple jewelry. Brushing her hair, she decided to wear it down. Giving herself a once-over, she thought she didn't look like a woman wanting to seduce a man, but also not like someone coming just from work.

What was it with people caring about their appearance all the time anyway?

She only noticed the red light blinking on her answering machine when she buttoned her coat. She went over to see who had called. If it was Carter to tell her he had to cancel, well, in such a case, so be it.

It wasn't Carter but Hastings, telling her he had two tickets for the opera next week. He wanted to know if she were interested in going with him. Also, he had something to tell her. So he was finally making his move.

Sharon sighed. She didn't want to know what it was. Her gut feeling insisted she wouldn't like it. Well, she'd call him back later, or even better, stop by his office tomorrow and tell him thank you, but she wasn't interested. Yeah, that would be best. It would be easier to tell him off at a place where everything reminded them of their jobs and responsibilities.

Realizing she had to hurry, Sharon made it to the restaurant with five minutes to spare. She was about to enter when Carter called out to her. Stopping, she looked around and spotted him only a few yards away, coming from the other direction.

"I'm impressed," he said, holding the door open for her.

"With what?" she asked, entering and waiting inside for him to catch up.

"That you're punctual."

She rolled her eyes, bore his scrutiny when he took her in. "You know, it's a myth women aren't able to be punctual. If it's up to me, I always am."

He gave a small smile. "So I see. It's a nice change."

"It seems you tend to date the wrong women."

"I rarely ever date, but I agree."

It fit with what he had told her before, that it wasn't his habit to seduce women. And yet, a good-looking man like him, with manners and money to spare, shouldn't have problems finding a date. It wasn't her business, but his. This place didn't have a host and he was obviously waiting for her to choose a table, so she led the way.

It was a big restaurant, noisy, with the clatter of pots in the background, and the loud voices of people trying to communicate. It wasn't a cozy or romantic place — one of the reasons she'd chosen it. That and it offered some of the best Vietnamese food in the city, at least in her opinion. Carter didn't seem to mind either. He followed her to a table beside one of the windows looking out on the street.

"Have you been here before?" she asked him when she opened her menu. She knew what she'd order, but somehow she didn't want to admit she went to this place every other week and knew the menu by heart.

"Yes, once or twice. Seeing you suggested it, I take it you've been here before as well."

"You're right." What could she say? She loved the smell of grease, curry and other exotic spices, liked to be surrounded by people without having to communicate.

"Too bad we didn't get the chance to meet before," Carter said with a twinkle in his eyes, making her forget all about dinner for a second. Was this man poison or an aphrodisiac for her senses? Damn her if she knew.

"Who says we didn't?"

He shook his head. "No, Sharon. I'd know if we had. I'd have noticed you."

Would he? She was never the only woman in here, never the most beautiful. Looking around right now, she noted a group of young women only a few tables away. They all looked to have Asian backgrounds, and they all were petite and dressed to impress. "You sound sure," she finally said.

"I am."

She decided to give him the benefit of a doubt, to play along, at least for the moment. "So would you have talked to me if you'd seen me here?"

The waitress interrupted them, then asked for their orders. Sharon raised an eyebrow and locked gazes with Carter. This discussion wasn't finished.

Focusing on the waitress, Sharon ordered a spicy chicken dish. Carter wanted beef.

"No, I wouldn't have," he answered as soon as the waitress was out of earshot. The disappointment settled in her stomach with a sudden pang. What had she thought? Flirting with...

"I'd have studied you, would've come to the restaurant again and again, in hopes of finding you here." He sounded earnest, yet his statement rubbed her the wrong way.

"So is this your way to go about relationships? Stalk your prey before you single it out and take it down?"

He sighed. "I know you don't know me well enough to really trust me, but I don't think I've ever given you reason to mistrust me on an instinctual level."

"It's not... Okay, I apologize." It wasn't mistrust, but something inside her had recognized early in the game that this man could be dangerous to her control, her heart.

"Accepted. To answer your question, haven't you ever met someone interesting, and gone to the same place again in hopes of spotting this person once more? It could be on the bus, in the gym, anywhere."

Yes, she had. As a teenager she'd fallen for the captain of the lacrosse team. She'd visited several games in hopes he would finally notice her.

"I might have."

"So you know that feeling. And to finish this thought, yes, eventually, I'd have spoken to you. And, yes, I'm sure. Now ask me something."

"Huh?" She brushed her hair over her shoulders, wishing she'd decided on a ponytail.

He watched her every gesture. "If we want to learn to trust each other, if we want to get to know each other, we should start asking questions, don't you think?"

He was right. Though, what would she uncover if she got to know him better? Would he lose some of his charisma, his charm, or would she want to know even more? It was a risk, but they couldn't go on like they had forever.

She gave him her best innocent smile, causing him to raise an eyebrow. "Tell me your favorite color, your favorite book and a memory of your childhood."

"Greedy."

Her smile widened. "I prefer to call it efficient."

They got their drinks, water for them both, and he raised his glass in a silent toast.

"I like red. It's a rich color, vivid. My favorite book is *The Power of One*. Now about my childhood..." He relaxed slightly, looking out of the window.

Has he noticed it's begun to rain and spotted that man trying to urge his dog to move faster? Most likely, he hadn't, and was lost in memories of his past. She faced him, waiting for him to speak.

He met her gaze again. "When I was about five, our dog died. I loved him as much as I loved my parents, maybe even more. We spent all the time together when I was at home. I was heartbroken, and my parents couldn't console me." He stopped, looking down at the table for a moment.

"That's a sad story."

He met her gaze. "Not really. That's life. And you didn't insist I tell you a happy one."

"Okay, I'll give you that. Please, go on."

"A few days after we had buried him in the yard, I told my mother I would never love anyone as much as I loved the dog. His name was Rusty, by the way."

Sharon ignored the impulse to reach out, to cover his hand with hers. "Your poor mother. How did she take it that you loved the dog more than you loved her and your dad?"

"My mother was a wonderful woman. She was very laid-back and down to earth."

So she was dead. Sharon couldn't imagine losing her own mother, although she'd never given much thought to losing her dad either, and it had hurt worse than she could've ever imagined, even though she'd been an adult when it happened.

Carter continued, and she cut off her musings.

"That day, she kneeled down in front of me, held me close and told me I might not believe her, but there would be a time when I would find someone special, a partner to share my life with. It would take its time, no one could hurry destiny, but it would happen."

Her heart beat faster as she contemplated whether he wanted to tell her something with this story. Surely not, or… "Did you believe her?"

He laughed. "No, I didn't, but I never forgot her words either."

"Did your mother really say partner?"

"As in instead of woman? So you picked up on it."

"Yes, I did. Cop, remember? It doesn't do to miss details. Sometimes it happens, but most of the time we're rather good with them."

His smile was as warm and open as she'd ever seen it. "I noticed. To answer your question, yes, she did. My uncle lives in San Francisco together with his partner, Ronald. While my mother's family was highly homophobic, it didn't transfer to her. And when I grew up, she used to tell me she didn't care who I was in love with as long as I was capable of love."

This was her first true glimpse into a man who had been an enigma so far. She had no trouble admitting to herself that she liked what she'd heard. It made Carter appear more human, more normal, although the more he said, the more questions she had.

When it came down to it, he was still the most controlling human being she'd ever met, and she hadn't quite figured out if it was who he was or what life had made him.

"Do you believe in destiny then?" she said. "I might be wrong, but so far you don't seem to have found the love of your life."

He almost always gave questions some thought before he answered them. It was another area of his life he had in a tight grip. Although there hadn't been a second of hesitation when he'd talked about his mother. No, she couldn't figure him out.

"It's true, I haven't, and no, I don't believe in destiny. I've seen a lot of people chasing after the concept of love without ever finding the one to spend their life with."

She agreed. She believed it was possible to love quite a few people in one's life, that there wasn't only one person who was right for. Love was one part of a relationship. The other was hard work. Her parents had clearly been in love, but their relationship hadn't only consisted of sunshine and rainbows. There had been anger, arguments and frustration, but they had dealt with it and trudged on, their relationship as strong as could be.

"Your turn," Carter said, pulling her out of her reverie.

"What do you mean?"

"I answered some of your questions, now I want you to answer some of mine."

"You didn't say this was how it's supposed to be."

"But I reckon you to be a fair person, and I think it's a fair proposal." There was a playful, amused note to his voice that made it hard not to smile back.

She spotted the waitress coming over with their dinner, the scent mouthwatering. They both thanked the young woman, who left quickly to serve the next customer.

"Okay, what do you want to know?"

She took up her fork and picked up a piece of chicken and some rice, her eyes falling shut as she closed her lips around it. The scent might be delicious, but the taste was nothing short of heavenly. When she opened her eyes again, she found Carter was looking at her, smiling.

"I didn't want to interrupt your private moment."

"It's…I guess I happen to love Vietnamese," she said.

"You don't have to apologize."

"I wasn't."

He inclined his head. "Now my questions."

Instead of asking them, though, he took a bite of his dinner, too. Typical, somehow. If he thought it would throw her off her equilibrium, he had to try harder. She waited, and continued to enjoy her own dinner in the meantime.

"Answer the same questions you asked me."

It was her turn to smile, something that came easier now. "That's lame. You could have thought up some original questions."

"Well, next time, I'll choose the questions and you can feel free to ask me the same."

"I'll hold you to it."

"Do that." He had taken time to answer his questions, and now he gave her the same time to find answers to them.

"I love blue. No special reason. Although it reminds me of better weather, a blue sky, anything but these endless East Coast winters, really. My favorite novel, I don't think I have one. I enjoy many books a great deal."

"Pick one."

"I would only name a different one next time you asked me." She was always surprised when people could readily state their favorite novel. She had read hundreds, liked most, but none of them had influenced her more than the others.

"Doesn't matter." The note of command in his voice was back.

"Your decision. In that case I'd say *The Shadow of the Wind*."

He picked up another piece of beef with his fork. "I don't know this book."

"If you want, I could lend it to you."

He nodded. "Thanks. I'd like that." The normalcy of the discussion, this evening, was almost weird. *"Never drink tea with a suspect,"* as her first superior had liked to say. Well, tea definitely wasn't involved here.

"What about your childhood memory?"

This question was the hardest. There were so many to pick from, all of them special, none of them more so than the others. Then she remembered Ava.

"You look sad," he remarked even before the feeling had taking root inside her chest.

"It's a sad memory. Anyway, I was ten, my brother was twelve, and we were friends with Ava, a girl living on the next street. She was eleven, so she was good company for both of us, although she was closer to James than she was to me."

Even after over two decades, she could remember Ava vividly, her big smile, her curly blonde hair, her eyes full of mischief. Life truly wasn't fair.

"One day when we were at home, there was a call, Ava's mother, asking us if we had seen her daughter."

She could see Carter already knew where this was going, and not sharing her qualms, he reached over, covering her free hand with his, their fingers linking as if of their own volition.

"No, we hadn't seen her. No one else had either. We were all frightened. They, well, they looked for Ava for five days."

It was a surprise that even after not having thought of Ava in years, tears still sprang to her eyes when she remembered her former friend. Tears were not a sign of weakness. It was a lesson her mother had tried teaching her time and again, confirmed by her father, who hadn't cried often but didn't try hiding his tears when they came either. She understood the truth of the statement, yet it had never quite sunk in. Now she was a cop, was supposed to be strong, to be above tears. It was not healthy trying to keep it all inside, but to lose the hard-won respect of her male colleagues? Not an option.

Carter gave her the time she needed to blink back the tears, calm a little. She cleared her throat.

"They found her in an abandoned warehouse a few blocks away."

"I figure she didn't die of natural causes?" His voice was calm, soothing her frayed nerves.

"No, she didn't. She was raped, then strangled." It was a harsh truth, but softening it with nice words wouldn't make Ava alive again, wouldn't make her death less painful.

"I'm sorry." The proper thing to say, yet it was such an empty phrase. Those words never made anything better, no matter what. How often had she told the families of victims she was sorry, feeling it, yet it didn't change a damn thing?

"Did they get the person who killed her?"

"Yes. They did. It took them nearly a year to find Ava's murderer, but they caught him. It was a priest originally from another community who had taken over when the local priest had died. You can imagine the scandal, I guess."

"You never know where evil hides."

"True." She hoped the vile bastard was still rotting in prison.

"What happened to Ava's parents?"

It wasn't the first time she'd spoken about Ava, but it was the first time someone had asked her about the girl's parents.

"Did you know people hardly ever ask about the relatives and friends of victims? Although they are the ones who will suffer the longest. Forever, really."

Carter nodded once. "It's easier that way. It costs people to deal with others' pain, and they'd rather pretend it's nothing that could ever happen to them."

"I agree. Anyway, Ava's mother started drinking. She died about ten years later. The father hooked up with his secretary, had another baby and Elena, Ava's sister, she was—no, she *is*—two years younger than Ava. She's a very strong woman. I admire her for not giving up when life around her fell apart. She's an attorney in Kansas City and rumor has it she's going to marry this year."

She took a sip of her water then looked down at her dinner, which had lost its appeal to her. She pushed the plate away.

"Don't."

"Pardon me?"

"This is a good meal. The past is the past and all the hurt you're feeling won't change a thing about it. Don't let it drag you down again. Enjoy this evening, enjoy being alive, this dinner."

She looked from him to her dinner and back, torn between wanting to argue, disregard him or admit he was right. "I lost my appetite."

"And you won't get it back if you push your dinner away. Sharon, I don't have to be clairvoyant to know this story shaped you, made you suffer time and again. Don't let it ruin tonight."

Reluctant, she picked up her fork and took a tentative bite. It didn't taste as good as it originally had but it didn't taste bad either. It was a good meal. Carter was right.

"I didn't mean to ruin the evening," she said.

"You didn't. I thank you for your honesty. So this is what made you want to become a cop?"

"Yes. I could see how the murder and the mystery about it tore at the people around me. Parents were overly suspicious, children were afraid and it broke Ava's family. I thought about it so damned often, trying to find out who killed Ava and why. To make a long story short, yes, she made me join the force."

Silence spread between them. It wasn't uncomfortable. Just, there wasn't anything particular to say at that moment. Often enough there was talk for the sake of talking—thankfully not tonight. Sharon relished being with a person who could accept periods of silence. She took another bite then looked around the room at the other customers.

"Do you ever wonder about their lives?" she asked.

"About the lives of random people? Yes. I think this, too, is human nature."

The rest of the evening they didn't talk about any more personal things—it was just small talk. If she'd ever allowed herself to think about dating Carter, she wouldn't have thought it could be so damned easy.

After dinner he insisted on paying, and didn't want to accept her refusal.

"Is it so bad if someone wants to treat you to something?"

"No, it isn't."

"Would you make the same fuss if it were a female friend?"

No, she wouldn't. She and Jenn invited each other to dinner all the time. But he wasn't a female friend, but an attractive man she was very aware of, one she could fall for if she weren't careful. It had been some time since she had really opened her heart to someone, and Carter was the wrong one to do so—at least, her warning bells cautioned her to keep a certain distance between them.

In the end she caved in, because she didn't want to argue any longer. After all, it was only dinner.

"You can pay next time," he said. She would hold him to it.

They left the restaurant soon after, pausing on the walkway. Sharon's heartbeat accelerated while she debated what to do next or if she wanted him to ask her for a nightcap. Okay, she wanted to be with him again, to feel the incredible rush she'd felt the two times she'd had sex with him.

Carter closed the distance between them and leaned down for a brief kiss. "I enjoyed this evening. Thank you. Shall I see you to the subway?"

That was it? He had to be kidding? First he all but seduced her upon meeting her and now it was 'thanks for dinner and goodbye'?

"I...no, thank you. I know how to take care of myself."

"I never doubted it. So it's goodbye then."

It was his loss, right? He stepped back, and she just knew he was aware of what she was thinking.

"It's still your decision," he said. "If you want to talk to me, call. If you want to meet for dinner, we can. If you want to have sex, it'll be my pleasure. And if you want to play...the same."

He was reasonable. Still, she wasn't used to a man treating her like that. She needed time to think.

"Goodnight, Carter." She turned around.

"Goodnight, Sharon."

Chapter Thirteen

What did she want?

It was the question Sharon had been contemplating for the last two days, not being able to find a good answer to it. Not only was there a difference between what she was allowed to want, seeing as they had never closed the Davis case, and what she wasn't, but the options Carter had given her came with different implications.

If she were smart, she'd either transfer the case to someone else because there was a conflict of interest, or finally forget about Carter. Simple, but, knowing her, impossible. So if she didn't want to give up the job or Carter, she had to decide what she wanted from him. Did she only want to trust him with her body, and if yes, how far was she willing to take it, or was she willing for her heart to become involved as well? Even more, could she protect it from being involved if she chose the former?

Being a reasonable adult, making decisions she could defend to others, to herself, shouldn't be so damned hard. If she could only get her heart, her mind and her body to be on the same page.

At least she didn't have much time to sit back and contemplate her love life.

Within the last couple of days there had been a breakthrough in another case, and they had nailed the victim's husband, who was now in prison, waiting for his trial. She'd also tried to find out who it was Davis might have talked to. Of course, no one had seen a thing—no one had any idea who it could have been or why someone would have argued with Davis that day. No one stepped forward to admit she was the woman in question. Soon, Sharon would have to decide if she should discard the notion there had been a second woman and follow other leads, or rather search for them.

Jenn's opinion was no secret. Her partner didn't say a thing but clearly thought she was putting her money on the wrong horse. Sharon was still convinced there was something to this story. There had to be. Furthermore, Jenn had avoided her as much as possible lately, which more than anything else was a sign Sharon's mood was unbearable to those around her.

Sharon had just come in from talking to one of Davis' colleagues, who had given her a hint which projects might have been contaminated, when she all but ran into Hastings, who smiled at seeing her.

"Just the woman I was looking for."

As long as he was smiling, he couldn't be pissed with her. At least that was something.

"What can I do for you, sir?"

"I need to talk to you for a few minutes. Let's do it in my office."

As a no wasn't an option, she followed him through the maze of corridors. Some people were throwing them looks, most of them uninterested, a couple of them speculating what it could be about. Sharon wondered herself but reserved her questions for later. Hastings opened the door to his office and let her pass him before he closed it. Was he about to bring up the fact she'd never called him back regarding the opera tickets? She'd wanted to. Actually, the day after his call, she'd tried to talk to him, but he hadn't been in and she'd forgotten about it since then.

"Please take a seat."

She did as she was asked, waiting for him to sit down behind his desk as well.

"Let's make it brief. I'm leaving the precinct."

Talk about dropping a bomb without any kind forewarning. Sharon hadn't known what to expect, but this, no. It hadn't even been a tiny blip on her radar.

"This is…a surprise. Where will you be going? What are you going to do?"

And why the hell was he telling her? Was he talking to everybody in person when a general announcement would save them all time?

"I'll start at the twentieth precinct next week. It's a promotion, so to say."

"I… Well… Congrats, sir." She had to get a grip now. She was no bumbling idiot.

"Thanks, Sharon." That he had addressed her with her first name again told her more than she wanted to admit. Telling her was personal to him. Dammit.

"Who will be your successor?"

"Captain Kelly from the first precinct. He's a good cop. You'll like him and his style."

She'd heard of Kelly, and what was said fit with Hastings' assessment, but at the end of the day, they'd have to see. Not that they had much of a choice anyway.

"I trust your instincts, and I wish you all the best, sir. If that is all…"

"No, it isn't. There's something else I'd like to address. It's actually related to the fact I'll be leaving the precinct."

Sharon had a sinking feeling in her stomach, and realized where this would lead now. She really didn't want to hear what he had to say. Her life, as it was at the moment, was complicated enough. She didn't need this. Didn't need him.

"I…"

"After I've left, I'd like to see you again."

She could claim not to understand what he was talking about, but they both knew she was smarter than this. "I don't know. I mean, we've worked together for several years, and…"

He interrupted her, a frown on his face. "Listen, if I read this all wrong, just tell me, and we'll pretend I never asked, but…I thought you liked our dinner last time. I know I have, and I'd like to repeat it, to get to know you better, especially now as it won't mean crossing professional boundaries."

Oh, she'd proven she was willing to cross the line — that was not the problem. It was that she didn't think she could fall for this man, that this could lead them anywhere. A month ago, who knew? Right now her mind was filled with another man. Still, if she gave up on this chance now, who knew if there'd be another? It was easy to deduce Hastings was the better choice of man, at least in the long run.

"I enjoyed dinner, too." It wasn't technically a lie, more like she was omitting part of the truth.

"Then why are you looking so unhappy?"

Just because Hastings was generally a less intuitive man than Carter was when it came to her, that didn't mean he didn't have sharp instincts, wasn't able to read people. It was one of many reasons he had made captain quickly.

"I'm not." She tried to smile. "This is just a big surprise, and while I'm happy for you, I'm not all that happy to lose you as superior, sir."

"As much as I like to hear it, I think you can call me Luke now without breaching any protocol."

"Let's talk about this next week...sir."

He chuckled. "You are incorrigible. So if I invited you to a date, say Saturday in a week, would you say yes?"

Yes or no. It was an easy enough question to answer. Yes or no? It was another case of weighing what she wanted to do against what she should do.

"I would say yes." She noticed the tiny flicker of surprise, hiding her smile. So he hadn't been sure of the outcome of this either.

"Good. How about I'll make a reservation? Do you have any preferences?"

"I doubt I'd like French cuisine. Everything else is fair game," Sharon said.

"Good. Expect me to call you about the details. Could you do me a favor, please?"

What was it now? Wasn't she already doing him a favor?

"Of course."

"Could you tell Reynolds to come to interview room two at three p.m.? You, too, please. I'll tell the others to be there. I'll make an official announcement then. So if you could keep it confidential until then, I'd be grateful."

"I will." Sharon was glad Hastings didn't try keeping her any longer. She'd be able to breathe more freely once she'd left his office.

She found Jenn in their office, bent over her desk, a frown on her face while she studied some pictures, most likely crime scene photos.

"Are you okay?"

"Yeah, yeah. Just some facts not making sense. Right now it looks as if two and two equal five."

Sharon shrugged out of her blazer. The time for winter coats was finally over. "If you need any help, let me know. By the way, Hastings wants us all in interview room two at three p.m."

Jenn looked up briefly. "Is it about him transferring to twentieth precinct and Kelly taking over here?"

Sharon snorted and walked over to their coffee machine. There was none left, but it would hardly brew itself. "Where did you hear that now?"

"I have my sources." Jenn grinned.

"And why didn't you tell me?"

"The same reason you wouldn't have told me more than that Hastings wants to see us all. Boss man doesn't want any information to leak early and we should respect that."

"True. But again, how did you know?"

"If you've got any kinds of sweets lying around, I want them and I promise I'll tell you everything. I could die for a healthy dose of sugar."

"That bad a morning?"

"Just this case giving me a headache. Reports starting to pile up on top of reports. Anyway…"

She held out her hand. Sharon rolled her eyes, opened her drawer anyway. While she didn't have a stash of candy, there were always one or two pieces around for whenever she felt the need. She handed Jenn a candy bar which her friend unwrapped with haste.

"Do you remember Aziz?"

Aziz was a former colleague who had left the precinct a few years ago.

"I do, why?"

"He transferred from fifth precinct to twentieth precinct last year. I ran into him when I passed by last week. To make a long story short, he heard about Hastings transferring and wanted me to verify if it was true."

Sharon wasn't surprised. People couldn't keep a secret for long if they were surrounded by cops.

"There's only one thing that is truly interesting, I think," Jenn said, biting into her candy, closing her eyes, moaning loudly. "God, this is better than sex."

It depended on the sex, didn't it? Sharon would prefer the sex she'd had lately to chocolate. She all but snorted. All roads might not lead back to Rome but rather to Carter, didn't they?

"You don't want to know?" Jenn asked her, making Sharon realize she'd zoned out.

"Pardon me?"

"You don't want to know what is interesting?"

"You'll tell me anyway."

"Party pooper. But yes, I will. Doesn't it make you wonder why Hastings told you and you alone in person this morning and will only tell everybody else this afternoon?"

"We ran into each other, that's all."

"Yeah, and I'm a Jedi. I'll tell you why. He's got the hots for you. Rumor has it the two of you are dating on a regular basis, and he's transferring so he can ask you to marry him soon."

Sharon could only shake her head as she let it sink in. "Total bullshit. We went to a deli together a few days ago. He caught me when I left the office late, and we walked toward the subway together. Anyway, he asked if I wanted to grab a bite, and we talked a little. He went home, I went home and that was it."

"I believe you."

"But?" This had come too fast, too easy.

"I didn't say there was a *but*." Jenn looked down at the pictures in front of her once more and sighed.

Sharon waited a moment, but nothing else was forthcoming. "Okay, in that case, let's get back to work." She sat down and booted up her computer.

Out of the corner of her eye, she saw Jenn looking up, and wasn't surprised when she spoke. "But Hastings still has the hots for you. I wouldn't be surprised if the chance to date you was part of his decision to accept the new job. I always thought he liked it here. Anyway, so how does it feel?"

"How does what feel?"

"To be desired by two men."

Hastings and Carter. How did it feel? Damned if she knew. "Right now it's more annoying than anything else. What is it about men not getting a hint or two or three?"

"Finally. She opens up." Jenn pump her fist in the air. "Anyway, it's the nature of men to be annoying. You often can't live with them, but you don't want to live without them either."

"I guess you're right." Sharon opened a file on her desktop and began to scroll through it. The hair falling over her shoulders annoyed her, and she got a hair tie out of the pocket of her jeans, quickly wrapping the strands into a messy ponytail.

"So who is it you want?"

"Jenn, please."

"No, really. Sharon, ask yourself who it is you really want in your life. Under these circumstances, you'll likely only get one chance with either of them."

Jenn meant well, but Sharon could hardly answer the question when she didn't know how. If she had a good idea what or who she wanted, she wouldn't be in this mess to begin with.

"You know, how about we try working for a change? I'm sure no one cares about these two men when it comes to murder."

"And here I thought all the world revolved around love, the resulting hate and murder."

Sharon rolled her eyes and went back to work.

After being on the phone and writing reports almost all morning, Sharon was still unsatisfied. She was up on her paperwork, and had scheduled another interview with Davis' sister this afternoon. She knew the young woman was sick of seeing her by now, but it couldn't be helped. No one had known the deceased better than her twin sister.

It was after twelve when she looked up for the first time to find Jenn had bought them sandwiches. The blonde sat down on the edge of Sharon's desk, unwrapping hers, tuna. How she could stomach the stuff, Sharon would never know.

"I know it's *still* none of my business, but, Sharon, don't go for the safe bet just because you think it's the wisest course of action."

"I don't understand." Or was it something she didn't want to understand?

"I know you like Hastings, but you're fascinated by Carter. One seems safe, the other…not so much. Although at the moment, you shouldn't go anywhere near either of those two. One is still your boss, the other's a suspect." Jenn laughed and took a bite. "Not that I think it would stop you from going after one of them if you felt like it." She paused to take another bite.

"Anyway, Carter is different, I agree. His profession is different, but don't run for Hastings only because you are trying to run from Carter. The three of you deserve better."

Even when she was mad at her, Sharon had to love Jenn. Although she still hadn't fully opened up to her friend, Jenn had her back, was looking out for her. Just as she would do for her. Out of impulse, Sharon got up and wrapped her arms around her friend.

"I appreciate your candid words, really. And I'll think about them. Promise. I don't know what I'll do. I don't know what I should do."

Jenn's hold around her tightened, then she let go, locking her gaze with Sharon's. "First of all, be flattered. Two hot men want your attention and not only that. If that doesn't give your ego a boost, I've got no idea what would."

Jenn looked at her sandwich, then at Sharon, sitting down again, for all the world not giving the impression she'd vacate Sharon's desk any time soon. Sharon unwrapped her own meal.

"How's it going with Brian?"

Jenn swallowed a bite, then put her sandwich away for the moment. "Good. Really good." She frowned. "And that's the scary thing, you know? I mean, he's a truly good guy. Not without flaws, but...good. Yeah, I know, that sounds like a broken record, but it's still the truth. Actually, he'd be the perfect guy for you, you know." She rolled her eyes.

"I'm not into pastors," Sharon teased.

"Me neither, but I'm into Brian. But what I meant to say is, you are the one who is usually doing things by the book, the one who does the sensible thing. Granted, you dated some assholes, but it never changed you. You are good. I... Well, my parents didn't think about sending me to boot camp without a reason. A very good reason. I'm sure I was hell to raise, and you know how many toes I stepped on by simply being me."

"And you're loved because you are who you are. You are life, energy. You are fun to be around and the best friend one could wish for."

"Brian said something similar the last time I met him. And with him...I feel calmer, as if it's okay to rest for a while. It's not that he tries to slow me down, but with him, I find not hurrying through life has its charms, too."

Sharon put a hand on Jenn's knee, squeezed. "Let's sum it up. You're happy, the relationship has the potential to go far and it scares you half out of your mind."

"That's about it, yeah."

Sharon sat back. "I wish I had any wisdom to impart on you now, but I don't. I've got no idea about healthy relationships. But how about you enjoy what you have for as long as you have it and play it by ear, going from one day to the next? You deserve to be happy, and sometimes the man who seems all wrong can turn out to be the right one, after all."

Shouldn't I take my own advice as well?

"Who would've thought, huh? Sharon Richards has a thing for what some people would call a really bad boy, and I'm dating a pastor. Life has a nicely fucked-up sense of humor."

"It keeps things interesting, don't you think?" Sharon said, allowing herself a smile.

"I think I'm happy you stopped denying there's anything up with Carter in the first place."

Jenn's phone rang, cutting the conversation short. Sharon was glad for the interruption. If anything was becoming clear, it was that she didn't want to strike Carter out of her life. She didn't know if this was a good path to follow, yet she didn't want to feel any regrets either. The same was true for her date with Hastings, although she'd be surprised if sparks started to fly.

"Yeah. Okay. I'll be over shortly. Don't get your briefs into a knot. Or were those boxers? Truth to be told, I figured you're more of a… Okay, I'll shut up. See you." Jenn had gotten up even before she'd put the receiver of her phone down.

"Dyson needs some help. I'll be back in time for the meeting."

Sharon nodded and waited until Jenn had left before she reached for her own phone. Making this call didn't seem as wrong as it would have a few days ago. Carter picked up on the fourth ring.

"Sharon. How are you?"

He'd recognized the number. She wasn't surprised. "I want to see you again." She bit down her lip, her foot tapping a nervous rhythm on the floor while she waited for his reply.

"All right. When and where?"

What did she want from him? He had told her to know what she wanted before they made contact. It was time to be honest with him and with herself.

"I want to…play."

It didn't take much to imagine a smile on his face.

"Good. Then how about you meet me at the club? At eight. Be on time and be sure it is what you truly want."

"I am sure."

"I hope so. I'm a patient man, Sharon, but when it comes to you, it seems my patience is sorely tested. You should know how much I want to play with you."

The surety in his voice sent a shiver of anticipation down her back. She had to smile at the rush of emotions. Relief over her admittance, anticipation for what was to come, a scrap of a guilty conscience, quickly suppressed.

"I don't make any decisions lightly."

"I'm glad to hear that. Now will you answer my question?"

She frowned. "Which question?"

"How are you?"

It was mostly a polite phrase, part of most conversations. It wasn't for Carter and she believed he expected an honest answer.

"I'm okay. Really. You?"

"Good. I'm looking forward to tonight."

So was she. There was a tingle low in her belly, mixed with a fluttering of nerves. A heady combination. "Me too."

"Sharon?"

"Yes?"

"Wear something comfortable. You wouldn't want something to irritate your skin after we're done playing." She closed her eyes, her breath catching as mental pictures invaded her mind.

"I will."

Chapter Fourteen

This time she didn't have to ask for Carter, as the man in question was outside on the street, leaning against the wall, smoking a cigarette. It was a warmer evening, and she'd only donned a short blazer. It was good to know she'd soon be able to put her jackets into the closet altogether and forget about them for a few short months. Walking up to Carter, Sharon returned his smile.

"I didn't know you smoked."

"I don't."

"Really? Because I'd have sworn this looks conspicuously like a cigarette."

"The smart cop is showing."

She snorted. "Nothing wrong with being smart, is there?"

"No, there isn't. And the cigarette, it helps calm the nerves."

"I didn't know you were even able to become nervous."

He straightened. "I'm human, Sharon. Just like you. And I wouldn't say nervous, but rather…curious," he said calmly, his voice as strong as ever. Apart from the cigarette and his own confession, there was no indication of nerves.

"It seems we're not that different in a way," she said.

"Which way?"

"We both keep our feelings internalized. We just like to deal differently with them." What cigarettes did for him was what Sharon found when she worked out really hard. "When I am unsettled by something, I hit the gym until I'm completely exhausted."

Carter stubbed out the cigarette against the wall of the building and actually walked the few feet to the next garbage can, throwing it inside. Joining her again, he stepped close, and Sharon could smell the smoke, although it didn't disturb her.

"You did a lot of thinking, didn't you?" he said, his hand coming to rest on the small of her back.

"I'm not sure I'd call it thinking, just learning to accept myself. I don't know if *this* is something I'd like to make a regular habit of, but…"

"You want to satisfy your curiosity. There's nothing wrong with that." He stopped, leaned down and kissed her, the contact soon deepening, making her hum from the pleasure of it.

"Do you kiss all of your play dates?" she asked when he withdrew.

He chuckled. "It sounds a bit like kindergarten, don't you think? And no, I don't. Sexual activities can be a part of play, but more often than not they aren't. And kissing… It's intimate, isn't it?"

"It is." She would've never kissed her last one-night stand—it hadn't been part of the unspoken pact. With

Carter it had been different from the very beginning. He'd torn down her walls without having to try hard.

"I guess the lines are blurring a little when it comes to you," he said.

"Is that a good or a bad thing?" *Do I even want to know?*

"I have no idea. But I'll find out. We'll find out. Shall we?"

He led them to the club's entrance and held the door open for her. Sharon couldn't help it. She began to question herself, her motives, again. Was this a good idea? How much pain could she tolerate? What if she'd be hurt in a way she wasn't prepared to bear?

Carter touched her arm, and she could feel the warmth of his hand through the fabric of her jacket. Or was it her imagination?

"Sometimes I only wish for it to stop," she said, while they walked up the first set of stairs.

"The relentless thoughts racing through your mind?"

"How do you do it? I'm sure you're not a mind reader."

Another smirk. By now she associated them with this particular man. "You're not the first person with this problem, nor will you be the last."

They reached Carter's room. He opened the door and walked in before her, switching on the light.

Had he entertained someone else here since their last time? She bit her bottom lip. That was none of her business. She'd never been a jealous person, and wouldn't start now with a man she fucked but didn't have a relationship with. *Yet*, a small voice inside her whispered.

"Let's introduce some more rules," Carter said without any preamble.

More rules. Sharon didn't let her trepidation show, but just waited for him to speak. His eyes lit up.

"Good girl. So you remembered. You may speak now."

"Which rules?"

"Which rules, Sir."

Her temper flared. She'd never addressed someone in the bedroom as sir, and she wouldn't start now. Only, it was part of the game. She had agreed it would be him in charge. His house, his game, his rules.

"All right," she eventually gritted out.

"Last chance."

"All right, Sir." She wasn't able to hide her irritation when he looked as amused as she was pissed. So be it.

"There'll only be one more rule. And it's the most important one."

"Name it…Sir."

"You'll only get to come when I say you can."

She'd heard of such games. Slowly, she shook her head. He ignored her unspoken irritation.

"I have utter control, over the game, your body and your orgasms. If you're a really good girl, though, you'll get to come. If you aren't, you won't."

She shook her head again.

"Do you want to end this here and now? You may speak, Sharon."

"No. I don't."

"Then you'll play by my rules. The only exception is your safe word. Are we clear on everything?"

When she didn't answer, he stepped closer. "I told you, last chance."

"Yes, Sir." She sounded like a petulant girl. Obedience wasn't in her nature.

"Good. See, it's not that hard, is it?"

It was harder than she was prepared to admit. The independent woman inside her cried outrage, while her mind rejoiced at the possibility of not having to make a decision for the next few hours. He would make her stop thinking — he had promised, and she'd hold him to it.

"Undress now."

He walked over to a single chair that hadn't been inside the room the last time, and sat down. She felt naked, even fully clothed, but it was part of this game. She'd have to get used to it.

He didn't say a word, didn't even move — he just waited for her to comply with his request. She'd done this before. She could do it now. Still, being the sole object of his unnerving scrutiny made the simple task of getting out of her clothes a daunting one. It was what he intended to achieve, for sure.

Fully undressed, Sharon remained standing with no idea what Carter expected from her next. Did he want her to move? To remain where she was?

He didn't give any indication about his immediate intent, so she went with the latter. His eyes were on her, moving over her body, but they didn't give much away. She assumed it was part of the game, but assumptions were always dangerous, a lesson she'd learned early on the job. Her hair falling down her back made her skin itch, yet she didn't reach around to try and scratch the spot.

A minute passed.

Another.

The silence, as well as her own uncertainty, began weighing on her. She was as focused on the man before her as he was focused on her. She could've cut the tension inside the room with a knife.

The relief she felt when he finally moved, finally got up from the chair, made her knees weak. Sometimes there was nothing worse than inaction, to be unable to do a thing about an unsatisfactory situation.

Stopping in front of her, he put a hand on her shoulder and let it trail up to her neck where he squeezed a little too hard for comfort. He chuckled.

"Don't worry. I'm not into breath-play."

Good. Neither was she. Not from what she'd read, anyway. It was still hard to admit to herself, but she'd read up about BDSM in recent days. Fascination and fear had occupied her thoughts for so long now that she had to know what was keeping her from sleeping at night. Although the tiny hope she might find herself appalled enough to step away, turn her back on this very different sub-culture, had proven futile. Instead, it had stoked her curiosity, had followed her into her sleep until she woke up aroused and frustrated.

He trailed his hand lower now, until he could cup one of her breasts. He closed his hand around it for a moment, brushing over it with the palm of his hand. It was hard not to react to the caress, to keep the moans inside. The only things she wasn't able to control were her breathing and her heart rate, as both of them had sped up.

"I want to hear your sounds of pleasure, of pain. Let it out. I don't want you to talk, but I don't want you to be silent either."

She swallowed and nodded. He took his hand away.

"Close your eyes."

She'd trusted him that way before, had given up a sense, knowing he wouldn't let her fall. It was still hard, although it came easier than it had the first time. True trust took a long time, but maybe they were on the way there. For a few seconds, nothing happened. The only indication he was still there was the heat radiating off his body.

Then he reached for both of her breasts at the same time, roughly tweaking her erect nipples. She hissed out as sharp pain coursed through her system, the surprise of it making her knees buckle.

He stepped away. "I will lead you to the chair. You will straddle it and hold on to its back. But remember, whatever I do, don't flinch too much. It's just a chair, it's not stable."

He was stoking her fear at the same time he was kindling her curiosity. While her mind understood the way he was manipulating her, her body didn't get the message, reacting just as Carter wanted it to. Taking her arm, he began leading her to where the chair was. She'd noticed it earlier, yet with her eyes closed, it was hard to calculate the distance. Carter was with her, but she didn't want to stumble anyway. Trust. She needed to trust him. Taking a deep breath, she straightened and just walked.

Two more steps, and he halted her, guiding her hands to the back of the chair.

"Sit."

She was already wet and the thought that she could leave a stain was ridiculous. Still, it made her uncomfortable.

"Sit. If I have to tell you again, there'll be a punishment."

She believed him and was sure punishment would be imminent if she didn't obey him. It was the one thing she shouldn't doubt or forget.

She sat down, her back straight, waiting for what would happen next. The temptation to open her eyes was high. Or how about moving her arms?

She could do both. If she did, he'd surely be quick with finding a blindfold and some cuffs or rope. At least that was her suspicion. If she didn't try, she'd never find out. God, was she so intent on finding out what punishment entailed?

Biting her lip, Sharon considered her options. She opened her eyes and put her hands on her knees before she looked at Carter. He was in front of the chair, looking down at her. His erection was straining against his pants, and it nearly made her smile.

"Did I allow you to move? To open your eyes? Talk."

"No, you didn't, Sir."

"Did I tell you there would be punishment if you disregarded my orders?"

"Yes, you did, Sir."

He turned on his heel, walking past her, but she didn't look where he was going. The sounds he made weren't an indication of what he was doing either. The blindfold appearing in front of her face and being quickly secured was not much of a surprise.

"Next time, punishment will be more severe. You better believe me. This is your last warning."

Cold. His voice was so cold. If they weren't playing a game, played with her own consent, she'd be scared.

"Are we clear? You may speak."

"Yes, we are clear, Sir."

How could she ever live with addressing him this way? This wasn't about respect but submitting to another.

She sensed him behind her, thought she could feel the heat of his body, then he lifted her hands, and it quickly became clear he had decided on rope this time. It was as good and smooth as rope could be, but she was sure it would leave marks around her wrists.

The air behind her stirred, Carter moved and her hair was lifted, brushed over one shoulder. His lips made contact with her neck, then they wandered down her back, a row of soft kisses making her toes curl, her desire unfold.

He stopped and stood up when he had only reached the middle of her back. *I better learn not to expect anything when it comes to him.* It was a lesson she should take to heart. Nothing happened for a while. Her heart wouldn't stop beating unnaturally fast. It would be easier to brace herself if she knew what to expect next, if it was pleasure or pain.

She couldn't ask. He wouldn't tell anyway. As she was left in a state of nervous anticipation, seconds ticked by and after a while she lost herself in cataloging the sounds and sensations.

She could hear her own breathing, could hear Carter's. There was the soft noise of the ventilation system. Someone moved in the hallway outside. There was a voice — no, two voices.

The rope around her wrists was uncomfortable, and her naked thighs digging into the sides of the chair began to hurt. She began to freeze as well, which made her want to suggest they move to the bed for a round of comfortable lovemaking. Would he even go for it? Would she want it?

No, she didn't make love with Carter—wouldn't. This was a purely physical thing.

Carter moved but she couldn't make sense of the noises, which frustrated her. She heard him move away before his steps approached her again, but she wasn't prepared for the sharp pain on her back following a whooshing sound. A whip? She wasn't sure, couldn't concentrate. She had trouble breathing, her nerve endings firing in alert.

Sharon didn't know if it was for a second or a minute that nothing happened, as she was focused on coming to terms with her physical discomfort. The next blow was just as hard. Remembering he had allowed her to make noises, she moaned.

There were five blows in total. After the last one, Sharon was out of breath, her whole back hurting in a way she could hardly fathom. The finger trailing down her back in a soft caress didn't register at once, but when it did, it was a counterpoint to the whipping of before.

"Good girl. Very good girl."

She wanted to curse him, yet in spite of it all she was still aroused, even more so than before. Her need was almost more uncomfortable than her pain. She wanted his hands on her body, his cock inside her.

She hadn't realized he had moved and was now in front of her again. He had to be kneeling as his mouth found hers in a kiss, passionate but controlling nonetheless. His tongue stroked hers, and this time her moan was one of pleasure. She tried to turn the tables, take control of the kiss. He pulled away immediately.

"No, this is my game. Not yours. You do what I please."

Agreeing to rules was not quite the same as accepting them, a lesson that would take time to learn.

"Get up."

Thanks to sitting in one position for some length of time, her hands still bound together, she had a hard time getting on her feet. Carter didn't help, and didn't ask if she needed any. Only when she was upright and had found her equilibrium did he take her hand.

"I'll guide you to the bed. Once on it, I want you to kneel down on all fours again."

Was this to be a repeat of last time? Somehow she didn't think so.

"I'm going to spank you, Sharon. For as long as I think you can bear it. If you think you can't take it any longer at any point, use your safe word."

Did he warn all his play dates of that explicitly, or was it because she was new to the game? Maybe she'd ask him later.

Reaching the bed, he left her alone with the complicated task of sitting down and managing a kneeling position. Now how to bend forward without ending up on her face in the process? It was humiliating to even think about it.

Carter's hand on her arm was a surprise, even more so how gentle it was with helping her lower herself so she could brace her weight on her elbows. It wasn't a comfortable position by any stretch of the imagination. It shouldn't be.

Carter left her to her own devices once again. While she'd come to expect the unexpected, it was another shock to her nervous system when a hard, even surface connected with her ass in a soft blow. Her mind suggested it was a paddle, but the thought whisked away as pain took over. She groaned and tears were welling up in her eyes. No, she wouldn't cry. Not now anyway.

The motion was repeated several times, the hits increasing in strength. Numbness and a pleasant warmth replaced the sting. She was reveling in the almost pleasant feeling when he inserted his hands between her thighs, urging her to spread them more. Complying, she moaned as one of his fingers slid between her labia, the single digit entering her, causing her inner walls to contract around it. The fire of her passion rekindled, she bit her lip hard so she wouldn't beg him to fuck her. God, how she wanted it, wanted him.

The next moment, the finger was gone. In less time than it took to curse him, he slipped his finger between her parted lips.

"Suck it."

She'd never had a problem with her own taste, so she treated his finger as she would his cock if he chose to slide it inside her mouth. While he didn't make a sound, she was sure he was enjoying the show, the feeling of her wet lips around his flesh.

For a moment, she was in control of him, the game, but he reacted swiftly, pulling away once more. Damn him.

"I want you to see."

Chapter Fifteen

Carter reached for her blindfold, removing it carefully. Even the dim lighting inside the room hurt her eyes, making her blink until she'd gotten used to it. A shimmer of light irritated her, making her look up, and to her surprise she found her own reflection thrown back at her. The mirror over the bed. She'd forgotten about it. Now she craned her neck so she could see better, wishing for a better angle. It didn't work, and she looked at Carter instead.

He was the calm she was missing. He was in control of his body and his reactions. Sharon, though, was a slave to her emotions, her body throbbing with need.

He picked up the paddle once again and raised his hands. It was worse when she knew when to expect the next hit, when she could see his hand moving downward quickly.

Again and again, never hitting the same spot more than two or three times. Soon, she couldn't watch any longer, the position too hard to maintain. All she could do was to hold on and give voice to her pain, following the rush of endorphins.

The best thing about it was the quiet inside her mind. She existed for the moment alone, and was more carefree for it. Without any reason, she was giddy. She wanted to giggle or cry out in joy.

The feeling was gone when she winced under the onslaught of another smack. Carter wasn't holding back. She didn't want him to. It hurt more than she'd ever be able to describe, yet expecting the pain, accepting it would come, gave her peace, made it bearable. Her tears were flowing freely now, her moans coming in a steady stream.

When he stopped, putting the paddle away, she had the irrational urge to tell him to go on. His eyes met hers, and he gave her a small smile.

"Your skin can only bear that much abuse."

Was it abuse when she wanted him to do it? Since she wasn't allowed to speak, she let go of the thought. There would be time for idle wondering later. Or not. It was hard to focus with different sensations confronting her at the same time. Her heated, hypersensitive skin began to cool down, which was unpleasant. Her arms ached from the constant strain.

It was a surprise she hadn't fallen flat on her face anyway, considering the force of the blows she'd endured. Her legs ached, and her stomach, too. She must have been more tense than she'd thought. Carter walked around the bed, then came to kneel down at her side. He helped her sit up, her body shaking like a leaf. Sharon had been sure she'd feel relief at the change of position, but she didn't. The pain signals coming from different parts of her body wouldn't abate. She doubted there was any kind of position she'd consider comfortable for the next while.

He began unwinding the rope, and Sharon sighed with relief when it was gone, although the sudden blood rush to her extremities reminded her of being swarmed by ants.

"This will itch a little while."

She looked at her wrists, where the rope had left its mark. It would be hard to cover this for the next few days, though at the moment, she didn't care much. Not even the thought of Jenn interrogating her left more than a passing impression.

"Drink something," he said.

He had gotten up. Her mind was too sluggish to keep up with anything. Taking the offered glass of water, she drank greedily. Her throat was raw from crying out, so the water provided relief.

"I want you to lie down on your back now. And so you know it, I'll cuff you to the bed."

She gave him a long look. He couldn't be serious, but he only shook his head.

"Lie down."

She could end it here but didn't. Giving her safe word would only make her wonder what she was missing.

Getting into position, she winced when her sore ass and thighs screamed in protest. Putting her hands over her head, she didn't try hiding her sigh when he secured her to the bed with handcuffs. It wasn't better or worse than the rope had been, just different, the ache of limbs being stretched beyond their means back full force.

Carter got onto the bed with her. "Spread your legs for me."

She cursed the instant flush, and was grateful he chose not to comment on it. He took his time studying her, and she had to force herself not to react to it. It would be less intimidating if he spoke, commented on what he saw, yet he didn't. She didn't need compliments, didn't even want him to pay her any, but this calm contemplation made her nerves flutter.

His eyes met hers.

"Do you remember the rules?"

Sharon nodded.

"Good. Just remember, I told you that you don't get to come unless I say so."

Her clit began to throb at the idea of him paying sensual attention to her body, and she hoped, prayed, he wouldn't avoid her erogenous zones altogether as he had done last time.

He didn't.

Leaning over her, supporting his weight with his strong, lean arms, he latched his mouth onto one of her nipples, sucking the tender bud. She moaned as the feeling transferred right to the center of her desire. It made her even wetter than she'd been, something she'd have deemed impossible if asked.

After some time, he switched to her other breast, while he roughly stroked the one he had abandoned. Sharon writhed on the bed, cursing the fact her movement was restricted. She wanted to touch him too, to drive him as insane as he was driving her. She feared that the punishment for speaking would be total retreat, so she kept her vocalizations to moans and tiny screams when he bit down on her nipples.

No man had ever paid such meticulous attention to her breasts, and when he kissed his way down her body, she knew they would be sore tomorrow.

Aroused as she was, it was still not enough to come, a fact she was thankful for. Though then he settled between her legs, putting both of them over his shoulders. Spread open, she could only let him go on and wait for whatever would happen next.

Carter had torture on his mind.

Latching onto her clit just the way he had done onto her nipples, he flicked the very tip of his tongue over her pleasure point, bringing her right to the edge of the abyss. Half a minute longer, and she would shatter for sure.

She wasn't allowed to come. She couldn't. Her body tensed, and she tried moving her legs so she could close them or... God, she didn't know. All she knew was he had to stop now or she'd be lost in a haze of sexual pleasure. She felt more than heard him chuckle before he sat back.

"Quite the dilemma, don't you think? It can be hard not to come." He reached out, pinching one of her nipples again. "You may speak."

"Please, please, just stop this. I can't bear it. I have to come, I need to come. Please."

She was babbling, begging, but she didn't care. He was still too close for comfort or not close enough. She couldn't decide.

"You need to come?"

"I...I..." *Damn this man to hell.* "I need to come. Sir."

He only smirked.

"Here's the deal. You'll wear nipple clamps, just because I think they will look good on you. And if you ask nicely then I might let you come."

Might, not will. She gritted her teeth as anger and desire waged war inside her.

"Do you want to try nipple clamps?"

She didn't. She was afraid of that particular sensation, especially after all the attention he'd paid to her breasts earlier. She shook her head.

"In that case, I can only advise you to stay strong."

He would truly continue his sensual assault if she didn't bend to his will. Well, it was a game, a scene out of time.

"Okay. Okay. Damn you."

"Didn't you forget something? Again." There was a distinct glint of amusement in his eyes.

"Damn you, Sir."

She had to laugh, in spite of herself, and it helped ease her tension. Looking at him, she had the feeling it had been his intention all along. Her tension having abated for the moment, she waited, trying to breathe steadily. She watched Carter reaching for his nightstand, getting a pair of nipple clamps out of the first drawer. Panic reared up inside her again. No, she didn't want this. Just…no.

Was this the time to end this game? It was her choice. Everything in life boiled down to choices. It was the nature of life having to make decision after decision, never knowing if one had made the right one. The path not taken, the one thing that could drive one insane if given too much thought.

"These are known as tweezer clamps," Carter said, holding the items in question up for her so she could take a good look at them.

"The name comes from the way they are built."

She'd rather have not looked. The clamps reminded her of tweezers, just as he had said, and were joined by a chain. If he pulled at the chain…God. Somehow this made her think of going to the doctor for shots. She didn't mind getting shots all that much, as long as she didn't have to watch the doctor pierce her skin. She hoped it would work the same way with the clamps. It should be easier to deal with them if she ignored them as much as possible, so she wouldn't twitch when they'd clamp some of the most sensitive skin on her body. She averted her eyes.

"No, Sharon. Look at them. I want you to understand what is going to happen to you."

Not what 'will' happen but what is going to happen. As long as she didn't end the game for good, he would apply these to her.

It couldn't be worse than being beaten with a paddle and a whip, could it?

She nodded her understanding, keeping her eyes on the clamps.

"Did you know a lot of women find these aesthetically pleasing?"

What did she care? He should know about her nervous anticipation. Was he dragging this out on purpose? Or wasn't he? She couldn't think.

"The tips are coated, in this case with latex. This way they provide a measure of comfort." She hardly listened when he pointed out the ring at the closed end that slid toward the end that would enclose her nipple. "They allow for increased or decreased tension. They are good for beginners."

He turned toward her. "I'm going to apply them to your nipples now. You don't have to worry. I know what I'm doing."

Sharon's breathing sped up, and she began feeling lightheaded. *This is silly, so why can't I calm down?* People were different. Some hated spiders and some were afraid of clowns. There was no accounting for one's fears.

He kept his promise and was careful. Lust shot through her body when he brushed against her nipple with his fingers. The metal of the clamp chain was cold against her skin. A shiver ran down her back.

He fastened the clamp quickly, giving her no time to contemplate the situation. The pressure on her skin came instantly, sharp pain radiating from a small point through all of her body. She bit her lip. She didn't cry out, couldn't, had no breath left to voice her discomfort. Needing to breathe, to focus, she took in as much air as possible, but Carter was quick and had already fastened the second nipple clamp. Tears shot into her eyes. She blinked so they wouldn't fall.

Her eyes closed while her body tried absorbing the new sensation. The pain reduced every second, until she hardly felt the clamps.

"Open your eyes."

She did. *Is that concern in his eyes? Surely not.*

"Is this okay? Speak."

"Yes, Sir."

"Good."

He reached for the clamps, one after the other, increasing the tension. *Shit.*

"Keep your eyes open."

It was hard, the urge to let them fall shut all but overwhelming. She managed.

"Still okay?"

Sharon refused to answer, to look at him. It would've been better if she had, as he lightly yanked at the chain connecting the clamps, fresh pain shooting through her body.

"Answer my question."

"It's still bearable, but barely so, Sir."

"We'll see about that. Lie back comfortably. Spread your legs for me again."

What was he intending to do now? Tighten the clamps, refuse to let her come? The options were plenty. She feared and wanted him to go on torturing her mind and soul, to make her mind recede until pure sensation filled it.

Settling between her legs, not hooking them over his shoulders this time, Carter slowly slid two fingers inside her, resting his thumb over her clit before rubbing it in slow circles. Instantly, she was close to orgasm again.

I won't come became her new mantra. Never would she have thought trying not to come would send her right to the edge even faster. If he kept this up, it would be a lost cause.

He yanked at her chain without warning, the sudden pain making her yelp. The impending threat of orgasm was all but forgotten as her muscles tensed and her back arched, a harsh cry escaping her.

He'd stilled his fingers inside her, cataloguing her every reaction. She gradually managed to relax.

"You're doing good, Sharon."

He started again with building up her pleasure, his motions steady, meant to arouse, to drive her mad. It ended just as before—her climax so close when it was replaced by pain. One time, two times, three times... She was surprised she had gotten used to the pain, that it wasn't as bad as it had been the very first time. It began to blend with the pleasure, even heightened it. She was in deep trouble.

"You're not to come."

Only not coming began feeling painful itself. She needed to release the tension. She would come if he didn't stop what he was doing within the next minute.

If she could only move away from him, deny him access. She couldn't, and no matter how often she pulled at the handcuffs, they wouldn't budge. This was cruel — physical and emotional torture. She broke into a sweat, her whole body throbbing while she tried to stave off the eruption of pleasure. Her legs began to ache from the tension in her body. Her back burned like the seven hells from sweat running over the bruises he had caused earlier, and her hair was plastered to her body. It shouldn't be possible to be so close to an orgasm while being uncomfortable in a way that was a distraction in itself.

Carter sat back on his haunches, and she opened eyes she hadn't realized she'd closed. There was fire in his eyes, controlled, yes, but not hidden, and looking down his body, she saw the erection straining against his pants. How could he possibly want her so much and do nothing about it?

"You're doing well."

She locked her gaze with him, wanting him to know she needed to speak.

"Yes, Sharon?"

"Please, fuck me. I need to come. I want you inside of me. I want that cock of yours inside me. Please." Usually she'd be revolted by such crude language. With cops, crude language was most often a given, but she tried to keep her language clean as much as possible apart from the occasional *fuck*. She hadn't been raised in a decent household to curse her way through life. Now she needed to get the message across.

"Please. I beg you. Please, please, Sir."

He didn't answer, which made her want to verbally lash out at him, and he hadn't forbidden her to speak either. Holding back was the better course of action. If he wouldn't give in to her plea now, it was unlikely begging or cursing him until she was blue in the face would help.

"How do you want me to take you?" he asked, pulling slightly at the chain connecting the clamps, making her wince.

She honestly didn't care as long as he thrust his hard length into her soon and allowed her to come. With dread, she imagined him fucking her while she wasn't allowed to come. She cleared her too-dry throat.

"I don't care for as long as you'll let me come. You will, won't you? Please. I need to come. I can't hold back any longer. I can't bear it." She was rambling, and wanted to stop but didn't know how. He put a hand over her mouth.

"Being allowed to come is a reward that has to be earned. You didn't do much to earn a thing so far and next time you'll have to work harder for it, are we clear?"

"Yes."

Right now, a *next time* was a long time away. She'd promise anything for relief now.

She watched with hungry eyes as he finally undressed and kneeled between her parted legs, his erection seeming to be as eager for action as she was. He took the time to apply a condom, then bridged the last bit of distance between them and took her without any subtlety. He didn't need any. She was as wet and ready as she could be, her muscles clenching around his cock. He set a fast, hard rhythm that was just right, and had her whimpering from the pleasure.

"Come now."

Sharon wouldn't have thought it possible to time an orgasm but it was. His voice, so deep, so rich, the movement of his cock inside her delivering just the right kind of friction — it was enough for her to fall into the spiral of orgasmic bliss. Her vision went black for a second, her body rocked by the force of the release, and when she heard him groan, it was all she could do not to pass out. She was panting, trying to regain her breath, while she willed her body to listen to her and relax.

Carter took only a minute to cool down, and in short order she was untied and the nipple clamps were removed. She turned, laying curled up on her side, spooned by Carter who offered her warmth and murmured soothing words.

"So, game's over, huh?" She yawned, suddenly sleepy, relaxed, sore in some places she'd expected and in some she hadn't been.

"Yes, it is. You were amazing, Sharon."

The tenderness of his voice was unexpected. She turned to look at him, but his eyes gave nothing away.

"I'll take care of you now, make sure there'll be no lingering bruises."

It was something else she'd read about after their last time. Aftercare. Some said it was the most beautiful part of the game — another reward. Was she prepared for the intimacy? Last time he'd done the same for her, yet he hadn't taken her quite that far. They hadn't been that close. Tonight she'd endured more, and the thought that he would treat her body with reverence and care didn't sit entirely right with her. Her emotions were too raw. She wasn't equipped to deal with his tender side.

"I'm not sure. I…I better get home."

To flee. Almost her first instinct in any intimate situations. There was a part of her that didn't want to leave, then she looked around the room and heard the moans and screams from other rooms. She needed quiet and peace now.

She sat up. "I…this…it's too much now," she tried to explain.

He nodded, and she found understanding in his eyes.

"Want to spend the night with me?"

The words needed a moment to make sense to her. "Spend the night? Here? No. I'm sorry, but…"

"Home. I wanted to know if you want to spend the night at my apartment. I could take care of you there, offer a not-too-hot bath and a warm bed."

Tempting. So, so tempting.

"I think I'd like it." She surprised herself with her admission. It was worth a try, right? She could still run any time she felt like it.

"Then let's get dressed and take a cab."

Chapter Sixteen

Carter helped Sharon with her clothes, and she was thankful as her hands weren't quite steady and neither were her legs. It only took them about five minutes to get dressed, but by the end she was exhausted, her body drained of all energy. She was glad she wouldn't have to face the subway on her own now. He'd called the cab before getting up, and she hoped it would be quick.

"I'll clean that up tomorrow," he said when he saw her looking around the room.

He took her arm and led her outside the club. They passed two patrons, or employees—she wasn't sure—but they didn't pay them any attention.

"What about your office?" she asked, the thought coming out of nowhere.

"Closed for the night and we've got security guards."

She nodded.

"How about you stop worrying, Sharon? Everything's in perfect order."

Worrying was what she did best, after all. It was exactly what she'd wanted not to do earlier, and Carter had made her achieve that goal.

"There's the cab," he said, leading her to it.

Getting inside, she winced when she sat down. *Shit.* The driver gave her a knowing glance. So he knew about the club? The building itself was as nondescript as they came, so it was likely he had picked someone up here before.

An idea formed in her mind. This was New York, after all. Taking a cab was a way of life. Who knew, maybe Davis had taken a cab the day she died, too, and what about the woman she'd met? It was a lead to check out tomorrow.

"I know you're thinking," Carter remarked, but when she looked over at him, he was looking out the window.

"Just an idea. About the Davis case."

"That's good. But don't forget it's late in the evening. You can deal with it tomorrow."

"I know. You're right. It's just..." She couldn't describe it, so she gave up on trying.

They reached Carter's apartment a short while later, the cab stopping at the curb. Carter got out first and shook his head when Sharon reached for the handle on her side. He ignored her eyeroll and opened the door for her. He paid the cab driver before he took her arm, entering the building.

The doorman greeted him with respect and a smile, and threw a curious glance in her direction.

"He's not used to the sight," Carter said when they waited inside for an elevator.

"Which sight?"

"That I'm bringing a woman home. It's not my habit, although you still seem to think it is."

"I never said so." Although he was right. A man that good looking could have women lined up to get a piece of him any given day.

"You didn't have to."

They were joined by another couple that got off two floors before them.

His apartment was as impressive as it had been the first time, and Sharon took in the sight of the city she hated and loved in equal measures.

"Give me your blazer," he said, leaving her alone for the moment when she'd handed it to him. She didn't care—not about her hurting body, either. The windowpane threw her reflection back at her and the single lone shadow was highlighted against the million lights out there. What was she doing here? It wasn't her city. This city could swallow her whole and no one would care. She couldn't explain her sudden melancholy, but couldn't find the energy to fight it either.

A second shadow joined the first until Carter stood right behind her.

"Here, have a glass of water."

"I…thank you."

"It's normal. After the rush comes the fall. It's the hormones."

"How?"

"Did I know? Just take a look at your face. Let me take care of you tonight, Sharon. Really take care of you."

This was harder than sex, and part of her yearned for it even more. It had been too long since someone had taken care of her physical as well as her emotional needs and had seen her truly vulnerable.

"Okay."

"I won't disappoint you. Come, let's get more comfortable." He turned around, walking towards the door. Sharon turned as well.

"Simon," she called after him.

She nearly smiled when she saw the surprise on his face that he couldn't quite mask.

"Sharon?" His expression became neutral again. They were both still unused to not wearing masks around each other.

"You haven't disappointed me once yet."

The smile he gave her was wider than his usual smirk, not guarded for once, the expression in his eyes softening. "I'm glad to hear that."

He held out his hand to her, and she walked over to take it. Something was shifting between the two of them. Whether that was for the better remained to be seen. He took the glass of water from her and placed it on the dining room table. She threw a last look at the city outside before turning her back to it.

He led her onto the corridor, opening one of the doors that had been closed the first time she was in here. The bathroom was huge, almost as big as her living room at home was. It was mostly white and black with a few splotches of color, which came from two paintings, some candles, towels. The bathtub was big, way bigger than her own. It would easily accommodate two. He started the water, added some oil. Lavender. He couldn't have known, but she loved lavender and found its scent soothing.

"Do you need help undressing?"

The no came automatically, but she was surprised to find how stiff her body was when she began to do it herself. Carter let her. Her decisions were her own again. He began lighting some of the candles before he dimmed the lighting and undressed himself. Next, he started some quiet music and turned to her.

"Would you like some wine or rather something else?"

"I'm not sure if I'll make it out of here awake if I have wine now."

The warmth inside the room made her drowsy again, even the physical discomfort doing nothing to make her feel more awake.

"If you fall asleep, I'll carry you."

She watched him pass her when he left the room. The door remained slightly ajar and, looking through the crack, she admired his lean body, his firm ass and muscular thighs. She wasn't too tired to admire an attractive man. She laughed, amused by herself.

He was back in short order with a bottle and two glasses. He told her to pour the wine while he stopped the water and tested the temperature with his hand.

"Perfect."

He offered her his hand. After getting inside the tub, Sharon sighed when the warmth enfolded her bruised and tired body. It hurt where heat met abused skin, but only for a moment before her body absorbed the warmth.

Carter got in next and sat down opposite her.

"Come here," he said, holding his arms open for her.

After crossing so many lines, what would be one more? She settled between his legs, letting her head rest against his chest. It was good, close to perfect. The hot water, the music, the man behind her. She couldn't remember a time she had been so much at peace with a man. Had she ever before?

"You can get out any time," Carter said after minutes of silence.

"I don't understand."

"This. If it gets too much for you to handle, you can get out."

Sharon twisted her head slightly. She could feel his heart beating. It was steady, and she smiled.

"You can do the same, you know."

"Why would I want to?"

To speak now was a risk. If she stepped on his toes, she could be booted out of his apartment fast. She hadn't known him long enough to predict how he would react. To remain silent, though, was not an option. That wasn't who she wanted to be. She wasn't a coward. "Because you're as afraid as I am."

He was silent for so long, she tensed — was sure this marked the end of the evening.

"Yes, I am. I didn't expect this to be more than sex, a delightful game."

"But it is," she said, relieved she wasn't alone in feeling that constant pull towards each other.

"I don't know what it is, but yes, it is more. I just don't know what exactly. But let's not try to define it right now. So far it was a wonderful evening. Let's continue it that way. No expectations."

She made a sound of agreement. No expectations sounded good to her. They sat like that for a long time, talking little. Neither of them tried to rekindle the passion of earlier. Sharon doubted she'd have the strength for another round. A few times they took a sip of wine, and as expected it made her even more drowsy. She didn't care.

So often she hurried through her life, trying to get just another thing done. She worked until the point of exhaustion and came home only to fall asleep on the couch. Later sleep eluded her once she made it to bed. A vicious cycle.

Here and now, doing nothing was perfect.

When the water cooled down, she sat up and turned towards Carter.

"I hate to…"

"I know," he said, sitting up himself.

He reached out, one hand at the nape of her neck, pulling her close for an achingly tender kiss. Her lips prickled where they touched his, his slight stubble scratching her cheek. There was a fondness for him that hadn't been present before.

If they were to go in different directions now, she'd miss him, think of him, and would wish he were back in her life. It scared her more than she could say, and she pushed the thought as far away as she could as she sank into the kiss. It was Carter who slowly withdrew.

"Let's get dry, then I'll take care of your back and thighs."

"That bad?"

"No. I know what I'm doing. But there are bruises forming, and they need treatment."

It sounded so clinical, and it was true — every stroke he had delivered had been deliberate, controlled.

He got out of the tub first, offering his hand once more. Two weeks ago, she'd have refused him. Now she took it without hesitation. He walked to a closet and got out a fresh towel. She laughed, which had him turn to her with a frown.

"I've got blankets that are smaller than this towel," she said.

"With most things in life, I want the best."

"And towels are among those things," she teased.

It was new territory for the two of them, tension replaced by ease. He hesitated for all of a second, and she loved that she'd gotten one over on him for once.

"Towels, yes. And women."

While it was a compliment, she raised an eyebrow. "Women? Are you going women shopping, too? Like, I want two of these towels, and could you wrap them around these three blondes?"

"You are silly," he said, his lips curving into a smirk.

He took the towel into his hands and wrapped it around her body. Then he ran a hand through her slightly damp hair and twisted it around a finger, pulling when he wanted her to look at him. Dominance was woven into the threads of his personality, and she'd do well to remember it. Although she didn't have a problem with it, seeing how he treated her with respect and let her make up her own mind.

"I'm more into redheads, you know. And right now I only want one."

"Is that so?"

"Yes."

As he had promised, he toweled her dry, then offered her a robe that was comfortable but much too big. It smelled like him. God, it shouldn't affect her that badly, but she'd have loved to take this thing home with her, to sleep in it so she'd have his scent blanketing her. She closed her eyes and silently counted to ten, telling herself to cut the crap. This mushiness was unlike her, but it had been a special night. Her emotions had ridden a constant roller coaster. It should be okay to cut herself some slack.

When Sharon opened her eyes, he was toweling himself dry, not in the least bothered by his nudity. She wasn't either. Quite the contrary. Leaning against the wall, she watched him, giving herself license to ogle an attractive man.

"Like what you see?" he asked.

"Uh huh."

"A bit unfair, don't you think?"

"What is?"

"That I'm all naked while you are covering your beauty."

"Not only did you put it on me, I can also remove the robe if you want me to."

He was done, so he put the towel back on the rack. He was the first neat man she had been with. All others would have thrown the towel to the ground and forgotten about it.

"Later, maybe. Right now I want you in my bed, then I'll take care of you."

While she felt good, very good at the moment, she suspected she wouldn't feel so stellar in the morning if she refused his help now.

His bedroom, like all the other rooms, was big, yet neat, comfortably furnished in light colors but not crowded. There were some pictures on the walls, and she suspected they were his family, friends, people he cared about. She hadn't expected that.

"My parents died in a car accident a few years ago. I miss them."

"I'm sorry."

"Don't be. That's the course of life. Come, lie down on your stomach."

It was with some reluctance she got out of the robe, although the room was warm enough. Lying down with her head on her arms, she began to drift as Carter rummaged around.

His hands on her back, applying cool salve, made her breath catch.

"Sorry, it'll feel better in a minute."

The slight sting, the cold of the salve, those sensations wore off in short order and were replaced by pleasant warmth. His hands — she loved how they were tender, yet strong. If it had been up to her, he could have kept this up for hours.

"Let's talk," he said when he removed his hands.

She turned onto her side. "That's a first."

"What is?"

"A man saying 'let's talk'."

"I think it's warranted in this case." He sat down with a pillow propped behind his back. Without waiting for an invitation, Sharon sidled closer until she lay with her head nestled against his chest. As if a dam had been broken, she wanted it all now. Who knew when she'd get to enjoy intimacy like this again? *Never take anything for granted*, a mantra that had served her well over the years.

"What do you want to talk about?"

"About what happened tonight. How far did I push your boundaries? Was there something that was too much even though you didn't use the safe word?"

"It was...okay, although the nipple clamps scared me at the beginning."

Slowly they talked it through. She trusted him that he would remember what she'd said and apply the knowledge the next time they wanted to play. In a way it made her feel more secure, believing he wasn't out to hurt her.

Trust. It was the thing hardest to achieve, the thing most feeble in any relationship. Once broken, it was close to impossible to regain. In all of her relationships, the trust had been gone first, the rest of the relationship dying a fast, or in two cases, a torturously slow death.

"What's bothering you?"

She hadn't meant to zone out. "Life."

He stroked her hair. "The thing you can't do a thing about. Life will happen whether you want it to or not."

She made a sound of agreement and began to play with his sparse chest hair. "I want this again," she said. "The peace of mind. The high."

"Are you prepared to deal with the fall, too?"

"It was the hardest part of it all." It was one thing to know her hormone levels were decreasing, but another to experience the sudden onslaught of sadness that nearly paralyzed her. He had been there for her, had sheltered her in that vulnerable state, had turned even such a moment into a good one.

"But yes, I want to do it again. With you."

He chuckled. "I'd be jealous if you went to another man with your needs."

She didn't rule out being with another man in the future, didn't rule out she'd be willing to play these kinds of games with somebody else. How could she? For the moment, though, she wanted the man she was with. She yawned. The day had been draining on many levels.

"Let's sleep," Carter said.

"Would be nice." He switched off the lights and pulled the pillow down again before he reached for her once more. Nestled in his arms, Sharon fell asleep.

Chapter Seventeen

Her growling stomach woke Sharon at four in the morning. She was surprised to find Carter wasn't in bed, his side cold. After donning his robe and a necessary stop in the bathroom, she went to look for him.

She found him in his living room, a single lamp beside the couch illuminating the darkness. He had his back to her, a book in his hand, but when she came closer, he put the book to the side and turned to look at her. He wore a thinner black robe which was belted at his waist.

"Can't sleep?" he asked.

She sat down on the couch beside him. "I should ask you the same."

"I woke up an hour ago, couldn't fall asleep again."

"Does it happen often?"

He nodded. "You?"

"More often than I care to admit."

She looked out at the city again. "Do people here ever sleep?"

"Sometimes." He smiled.

Her stomach growled again.

"I see. I should've fed you earlier," he said, amusement tinting his voice

"I'm capable of feeding myself and wasn't hungry earlier."

"But now you are. I can heat us some frozen pizza."

So a man with his eclectic tastes likes frozen pizza? I should rethink my prejudices. "Do you have pepperoni and mushrooms?"

"I see you're a woman after my own heart."

They walked over to his kitchen together.

"I wasn't born rich, Sharon. I grew up with a brother and sister, in a loud and noisy but wonderful home. My mom made her own pizza, and there was always plenty of pepperoni, mushrooms and cheese. I never bothered to ask her for the recipe, but having some, even frozen, reminds me of her."

It was one thing to know the bare facts of the man, like the fact his parents had died, but quite another to hear him talk about them. His calm behavior couldn't belie the fact he had loved them, was still missing them.

"My mother has never been a good cook. But I loved it when we ordered pizza," Sharon said, rewarding trust with trust.

"Maybe we should try our hands at a self-made pizza at some point."

The thought of the cop and the sex club owner with their hands covered in flour and no idea what to do next was entertaining.

"We'll see."

Pizza heated in the oven, eating in the middle of the night—it reminded her of college. She'd never been one to pull off all-nighters on a regular basis, but before finals, she and her roommate had scrounged up some food and devoured it at all possible hours before they tried cramming in even more information into their tired brains.

The last time she'd heard from Annie, her former best friend had wondered how Sharon could have thrown away her college degree to join the force. That from a woman who had married the next best lawyer and had had two children in three years. Rumor had it Annie was divorced, but Sharon was beyond caring. Friends supported each other, no matter their decisions. Annie hadn't, so she wasn't worth another thought.

"That bad?" Carter asked.

"No, I was thinking about a former friend. We used to have midnight snacks. She never understood how I could become a cop."

"Not a true friend then. Did she know about Ava?"

How was it possible that after a few weeks he knew her better than one of her best friends ever had?

"No, she didn't. She still should have supported my decision."

He nodded. "Yes, she should have."

After dinner she was ready for bed again, and she was glad Carter said he wanted to sleep some more, too. She wasn't afraid of sleeping in a bed that wasn't hers. It just was nicer to have the company and warmth.

When she woke up next, Sharon was still lying on her side, and there was a hand on her naked stomach, stroking the skin lightly. Her mind was so sluggish, it took a few seconds to understand it was Carter's. More than anything else, the fact that her instincts hadn't protested the touch told her she was comfortable. He had to know she was awake now, but she didn't speak, wanting to see what he'd do next. She didn't have to wait long, as he trailed his hand up her chest and cupped a breast, his movements languid, slowly stoking her desire. The fingertip brushing her nipple had her breath catching as lust raced through her body, settling at the apex of her thighs.

He moved his hand to her other breast, kissing her shoulder. While his movements were slow, his caresses tender, the erection nudging the small of her back told its own story. He wanted her, and God help her, she wanted him, too.

"Turn around. I want to kiss you."

Rolling over, Sharon opened her eyes, and found he had switched on the lamp on his nightstand. He smiled, cupping her cheek before joining their lips for a soft kiss.

Her heart missed a beat. There was a tiny flutter in the pit of her stomach, and if she didn't want to fall even more for him, she'd have to withdraw now. Right now. She couldn't. Instead she returned the kiss with equal gentleness.

Their kiss deepened, both of them in no hurry to rush this encounter. She wanted him inside of her though, so she lifted her leg and slung it over his waist. He shook his head, and reached for his nightstand to get out a condom. Once he'd put it on, he positioned his cock at her entrance, slowly sliding in.

They groaned as their union was completed. His eyes remained open, and so did hers. This time she wanted to see him, to connect and make love. There was moment of stillness, then he slowly began to move, the feeling exquisite. She moaned, a smile on her face while she met him thrust for thrust, their bodies in tune with each other.

Rough she could handle, but she wasn't sure if his tenderness wasn't going to break her. He didn't speak and neither did she. Words were superfluous when their bodies were doing the talking for them.

Carter's hand made its way from her waist to the juncture of her thighs, finding her clit, rubbing it lightly. Her breath hitched, and her eyes fell closed as her body tried to absorb this new sensation. She didn't want to come yet. Last night she hadn't been allowed to come, now she didn't want to. The irony wasn't lost on her as she tried to distract herself.

Carter would have none of it though, his kisses insistent, penetrating her mouth as deeply as his cock was penetrating her body.

Good. So good. Needing to see him, Sharon pulled away. She opened her eyes, and she found he was looking at her too. For the first time, there was true emotion in his eyes. If she hadn't been drawn to him before, she clearly was now.

"Come for me. Please," he said, his voice rough and husky.

Even if her mind wanted to prolong the experience, her body obeyed, gentle waves of pleasure cresting, coursing through her body for a long time.

He stopped all motion and reached up to brush a strand of hair from her face before he pulled out.

"I want you to come, too."

"Not that important."

She'd often felt the same, thinking that giving pleasure was more important to her than receiving it. To hear it from a man was still something new. Using her training, she pushed him onto his back before sliding down on his erection, joining them again.

"It's important to me."

She enjoyed each second of making him lose control.

* * * *

Sharon needed three hours to find the right cab company. Thankfully, it only took her a few minutes to convince the owner to send his cab driver to the department later in the day. It was only a small victory, but each piece of a puzzle was valuable.

Putting down the phone, she sat back, reaching for her coffee. The slight movement made her flinch, as her arms were aching and her ass was sore. Still, the memories only made her smile.

"Being distracted on the job?"

"Hey, Jenn. What's up?"

"Not much. You remember the case with the bank robbery gone bad? We found the mask of that jackass bank robber. In an abandoned building near the bank. Too bad we can't prosecute a mask."

She sat down and took a look at Sharon's half-eaten sandwich which Sharon shoved over to her.

"Thanks. This is just maddening. We'll try to get some DNA from the mask, still..." She took a bite of the sandwich, looked over at Sharon and her eyes widened slightly. "Care to explain?"

"Huh?"

"That." Jenn pointed in the direction of Sharon's neck. Sharon reached for the spot, but couldn't feel a thing.

"What are you talking about?

"There's a hickey."

"There's not."

"Well, right now I'm the only one with a clear view of your neck, and let me tell you, that's a hickey."

Sharon got out her pocket mirror. Jenn was right. There was a tiny hickey on her neck. She couldn't even remember when it had happened. Although it was better to be caught with a hickey on her neck than with the fading bruises around her wrists and on her back.

"You've got sharp eyes." She was glad she'd opted for a snug sweater that would keep her wrists covered today.

"I know. So, who was it? Hastings or Carter? Want me to guess?"

"Jenn."

"Too late for secrecy. You can't close Pandora's box."

"What if it was neither of the two?"

That gave Jenn pause for a second, then she laughed. "I don't believe a word you're saying. So are you going to tell me? Or should I call and congratulate Luke?"

"I don't believe you'd do it."

Jenn had a big mouth, but when it came down to it, she would never betray a friend. "Touché. Anyway, I think it was Carter."

"Do you?"

"Yes. And now tell me. How is he?"

"You are impossible. Play nice or I'll find your Brian and warn him off."

"You couldn't. He's in love with me." Jenn's smile faltered, and she began playing with a paperweight. "It scares me, you know. Today he loves me. I love him. But what happens if that changes? I...I don't think I've ever truly loved a man before."

"You'll figure it out, Jenn. There's nothing else you can do. That's the nature of life and love." Sharon got up and smiled at her friend. "I've got to leave for a while."

"Have fun. But tell me, do you have that thing with Carter figured out yet?

Sharon shook her head. "But I will."

* * * *

The cab driver arrived at the department the same minute Sharon came back from investigating a lead in the case of a murdered housewife. Mustafa Jamal, a man in his forties, was wringing his hands when she took him to her office, his gaze flickering around. *Why is he so nervous?* He didn't have a criminal record in America, but she had no idea how his life had looked back in Morocco.

"Mr. Jamal, I don't want to keep you for long. I just need to know about this one taxi fare. Then you'll be free to go."

"It's okay, Miss—I mean, Detective."

His smile was too broad. He didn't believe her. It was almost as if she could smell and taste his fear. It was too bad she couldn't take his fear away, but she could make it quick for him.

"I need you to tell me about your trip to the club."

"You mean the sex club. My boss told me you want to know about that woman. It's not right, you know. People shouldn't do such stuff to each other." He shook his head, looked down at his hands, then at her. "There's hurt, a lot of hurt in this world. Why do people hurt each other that way without a reason? This is crazy."

Sharon let him ramble. Hadn't she asked herself the same questions not long ago? "Would you please tell me about your guest now? That's all I need to know."

Mustafa looked at some point over her shoulder and sat very still now.

"She was beautiful. Blonde lady. Blue eyes. I like blue eyes. She didn't talk much at first. Just gave me the address. I didn't know that address. She told me it was a club."

Why would Marlene have told him about it?

"When I asked her what kind of club, she laughed out loud. Told me it was a sex club where people hurt each other. She wasn't happy about it. I asked her why she went there when she didn't want to be hurt, and she said she didn't want to go there, but had to."

It didn't make sense. From all she'd heard so far, Davis had gone to the club on a regular basis. She'd enjoyed that kind of lifestyle. Why the sudden apprehension? Had she had any idea what was expecting her there? Had there been a threat, after all?

"Did she say anything else?"

"No. When I asked her what made her go there, she said it was an obligation. That's the right word, isn't it?"

"It is."

No sense at all. But where to start looking for the answers?

"You know, she looked so nice, too. So normal."

"What do you mean?"

"These women there. They wear leather, right? Dark things. This woman, she wore a white dress, with…points."

"Dots? Polka dots?"

"Black, round points."

Sharon nodded in confirmation. "Why do you remember her dress so clearly?"

It had been almost a month since this trip. If anyone had asked her what she'd done exactly a month or two prior or at any other specific day, really, she wouldn't be able to remember. At least not that clearly.

"She was beautiful. Sad. So sad." He looked away, then at her again. "My wife looked so sad after our son died."

Every life told a story, some with more drama, some with less. This man had obviously suffered more than any person should suffer.

"I'm sorry," she said, those two inadequate words tasting bitter on her tongue.

"It was a long time ago." He cleared his throat and looked around the room again. "Is that all?"

"Yes, it is. Thank you, Mr. Jamal. I only need you to write it down and sign it for me, then you're free to go. If there's anything else you remember, you can call the precinct or my cell."

He nodded and quickly penned down his statement, clearly wanting to be out. When he was done, she handed him her card. He crammed it into the pocket of his jacket without looking at it. The chance he'd call was slim to nonexistent, but one never knew.

She stared into the distance for a long while after he'd left. What she had heard didn't fit the pattern at all. Whenever she thought she had at least the basics of what happened, something shook the pieces of this particular puzzle around, the picture emerging making no sense.

Either she had had the wrong picture of Marlene Davis all along, or something had happened that changed her behavior. And where was the dress? She had been dressed all in red when they had found her. She'd have to think about it. Right now, she had a report to write, then she had a late court appointment. Afterwards, she might call Carter. Or not. He'd said she should call whenever she wanted. She'd see if she'd want to or not.

Chapter Eighteen

Her mother was already waiting for her. Sharon had to smile. She hadn't expected anything else. Whenever her mother agreed on a time, she'd be early. It was a law of nature in their family, at least on the female side. The one time her mother hadn't managed to meet her at the agreed time, Sharon had been worried sick, the eight minutes her mother was late among the longest of her life.

"Sharon, darling, you look great."

The older woman hugged her, refusing to let go of her for a long time. Although her mother was half a head shorter than she was, Sharon still relied on her strength, wishing she possessed an ounce of it.

"Where's your own Mr. Handsome?" Sharon asked when she let go of her mother. People liked to say she looked a lot like her mother, but she wasn't so sure about it. Her mother was short, petite and had dark eyes in contrast to Sharon's green ones. The hair color was the same, as was the smile. At least her dad had said that more than once.

"Henry's doing some sightseeing on his own. He thought we might like to catch up a little."

"He's right."

Sharon and her mother had agreed to meet at the Empire State Building to take a walk and have some coffee and dinner at Sharon's apartment later. That they would spend the first part of the day alone was a plus.

Sharon took her mother's arm and led the way to her favorite coffee shop. It was a good day — not too warm, not too cold, the onslaught of tourists not as bad as it would be a month from now. While they walked, her mother told her all the news from home. Sharon was content to listen. She really needed to take the time to visit home again soon. There would always be excuses why it was a bad time, so she'd better not wait for the right time.

Inside the coffee shop, her mother took a seat while Sharon got them some coffee and a slice of cheesecake to go along with it. It wouldn't be a fraction as good as her grandmother's, who had been a first-class baker, but it had to do.

"Who is he, darling?"

Her mother wasn't even looking at her. She was stirring her coffee. *What the hell?*

Sharon could try to lie, to evade the topic, but it wouldn't work. Not with her mother. She'd tried it often enough. "Someone I got to know through work."

"Is he a cop?" Now her mother's eyes found hers and held her gaze.

"No, he isn't." The thought of Carter as a cop had her smiling.

"Sharon, while I don't want to pry, I want to know my baby girl is happy and that the new man in her life is treating her well. So tell me everything."

Her mother meant well, and she was a tolerant woman, but Sharon doubted she'd like to hear the man her daughter was dating was in the sex business and liked to beat up her offspring, who in turn enjoyed it.

In the last few days, she'd met Carter twice more. Once for a session involving handcuffs, a flogger and hot wax in his club, the other time for dinner in a restaurant and a round of lovemaking in his apartment. Both times she'd stayed the night.

It would be a lie if she said she wasn't getting used to it, to him.

"He's a businessman, has a lot of money. Although that's not what attracted me to him. He knows what he wants, is rather direct... Gosh, it's hard to describe."

"But he respects you and there's no indication he has any intention of cheating on you yet."

"Mom."

"Hey, I thought your last boyfriend was a nice guy. I learned my lesson."

Sharon snorted. "Me too." She got a text message and reached for her phone. "Sorry, it could be work."

It wasn't work but Carter, who wanted to know what she was doing, and if she were interested in meeting for lunch. She'd forgotten to tell him her mother would be in town. Not that it was any of his business, or was it?

She texted back she was having coffee with her mother, and would get back to him later.

"Sorry, Mom. It's..."

Another message. Carter wanted to know if they cared for company. What the hell? What was he aiming for? They hadn't known each other for long and weren't in any kind of traditional relationship. He wasn't pushing her on anything when it didn't come to playing, and now he wanted to meet with her and her mother.

"What is it?"

She looked up at her mother. "Nothing."

"Doesn't look like nothing to me."

"Carter. Simon, he wanted to know if we were interested in having coffee with him. It's not that I'm ashamed of him or anything like it, but we're not... We haven't been together for all that long."

"Sharon, relax. This is him proposing to have coffee with us, not me inviting him for dinner and an interrogation. If it doesn't make you too uncomfortable, I'd like the chance to take a look at him, though."

Sharon broke eye contact, her gaze drawn inwards while she tried getting her emotions under control. If it came down to it, her mother hadn't even met half of her boyfriends, and Carter wasn't her boyfriend. Or was he?

"Sharon, you don't have to."

"No, it's okay. But I have to admit this feels a little strange to me."

"I understand. And as soon as it gets too much, you'll just send him or me on our way, okay?"

Sharon laughed and took a deep breath. "You are wonderful, Mom. You know that, right?"

Her mother's hand covered hers. "I'm not. But I like to treat people as I want to be treated myself."

"I know. I know." She suppressed a sigh and quickly texted Carter the address.

He arrived less than twenty minutes later, and during that time, Sharon was distracted, wondering about his agenda, about her mother's reaction to a man she didn't understand herself.

Her mother, although she had to be aware of her predicament, didn't give any indication that she noticed. Instead she talked about her impending marriage, the fact they only wanted to invite close family, where they wanted to go for their short honeymoon. Sharon listened even when her heart wasn't in it. She cursed the fact she had her back to the door, so she wouldn't be able to brace herself for the moment Carter appeared.

God, this was worse than prom night had been when her whole family had waited for her date to appear.

As it turned out, she didn't need to be able to see the entrance. Her mother stopped mid-sentence, took a look at her then the door again.

"If that's him, then…"

"Mrs. Richards?"

It was Carter, his voice making the hairs on Sharon's neck stand up.

"I am. And you must be…"

"Simon Carter, pleased to meet you." He had a small bag with him, which he placed beside the table. When he offered her his hand, her mother took it without hesitation.

Sharon watched him, all kinds of thoughts running through her mind in the few seconds she was free to do so. Damn him. Would she ever be able to look at him without desire coursing through her veins? Did she even want that? At least in her opinion, he looked delectable in tight-fitting black jeans and a black turtleneck.

"Sharon, I hope you don't mind too much," he addressed her.

She did. She didn't. Damned if she could decide. All she knew right now was that he was different today, a little less guarded, or maybe just showing a different mask for the sake of her mother. It was still him though.

"I'm not sure, to be honest," she said, indicating the place between her mother and herself for him to sit.

"I understand," he said. "I'll get myself a coffee and be back."

Her mother waited until he was out of earshot before she spoke.

"Handsome, clearly intelligent and there's a bit of bad-boy charm underneath the polish. Interesting."

Sharon shook her head. "How are you doing that?"

"I'm doing nothing, dear. I'm sure you were aware of all this the moment you met him, too. I only vocalized it."

"I think you described him well."

"Thank you. You know once upon a time I spent a whole week considering joining the force myself." Her mother laughed, looking in the direction Carter had vanished, her lips pursed. Following her mother's gaze, Sharon chuckled.

"Please don't tell me you're checking him out."

"He's got a nice ass."

Sharon closed her eyes for a second. How was she to survive the next hour?

"Sharon, again, relax. I'm not out to embarrass you, and I doubt this very nice-looking man over there is either."

"Uh huh."

The road to hell was paved with good intentions. Carter was back a minute later, taking the seat Sharon had offered earlier.

"What brought you here?" Sharon asked. "Don't you have work to do?"

She knew how she sounded, and hadn't intended to react this way. It just poured out of her. Carter gave her a slight smile.

"I know I've got no business being here, Sharon. I'm sorry. I only wanted to let you know I'll be out of town for a few days. I thought it would be nice to tell you in person and not over the phone."

"I see. Thank you." They had agreed on a date tomorrow. A date at the club. She'd been looking forward to it, as much to the game as to his company afterwards. The slight disappointment still came as a surprise. But anyway, what kind of business would have him leave town?

Suspicion uncoiled like a snake in the pit of her belly. She quickly suppressed it. Not only could he hardly tell her here with her mother around, but it was none of her business to begin with.

Or was it why he wanted to meet her here now? Because she couldn't try to pry for any information? Bullshit. He hadn't known she would be meeting with her mother. The chaos in her mind made her grit her teeth.

Her mother's laughter made her realize she hadn't listened to the two of them talking. She willed herself to relax at least a little, and took the opportunity to watch Carter interact with someone on a purely social basis. He was still a little guarded, as was his nature, but his pose was relaxed, he was ready to smile at any given moment and his eyes twinkled with humor.

Her heart gave a tiny flutter, and she wanted to reach out, to trace the shape of his lips with her fingers. Not here. Not now. What had happened to impulse control? He was an extremely good-looking man, that was…

Was it really such a wonder she'd fallen for him? This man had looked into the abyss of her darkest desires, and had helped her to accept them with care.

"I'm going to marry soon," her mother said.

Sharon's head whipped around to her.

"My congratulations."

She hadn't told Carter about her mother remarrying. Why should she have? They weren't that close yet, maybe would never be.

"If Sharon decides she wants to bring a date, you'll be very welcome."

It was the ultimate sign her mother accepted her dating Carter. Still, she wished she hadn't all but invited him. Although this was only a reminder that she couldn't live two lives. One as a cop, a daughter, a friend, the other as lover to a man with refined tastes. At some point she had to let the two lives merge or let one go.

Which one she would discard if she needed to choose wasn't even a question. She wouldn't give any man that much power over her, no matter how much it hurt.

"Thank you," Carter said.

"So Sharon said you two got to know each other through the course of an investigation?" An innocent question with the potential to lead to an inferno.

"We did. From what I could see, Sharon's very good at her job."

Her mother smiled. "From what I've heard, she is. So far she has never let me accompany her to any of her investigations, though." The light laugh assured Sharon her mother was only kidding.

"It's against any and all regulations and believe it or not, I want you safe, Mom."

"I want you safe too, my darling." She focused on Carter again. "Have you been living in New York for long, Mr. Carter?"

"Please, call me Simon."

Her mother inclined her head. "I'm Martha."

"Yes, I have, Martha. I've always felt at home here. I can't imagine living anywhere else."

"Funny. I couldn't imagine living here at all."

For the time Carter stayed, their conversation remained lighthearted. Sharon mostly listened, all the time wishing this would finally be over. It wasn't that there was any awkwardness or tension between her mother and Carter, just that Sharon couldn't be sure that it wouldn't change any second. After all, there were things Sharon would rather not have her mother know.

Finally, Carter looked at his watch. "I'm sorry, I need to catch that plane." With an apologetic smile, he got up, said goodbye to her mother, then leaned down to kiss Sharon's cheek. "I'll call you."

"Sure. I'd like that."

He left without turning back once. Sharon wished she hadn't followed his movements either. She was stronger than that.

He was hardly out of the door when her mother spoke. "Now I've seen you kiss your boyfriends more passionately."

Sharon rolled her eyes. "Thanks for the reminder, Mom."

"It's human, dear. And yes, I understand you haven't been together for that long. I understand, too, that the last thing you expected for today was for your mother and your boyfriend to meet."

"To say the least."

Her mother's smile faded, and she reached out to cover one of Sharon's hands with one of her own. "So far, I like him. He's less charming than your other boyfriends were, but I think he's more sincere. And he's a real looker." She gave Sharon a speculative look. "Out of clothes as well?"

"Mom. Please. You're starting to sound like Jenn. And to be honest, I think that is a scary notion."

"Talking about Jenn. How's the girl?"

Her mother had known Jenn for years, and Sharon and Jenn had driven up to Vermont for a weekend once or twice during that time.

"She's good. But you won't guess who she's dating lately."

Though Sharon was usually not one to gossip, it was easier to talk about Jenn than to contemplate her own love life.

Chapter Nineteen

Simon hadn't called. Not since that day meeting with her and her mother. Not the next. He didn't owe her an explanation, but more than "*I need to leave for a few days*" would have been nice. That he didn't explain a thing around her mother, good, but that there wasn't a life sign from him afterwards disturbed her. What were cell phones for? If there weren't time for a call, why not send a quick text?

Although this didn't annoy her as much as the fact she'd tried calling him twice. Or rather, she'd punched in his number and had disconnected before it even rang for the first time. She had some pride left, hadn't she? To hell with him. If he wanted something from her, he would call.

Heading for the shower, Sharon was glad her mother had left the city earlier in the evening. It was one thing to be in a bad mood, quite another if her mother were privy to it and knew what was bothering her.

"He'll call," she'd said at least three times. How her mother had known this was what had her panties in a knot, Sharon didn't know and didn't ask.

No matter what her mother said, she hadn't been convinced then, and wasn't convinced now. Damn this man. If he wanted to call this thing between them off, he could. No big deal. To just disappear, though...just no.

Sharon was in bed a bit before midnight, still awake a little before one in the morning, when her phone rang.

"Yes?"

"Sharon, it's me." Simon. Sharon counted to three to prevent herself from snapping at him.

"Hey, how are you? And you're calling way late if I may say so."

"I'd have called earlier if it had been possible."

It wasn't exactly an apology, and hadn't she heard these words before? One of her ex-boyfriends had been a pro at this kind of non-apology. She hadn't expected such bullshit from Simon. Suddenly tired, all she wanted was to hang up, turn around and sleep. Only she wouldn't sleep. It was an emotional kind of exhaustion, not a physical one. There was no sense in lying to herself.

"I see. Well, you didn't have to."

"I wanted to."

She admitted to herself that he sounded tired. It made her ire thaw a little. "Listen, Carter. It's late and..."

"So it's Carter again. Tell me, what's worse, that I dared meeting with you while you were with your mother or that I didn't call for two days?"

"I'm tired, Simon. Too tired for games. And it's actually both. I'm pissed at both. I don't understand the one and don't understand the other. I know I have no right to expect a bloody thing from you, but I'm human. And I'm a cop. Suspicious behavior puzzles me and makes me curious."

Sharon fell silent. It was the first time she'd had such an outburst when it came to a lover, and right now she didn't regret it. While she didn't mind the games they played in the privacy of the club, she didn't want to play any games when it came to her life. She wouldn't ask him where he had been, but she wouldn't pretend that she didn't care either.

"Thank you."

"What for?"

"Your honesty."

She snorted. "As I said, I'm tired."

"I didn't mean to barge in that day with your mother, Sharon, but I really had to leave. I thought it would be worse if I just left a message. And it all was too complex for a text message anyway."

"You don't owe me any explanation."

"No? Then let me tell you a story. You know I've got a brother and sister, right?"

"I do, but..."

"Will you listen?"

It was the first time he had given any indication of being troubled by something, and angry as she was, she wished she could be with him to offer comfort. Not that she had any idea where he was in the first place.

"I will."

"Good. My brother is gay. No big deal in my family, as I told you before. He's in love with a wonderful man named Garrett. They've been together for fourteen years next month. Andrew, my brother, called me the day I left. Garrett was just diagnosed with HIV. They don't know yet how he got it and my brother's test was negative, but he has to take another one in a few months. We all know that it is possible to live a long and good life with HIV these days, but it was and is still a shock. Andrew needed a shoulder to cry on, so I took the next plane to Chicago."

Sharon swallowed, lost for words.

"Simon, I'm..."

"Don't say you're sorry. There's nothing to be done. But this taught me one thing. Nothing in life is for certain and you better go for what you want today because it could be gone tomorrow."

Didn't she know it? She twirled a strand of hair around her finger. "And what is it you want?"

"You. I want you to think about a relationship. A real relationship. You don't have to answer me today or tomorrow but soon would be good. And for right now, you could let me in."

The words took a moment to register. He was here, at her apartment? Right now? She hadn't even told him where exactly she was living, which was odd considering what else he knew about her. Out of the blue she remembered a call in his presence from the company that wanted to schedule the delivery for a new wardrobe. She had given them her address, and he must have remembered. There wasn't much that he missed.

"Sharon, don't make me beg."

The tired voice was what finally got her into gear. Ending the call and getting up quickly, she walked through her small apartment, idly wondering what he would think about it.

She opened the door, and there he was. No, he would wonder about nothing right now. He looked as tired as he'd sounded. He had to have come here directly from the airport, as he had his luggage with him.

"Come," she said, stepping to the side so he could enter. Why had he called instead of knocking or ringing the bell? It was a question for later. She closed the door behind him.

"Thanks for letting me in."

"What was I supposed to do? Let you stand out there?"

"You could have. You sounded angry enough."

"Let's not argue, yes? Can I offer you something?"

He dropped the bag right where he was and pulled her in for a kiss that was almost desperate. He was cold, and the hands on her shoulders, touching her neck, made a shiver run down her back. As tempting as his kisses were, as easy as it would be to retreat to her bedroom and make up in the best way possible, she should get him warm. Never mind — she'd never been one for make-up sex. She had to resolve a conflict before she could fully give herself to a partner. She pulled away reluctantly.

"Let's get you warm. I could run a bath if you like."

"I honestly only want to go to bed. I want to stay here with you. If you'll have me, that is."

It was her choice, the ball in her court. It was the first time he had directly barged into her private home life, and at the moment, she wasn't sure if she liked it or not. She wasn't prepared for his presence here. Although he hadn't chosen the blow that had been delivered to him.

"Of course, I will. Do you need anything?"

He ran a hand through his short hair, contemplating. "No. A short stop in the bathroom and you can forget I'm here. Just go back to bed."

As if it were so easy. She showed him to her bathroom then walked back to her bed where she sat down, waiting for him to join her. If she'd known he'd be here, she'd have cleaned beforehand and changed the sheets, which was ridiculous as it was obvious the state of her apartment or her sheets was the last thing on his mind.

When he came to join her, he'd shed most of his clothes and was only wearing a pair of briefs. Even tired as she was, tired as he looked, there was still a surge of desire coursing through her body. It was as if she couldn't help it.

They didn't speak, and he slid under the covers with her. When she thought he was comfortable, she reached out to switch off the lights. It was a surreal situation, and it would really hit home for her in the morning when she woke up and he was there.

A few minutes passed. He was lying on his back, completely still. She could only guess at his thoughts. Reacting on impulse, she turned onto her side. He opened his arms for her, and she snuggled close. He was already warm, his presence offering instant comfort.

"Do you want to talk about it?" she asked quietly.

He chuckled. "Didn't they tell you it's about the only question you should never ask a man?"

"Says the one who insisted we talk that first night in your apartment. You're not just any man. And I don't care what people say. I've started to think I care for you, though." Her confession made her heart beat faster. But she hadn't lied. She did care for him. He was more than just a lover, a convenience to scratch some of her itches.

"I'm just sad," he said after a minute. "My brother and his partner were happy. It wasn't and isn't the perfect relationship, they had their share of arguments, but at the end of the day, yes, they made it work, and were happy."

"And they have no idea how this has happened?"

"I believe Garrett when he says that he was faithful to my brother, and the best bet is the blood transfusion he got when he had surgery a few years ago. A ruptured appendix. They only just saved him in time."

And for what? Sharon knew it was possible to live with HIV. It wasn't the end of the world for people any longer. Sooner or later it would likely determine the cause of death, but one could live an almost normal life if it was diagnosed early enough, if one got the right medication and lived carefully. Still, she couldn't imagine getting such a diagnosis.

"Will they be able to cope? Will they try to find out and sue?"

"Andrew is angry. He would go on a war path if possible, but Garrett doesn't want to hear a thing about it. He says nothing will make him healthy again."

"Do you think they will make it?"

"I don't know. I hope so. Right now they're at odds with themselves, each other, the world. I promised to help as much as I can, to make sure they'll get their hands on the best medication, but..."

"It doesn't feel like it's enough."

"Yes."

"That's all you can do. That and offering an open ear when it's needed. Simon, I'm sorry, I really am."

"Thank you. And thank you for letting me stay the night."

"The least I can do."

They fell silent again, but Sharon was unable to sleep. Simon's breathing hadn't evened out either. If she felt helpless now, was uncertain what was the right thing to do, how must it feel for him? Finally, she sat up in bed, unsure what she wanted to do, only that she couldn't pretend to be asleep any longer.

"I'm sorry for keeping you up," he said quietly.

"Nonsense."

When she leaned over to kiss him, he reached for her and pulled her on top of him. This time she didn't try to stop him and gave in to his need to connect. If that was what he needed, she'd gladly give it to him, especially as her own desire was woken by his tongue battling with hers, his hands gliding along her back.

"I want you," he said. "Please."

She answered by pushing her tongue inside his mouth, being the aggressor for once. In short order they had divested each other of their few clothes, and she was glad she had protection right at hand. Their lovemaking was aggressive, a constant give-and-take. There was nothing controlled about this encounter, something she relished as much as she did their other kind of intimacy.

Tonight they were two people caught in the throes of passion, stripped of all masks. At one point she left scratch marks on his shoulders, but he didn't seem to notice. When he came before her, he hardly took a breath before he pushed her to her back, settling between her legs, licking and nibbling until she cried out her own release.

They fell asleep soon afterwards, a tangle of bodies and sheets.

* * * *

Sharon should have turned off the alarm. It woke her, them, way too soon, and her eyes were swollen when she opened them to get the noise to stop. Carter — no, Simon — had still been asleep, too. He sat up with a sigh, rubbing his eyes.

"Morning, sleepyhead," he said with a smile at her appearance.

"If you make one unseemly comment about my looks in the early mornings, you'll…"

"Have to die? And you might remember I've already seen you in the early morning."

But never like that, after a too-long night, with only the barest minimum of sleep. The way he looked at her, though, he didn't care.

"I'll have a quick shower, then you'll have the bath to yourself and I'll prepare some coffee."

He nodded, and she left him behind, wondering what he might think about an apartment that was so unlike his own.

She'd just started the water when he joined her.

"How about we share the shower and make it a longer one?"

This man was insatiable, and she enjoyed every second of it. After having sex in the shower, they had breakfast in her small kitchen, while he shared stories about his dorm room in college. Time passed much too quickly.

Eventually, Sharon had to leave for the office, and Carter convinced her to share a cab with him. He let her out two blocks from the precinct. She walked the rest of the way, enjoying the first rays of morning sunshine warming her. Today most people looked more relaxed than usual, the good weather mellowing their moods. It wouldn't last for long. First they'd get used to the warmer temperatures, then soon they'd complain about the heat. If there was one thing people were way too good at, it was complaining.

Jenn greeted her with a wave when she entered the office.

"Way late today, dear."

"Half an hour, if at all, and what is that?" she asked, pointing at a bouquet of flowers in the middle of their desks.

"Oh, it's for you, but you weren't there, and I thought we could share these."

Carter had sent her flowers. When had he ordered them? They were beautiful, yellow roses mixed with three orchids. An unusual combination. She reached for the card, surprised it wasn't signed by Carter.

"Who sent them?" Jenn asked.

Hastings. She'd almost forgotten about him.

The note accompanying the flowers read, *They are unique, just like you. I'm looking forward to our date. Luke.*

Sharon put the note to the side.

"You're making a face as if your mother just drowned."

"Jenn."

"Sorry. You know I love your mother and want her to live to a hundred years and more. But now who sent these?"

"Hastings."

"Oh."

Sharon looked at Jenn. "Yeah. Oh. But it's not like you to be speechless."

"Yeah. But this poses a problem, doesn't it? From what I understand, you want Carter. From the hickey you're sporting—once again—you're doing Carter. Now Hastings wants a piece of you as well. I guess you still think you shouldn't want Carter, but you are an honest soul and can't pretend you don't. Now you have to find a way to let Hastings down."

It came too close to the truth of the matter. Only Sharon had promised herself to give Luke a chance. Why did it feel like a betrayal then?

Because Simon wanted a relationship with her. When they had said goodbye this morning, he had told her to let him know, and he hadn't needed to clarify what he was talking about.

What would Simon think if she went out with Hastings? Was it even any of his business?

There were no good answers, and there was no chance in hell she'd tell Simon about Hastings right now.

"Sharon, you listening?"

No, she wasn't. She had to find out what the best course of action was.

"Sorry, Jenn."

"Why don't you call Hastings and tell him thank you but no? Yes, he'd probably be best for you, at least looking at it from the outside, but the only thing that matters is how you feel about it. And your face tells me everything."

"It doesn't."

"It does. So you want to pretend you're not in love with Carter?"

In love? Who is talking about love here?

"Deer in the headlights, hon. But for the sake of the argument, let's say you don't love Carter, just do the hanky-panky with him." Jenn stopped, shook her head. "Nah, you know, somehow I don't believe it. How does it work with you two anyway? Is he whipping you into shape?"

"Funny, Jenn. Very funny." Jenn was only teasing her. Yet it was almost tempting to tell her the truth just to see her friend's reaction.

She wasn't ready for such a move. It seemed she wasn't ready for quite a few things, one of them trying to figure out what she wanted from Simon, how much she wanted to give.

Jenn interrupted her musings. "Anyway, did you get any closer to finding out what happened to Davis' clothes?"

Talking business — that she could do.

"No, it's as mysterious as it's going to get. Why would someone enter a club in a dress with polka dots and end up dead in red leather? True, she wouldn't have worn the leather at work, but no one ever saw her in a cute little dress either. I don't get it."

"How long will you follow dead leads, dear?"

It had been several weeks now. Jenn was right. It was more than time to see about other investigations. Davis shouldn't have priority any longer. Still, she wasn't ready to let go yet, not even a little. How could she rest and maybe contemplate something more with Simon for as long as he wasn't cleared as a suspect?

"It feels like there's something I should see but don't. It drives me nuts, Jenn."

"But forcing it won't help. And there are three other murders that need your attention." Jenn lifted her hands in defense before she could speak. "I know you're working on them, but you can't deny they're not getting the attention they usually would."

Jenn was right, yet it didn't change a thing.

Chapter Twenty

Sharon waited until Jenn had left the office before she called Hastings, her fingers playing with the cord of the phone. He answered the call on the second ring, and she didn't need to see his face to know he was smiling.

"Sharon. That's a nice surprise."

And it wasn't the opening she had waited for. With no good idea what to tell him in the first place, she'd hoped he'd give her something she could react to, like a simple "Hey, how are you?" to ease her into the conversation she wanted to have with him.

"I...called to thank you for the flowers. They're beautiful."

"Good. I'm glad you like them. As I said, they reminded me of you. I've got to admit I was a bit worried about what you'd think about the fact I sent you flowers but decided to risk it, anyway." He laughed out loud. "So, yeah, your call is very much appreciated."

His frank and honest behavior made her feel even worse. While she wasn't in a committed relationship, she wasn't a free agent either. Would Hastings still want to send her flowers, invite her to dinner, if he knew she was seeing someone? A someone who could, no, should be considered a suspect? A someone with whom she shared a different flavor of lovemaking? Somehow she doubted it.

Hell, even if she went out with Hastings, kissed Simon goodbye and started something with her former boss, could she ever bury the knowledge that she liked to submit to a Dominant in bed? While she and Simon had shared quite a bit of vanilla sex, as he liked to call it, she wouldn't want a steady diet of it either. Not any longer.

Sharon rubbed her aching temple. "It's a really thoughtful gift." *God, he deserves a better woman than me, one who truly appreciates him for what he is.* "So, how's life at the new precinct?"

"Good. Different." He chuckled. "I think most of the people here still hate me. But that's okay. It's better they slowly find out I'm not the hard-ass they think I am. After all, it wouldn't do for them to think I'm their next best buddy either. I'm not and can't be. Anyway, I'm still missing you all. But don't tell that to Reynolds and the others. They would start to think I'm one big softy."

She smiled. He was right about Jenn. She'd have a field day with such information. It would be even more effective than sending a memo to everyone concerned.

"Your secret's safe with me. But believe me, you're missed here as well."

"Kelly's a good guy."

"He is, and I'm sure he'll do a fine job here, still…we all got used to you, too." The new captain was all about efficiency, at least that was the impression she'd gotten over the last few days. He would support them, but she doubted he'd have their backs like Hastings would have. Well, not yet anyway. Which was another reason to close the Davis case before Kelly insisted on putting it on the backburner.

"Are you trying to tell me you miss me, Sharon?" Hastings teased.

She did. Although on a strictly professional level. "I do."

"Well, it's convenient we'll see each other in two days then. And I'm really looking forward to the date."

She couldn't return the compliment, no matter how much she wished it was different. "Luke, what if you're mistaken about me?" A little warning was only fair, wasn't it?

"What if I'm not?"

He was right, and it was the reason she'd agreed to the date in the first place. It had happened before, people knowing each other for quite some time becoming lovers, with sparks starting to fly way late in the game. What were the odds, though? She shook her head.

"I don't want to hurt you." He deserved the truth, at least as much as she could give him without incriminating herself. Her job was still on the line and one wrong word could finish her career.

He sounded instantly concerned. "Sharon, do you want to cancel our date? If so, just say it."

This could be her way out. A simple yes, and she could forget about this mess. And what if her instincts were mistaken on that one, and Hastings was her shot at happiness?

"No, I don't want to cancel. It's just…"

He was a couple months too late, and Sharon wasn't sure she could turn her back on what she'd found with Simon.

"Then what is it? Is it that I want this more than you seem to? I'm not stupid, Sharon. But I want to give this a try, would love for you to give it a try as well."

"I really didn't call to cancel." She hated herself for lying to a good man.

"Good. And as much as I hate to cut you short now, I've got a meeting with my boss at ten. I'll pick you up at seven-thirty?"

"Sure. Sounds good."

She said goodbye, put down the receiver and looked at the flowers again. One man sent her flowers, another cracked the whip. By all means, this shouldn't be a hard choice.

What if normal was simply overrated? The standard for normal was based on average human behavior, but who said behaving differently was a bad thing for as long as it didn't affect another's life in an unwanted way?

When Jenn came back an hour later, Sharon didn't hear her enter the office. The arms embracing her from behind were a surprise. "You know you're basically hugging a chair now, right?"

"Lame one, Shar."

Jenn rounded the chair in question and sat down on Sharon's desk. "And it's still better than hugging a tree," Jenn said.

"There might be some grander purpose in hugging a tree."

"Yeah. There might." Her friend looked unusually serious, and Sharon braced herself for what was to come.

"Just get it out, okay?"

"Sure. All morning I've been thinking and actually, I'm sick and tired of seeing you look so sick and tired. I'm feeling as if I could kick Carter's, then Hastings' ass. You're not looking happy. At all. Being in love or maybe only in lust with someone should make you feel good."

"Even if the man in question is a suspect?"

"No one really believes he's a suspect. And if it's the investigation, then by the love of what is holy, claim bias and have someone else take care of this."

Sharon picked up a pen and began doodling on a sheet of paper lying before her.

"Not going to work. If someone else went to investigate this, they might find out I was at the club a few times, that I…spent some time with Carter and not in his office."

It took less than a second for the implications to hit Jenn. Her friend whistled lowly under her breath. Sharon focused on her doodling. She didn't quite want to know what Jenn was thinking.

"Look at me, girl."

When Sharon did, she was faced with the cop she knew her friend to be. Under all her flippant behavior, there was a top-notch cop who wouldn't take shit from anyone.

"Jenn, this is not an interrogation. I'm talking to you as my friend here."

"I know, just…all teasing aside. I didn't think you had the guts for it."

"I didn't think I had either. But I was curious. And it was good. It is good. Have you ever found something you needed although you didn't know you did?"

"I found Brian. So yes, I do. Anyway, it explains quite a few things."

"Like?"

"Wearing turtlenecks or something long-sleeved when you'd usually go for a shirt."

So when she had thought she was hiding what she'd done, she had been advertising it. Maybe not the exact nature of her doings, but enough to put another cop's instincts on alert. She should have known better. Only she'd been too preoccupied to think that far and what could she have done differently? Buy expensive makeup, maybe?

"He's not really hurting you, though, is he?"

"No, Jenn. If at all, I'd say Simon is the perfect gentleman. It might sound strange in this context but no one, and I mean no one, has ever taken care of my needs in the way he does."

"So it's Simon now, huh? And anyway, I'm glad to hear it."

Jenn covered Sharon's hand with her own, and Sharon stopped her restless motions with the pen. "If Carter's good for you, then he is. Just you don't look too happy right now. Allow me to be worried. I've seen you date too many scumbags, and I really hope you're not wrong about Carter. From what I've seen he's an okay guy, and anyway, if he is it, if he is the one who gives you what you need, then go for it. Well, after the investigation has run its course, one way or the other."

Sharon looked away and sighed. "I promised Hastings to give a date a chance."

Jenn raised both eyebrows at once. "A date with Hastings? When and why?"

Sharon wished she could take back the words. She had forgotten she hadn't shared her plans with their former boss with Jenn. "Dinner in a few days. Nothing fancy."

"But you don't feel good about it either. Geez, girl. Are you sure you want to do that? If I understood you correctly, you're into Carter, you want the man and badly. Dating another man can't lead to anything good."

"It's only dinner." If she could only believe her own words.

"Yeah, and it's not as if Hastings has had his eyes on you for the last few years. His second name could be Crush."

"Jenn, you're not helping."

"No, your conscience isn't helping." Jenn shook her head. "Anyway, I'll sew my mouth shut. And if you need a shoulder to cry on, you know where to find me."

"I do. And the same goes for you."

"Yeah. Yeah." Jenn walked back toward her desk, sat down. "So there's truly something to pain, huh?"

"Yes, there is. It enhances the pleasure, and I've never known such a peace of mind."

"Hmmh, you think it would work if I suggested it to Brian?" Jenn cracked a small smile.

Sharon laughed out. "You never know."

They shared a smile before they went back to work. Nothing was solved, she still felt bad about the whole situation, but at least she had a friend she could count on.

* * * *

"No. I'm sorry, I already have plans on Saturday."

When she'd called Simon earlier, she hadn't counted on the fact he would be busy on Friday. Heck, she wasn't even sure what she'd wanted to achieve by calling him, trying to meet him before her date a day later. How could she possibly enjoy herself when she'd go out with another man the very next day?

But as it was, Simon had a meeting with some realtor about a building he would like to acquire. She hadn't counted on him offering Saturday instead. Now she'd had to tell him she wasn't available, only she couldn't quite tell him the reason. Well, she could, but she doubted he would like her plan.

"I'm going to meet with a friend for dinner," she said, even though he hadn't asked what was keeping her busy. It was true, in a way.

"Too bad. That would leave Sunday, if you're interested."

"I am."

"Good. Will you meet me at the club? I'd appreciate the distraction after this week." He wasn't the only one. It was hard to admit, even to herself, but the whole week she'd felt the strain of the investigation, and now the idea of Saturday had her stomach in knots.

"Yes. I'd like that." Too much even.

"Then it's a date."

"It is."

"I miss you, Sharon."

It was the first time either of them had uttered such a statement, and it made her heart flutter. It was true, with each passing day she got used to him a bit more. He was slowly tearing down her walls. After her last failed relationship, she had vowed not to let anyone come that close again, to keep a distance between her and her partner until she was a hundred percent sure he wasn't just another man about to screw her over. Now Simon had wound his way into her heart without even really trying. Maybe that was the trick. That happiness would find a person when it wanted to find them and not when they went looking for it.

"I miss you, too," she said quietly.

"Call me tonight?" he asked.

"Why don't you call me?" She understood why he wanted it to be her to make contact. It should be her choice. By now, though, he should know their affair was a two-way street.

"I will. Talk to you later, then."

He ended the call, and Sharon found herself smiling.

* * * *

When Sharon stepped inside her apartment a bit before nine in the evening, take-out in hand, the first thing she did was scan her missed calls to see if Simon had called. The whole day she'd thought about him at random intervals. Would he do as he had said? So far he hadn't called, and she chided herself for being disappointed.

Rolling her tense shoulders, Sharon put her meal into the kitchen then got out of her coat. It had been a good day. She had solved a murder and got a good lead in one of the other investigations. She owed the other detectives a big thank you. They had busted their asses on the case of a dead vagrant.

With luck, her workload would be reduced to the murder of a musician and the Davis case tomorrow.

Whenever she thought of Davis, she still had the feeling she was missing something crucial. Damn.

Inside her kitchen, she put the food onto a plate. Vietnamese. Simon would approve. The thought had her shaking her head at herself. She sat down in front of her TV, and she'd finished half of her meal when her phone rang. To her chagrin, she found herself smiling again.

"Hi," she said.

"Hi."

She reached for her remote to mute the TV.

"What are you doing?" he asked, his voice warm in a way she hadn't thought him capable of when they first met.

"I'm having dinner, was watching some TV. And shouldn't the question be what I'm wearing?"

He chuckled. "While phone sex can be a nice diversion, I prefer the real deal."

"Me too."

"So, what are you having?"

"Vietnamese. And before you can ask, I was watching reality TV. Sometimes I'm too pathetic for words. What are you doing?"

"I just came home from the club. Now I'll be having some dinner, running a bath, reading a little."

She'd love to join him, a thought she hadn't had in a long time when it came to a man.

"Sounds good."

"It does. So tell me, how's work going?"

They talked for almost half an hour, and when she hung up, she sighed. If she wanted to give Hastings a fair chance, she should stay clear of Simon in the meantime, as she was falling way too hard.

Chapter Twenty-One

"You look beautiful."

Standing in the door of her apartment, Sharon smiled at Luke's compliment, debating whether to let him in or not. In theory she was ready to leave, but she'd rather look for her coat and purse without having to hurry and seeming rude because she'd left her date waiting outside.

Would her mind ever wrap around the fact she was about to have a date with her former boss? By now, to her, he should be nothing more than a good-looking man, one working as a cop, just like she did. He was compassionate. His laughter was genuine and unashamed. From all she knew, he was the quintessential nice guy with a few rough edges making him human.

It was a shame nothing inside of her reacted to him in any way. Hell, she wasn't blind. He looked good in that pair of tight blue jeans, a nice shirt and a jacket. Casual, but not too casual.

"Would you like to come in for a moment? I only have to grab my coat and purse."

"Sure."

She turned her back to him, feeling his eyes on her as she made her way to her living room where her coat hung over the back of the couch.

"Is the dress new?"

She turned to him, looking down at the short green dress. It was made for a date, but not overly seductive.

"No. I've had it for years. But it's not quite the right thing to wear at work. And I've always liked to keep my dating a private matter."

On her first job, she had been paired with a woman two years older than she was. Louisa had been a witty, dark-haired, dark-eyed beauty. She had been a good cop, and they got along well. One night the older woman had appeared at the precinct in something that was hardly worth calling a dress. She'd met with a date there, a cop from another department. The men had ogled her. There'd been some whistling. It should have been the end of the story, but it wasn't. Talk and gossip hadn't abated, neither had the lewd comments. Louisa had lasted two months before she had asked to be transferred. It had taught Sharon a lesson for life.

"It's better that way," he said.

Sharon threw Hastings a brief look. "You sound like you got your own experiences when it comes to interdepartmental dating."

"I do." He smiled. "But you know, Sharon, you should pay more attention to the gossip."

She grabbed her purse, joined him. "Why would I want to do that? I'm not all that interested in gossip in my private life and even less when it comes to work."

"That's honorable of you. But if you were, you'd know my ex-wife is a cop."

She closed her apartment door behind her, glad to be out, even though Luke wanted to take her to dinner, not ravish her on the couch. Not that she doubted he'd take a chance if he saw one.

Right now, she would gladly send him on his way without a second thought, but the night was still young. What if it happened? Would it be okay to sleep with another man, seeing as she and Simon hadn't discussed the nature of their relationship yet? She didn't think so. Everybody's personal value system was a different one, but to her that would equal cheating.

While they walked toward the next subway station, Luke took her arm. It was okay, but the reduced distance didn't make her heart beat faster.

"How bad is it when you divorce a fellow cop? And did you work in the same department?"

"Thank God, no. She was with Internal Affairs. I was already working homicide investigations."

"Internal Affairs? No one dates people from Internal Affairs," she teased.

"Well, believe me, I learned my lesson. You'd have thought this woman had swallowed the whole damn rule book, and sometimes I started to think I must have broken them all at least twice."

Sharon laughed out. "Did you?"

"No. But it wasn't as if she believed me."

They passed a couple arguing in the middle of the street, her hands raised, his curled into fists at his side. That was something she wouldn't have seen in the middle of their small town back in Vermont. People there liked to believe their lives were private, although they all knew that every secret worth its money would be known town-wide within a day.

Here, people didn't bother with privacy. They were all so used to the constant presence of others that they hardly ever acknowledged the fact they weren't alone.

She met Luke's gaze, and he only shook his head. As long as these two didn't start to harm each other bodily, there was nothing they could or should do.

"You know, I wasn't a perfect husband," he continued. "Too many evenings I preferred to work a little longer instead of spending time with my family. I wanted a career, I wanted murderers in prison. Somehow my family was a constant, and I thought they would always be there, waiting for me. Stupid, I know."

"So she left you?"

"Yeah. One day, in the midst of just another heated argument, she went silent, and it scared me more than any screaming, any violence would've done. She told me she couldn't do it any longer, and had finally realized I wouldn't change. She asked me to move out, and I did."

He fell silent, obviously traveling down memory lane.

"What happened then?"

"We filed for divorce, and work was hell. People either believed it was my fault, although it was mostly the people from her department, or they thought it was her fault. I could've sat it out, especially as people were favoring me in the role of the saint, but it wouldn't have been fair. I asked for a transfer and got one quickly."

Hearing this, Sharon was glad she'd never considered marriage. Too often it meant ending up with a broken heart.

"Are you two still in contact?"

"Yeah. We'll never be friends, but at least we manage to be civil around each other. It has to be enough. As long as our son is okay with the situation, I'll be, too."

Sharon hadn't known he had a son, but it wasn't as if she had thought much about him outside of his role as her boss. Still, it wasn't much of a surprise. He was the kind of person she envisioned as a family man, going home to his wife and kids in the evening. Why did he want to date her then? Marriage and kids were nothing she was considering right now.

Sharon pushed her thoughts to the side. "Hey, I know this means nothing, but I think you're a good man. Don't doubt yourself."

He stopped, his gaze connecting with hers. "Thanks, Sharon. It means a lot hearing that from you. And I'm glad you agreed to go out with me tonight, too."

She pushed the guilt that wanted to come to the forefront away once more. There'd be enough time for that later. She eyed the people around her, always looking out for Simon. It was stupid to expect him here. It didn't change the fact she wished he was. Wasn't it the last thing she should wish for?

In contrast to her dinner date with Simon, Luke had chosen what could be considered a restaurant meant for dating. It was cozy, but the dim lighting, the pictures on the walls, all advertised love and romance. Stepping inside, Sharon looked at pictures of kissing couples, of people walking hand in hand along a deserted beach. All the prints were black and white, contrasting nicely with the furniture that was exclusively in warm colors, mostly dark red.

It was too cozy for Sharon's liking.

The maître d' saw them to their table, which was placed in the middle of the room. It instantly made her uncomfortable. She always wanted to know who or what was at her back. Still, she smiled and let Luke take her coat. Looking around the restaurant, she noticed there were only two empty tables in sight. With an approximate total of thirty tables, that meant a busy night.

"No need for the cop's eyes here tonight," Luke said, taking his seat.

"I'm sorry. But I can't help checking out my surroundings. It's a habit."

"I know. I had to learn not to do it when it came to dates. Although the promotion to captain helped. Nowadays I'm mostly shuffling papers as you know."

Sharon smirked. "May I tell you that you're doing a great job with shuffling these papers?"

He smiled. "Smooth talker."

The waiter came over, took their order for drinks and handed them the menus. While they perused what was offered, they were mostly silent. Only when they had given back the menu and the waiter was gone did they continue their small talk.

Conversation was easy if not utterly engaging. It wasn't Luke's fault—that much was sure. It was her own uncertainty putting a damper on things.

"I better not mention I didn't think you'd ever go out with me."

Sharon locked her gaze with him. "Why?"

"Do you know people call you the 'ice queen' around the office?"

Sharon shrugged. "I do. Let them. Better have them fear me a little than dealing with no respect at all."

"Did you also know I can give you five names of detectives that would love the chance of a date with you?"

"No, I didn't. I've got to admit I'm not interested, though."

She was flattered, a little, but right now her interest in dating was close to zero. Not that she'd want to go out with a colleague — even less with someone beneath her own rank. Those relationships never worked out. Well, she knew of exactly one case, but by now the man had been promoted to captain and his wife, a lieutenant, was at home, taking care of their three children.

"Somehow I'm happy to hear that."

She realized her mistake at once. No, she hadn't meant to say she might be interested in dating him. Damn it. This could be her chance to set him straight, to try and bow out of this with at least a little grace. Looking at him, his hopeful gaze, she couldn't do it, couldn't bring herself to let him down, not even gently.

His smile was kind, but her own was forced.

At least he didn't make any more moves all through dinner. They talked about work. He told her some childhood stories, while she talked about the time she'd moved to New York. Had she been a fraction more relaxed, it would've been a good evening.

"How about dessert?" he asked after he had finished his steak and she her pasta.

She shook her head, put a hand over her stomach. "No, I'm so full I feel I could burst any moment."

"Funny. It's what women always say. I like to think a little bit of dessert will just slip through the cracks."

"I doubt that." Especially as she had eaten more than she wanted and her stomach was still in a slight knot over her inability to relax.

"But they've got cheesecake on their menu. I know I'll try it."

"Then do. I'd like some coffee, though."

"And you can try some of my cake if you'd like to."

Why do some men think they know what's best for their date? She was able to make up her own mind, thank you very much.

"That's a deal," she said despite her misgivings, knowing he only meant well.

She had to admit the cheesecake looked delicious, and from the way he became still, his eyes closing for a second, it tasted that way, too.

She was content with her choice of coffee, its strong aroma rejuvenating her in a way no sweets could.

Luke put another bite of cake onto his fork, held it out to her. Hoping he didn't realize her inner struggle, she took the offered bite. The cake was good, tasty, yet she didn't find any enjoyment in it. It was the theme of the evening. No matter what Luke offered, she found herself unable to say no, to hurt him, even if it meant she was hurting herself in the process. Even more, she was keeping the man's hopes up when there was no real chance anything could happen between the two of them.

When she looked up, she found Luke's eyes were on her, the longing in them making her insides go cold. If she hadn't known it before, she was now fully convinced this evening had been a bad mistake.

She broke their gaze, and he sat back. It might have been her, but this began to feel awkward.

"Sharon, why do I always have the feeling I'm doing something wrong?"

She looked at him and he was frowning. "You didn't. Really. It's me."

"You can talk to me, whatever it is."

"It's nothing."

A lie. Another bloody lie. She wanted to say one thing, but another one was coming out of her mouth. She wished she could flee here, find Simon and meet with him at the club. He would make her forget, ease the tension. No—just no. She'd see this through now. There was no safe word for this kind of situation.

"I'm not sure I believe you."

"You didn't want to believe I was feeling full, either."

He nodded, reaching for his own coffee but not drinking. "Good point. I apologize."

"Don't. I didn't need to accept the offered bite. So tell me, have you been here before?"

It wasn't the best question as he might think she was inquiring if he liked to bring his dates here, but so what? Anything to fight the awkwardness.

"No, it's the first time. I...and if you laugh at me now, I'll be pissed. I asked a colleague for a tip where to go for a date."

Sweet. Too sweet for her.

"Your secret's safe with me. Didn't you tell me yourself that if your subordinates learn their boss has a soft side, they'd never let you live it down?"

He scowled. "I'm not a softy."

"Of course not."

To Sharon's relief, the rest of the date passed with light banter, and she could breathe easier once they had left the restaurant. She'd have preferred if he had let her pay her part of the check, but he had insisted it had been an invitation. On the one hand, it was pleasant to have men wanting to treat her to something nice, but on the other hand, she liked to make clear she was an independent woman and could provide for herself.

"I'll see you home."

Luke's voice brooked no argument. Sharon would rather have made her way home alone, but what could half an hour more hurt?

A lot, as she wasn't sure about his intentions once they arrived at her apartment.

By now it was way after eleven, and the city was becoming alive once more. Most musicals and theatre shows had ended some time ago, and people were now on their way home or on to the next stage of entertainment. Some began to head for the clubs whose businesses would only really perk up in another hour or two.

Sharon had gone clubbing with Jenn a few times. It had never been for her. She'd been more interested in watching the people than in dancing with the men or women coming over asking for one.

The subway was crowded, making Luke and her stand so close she had to look up to talk to him. It wasn't hard to read his thoughts, and she made as little eye contact as possible. What if he decided to go for her, to kiss her while he had her right where he wanted her? The last thing she wanted was to cause a scene right here and now.

Damn life for having a habit of being cruel. Half a year ago, she would've reacted differently to this date, differently to him. That there hadn't been a single spark all evening wasn't due to the fact she didn't find him appealing but the fact there was another man who made her stomach flutter without trying. She couldn't turn back time, and she wouldn't want to.

Finally they arrived at her apartment. It was time to send Luke on his way, disappointment be damned.

"Listen, Luke…"

"Yes, I thought this was a nice evening, too, but I'll see you upstairs. I insist."

"You know I'm not some damsel in distress, but a cop, right?"

"I do. But my mom likes to point out she raised me well. I'd like to think she's right about it."

Gritting her teeth, Sharon led the way. Would he insist on looking inside her closet and under her bed for monsters, too? If she wanted him to understand this was going nowhere, she had to be honest. Right. Now.

"Would you like a cup of coffee?"

"Yeah. Thanks." His eyes lit up, his stance widening.

Okay, so he thought this was the prelude for making love. Fine. It wasn't. She'd deliver the news with the coffee. *It'll be better than 'thank you for dinner but I'm screwing someone else and am not interested'* right in front of her door.

Luke leaned against her kitchen counter while she filled her coffee maker with water, and added the filter and powder. In situations like this, one of those fully automatic coffee machines would come in useful. Maybe after her next pay raise. Simon had one of those, and she had started getting used to it.

"You've got a nice place here," Luke remarked, pulling her out of her reverie.

Sharon looked over her shoulder. "It's nothing special. But I like it," she added with a smile.

"I bet most items in here have a special meaning for you."

She followed his gaze. He was right. The vase on a shelf left of her TV was an heirloom from her grandmother. It was glass, painted with black flowers and pink swans. By all accounts it was ugly, but she loved it for the fact it would forever remind her of the woman who had told her the dirtiest jokes while simultaneously teaching her how to knit. How often, when they had visited her grandmother, had they brought her flowers, which she had put into just that vase? As her grandmother had said once, laughing at herself, she couldn't part with this vase as it had been a gift from her beloved late husband.

Then there was the black and white picture of her parents, her brother and herself, taken when she was eight years old.

There weren't many things she kept, but those she did had a special meaning to her, like the quilt made by her mother, a bookend from her father, a picture she'd drawn when she was five. Little things, but they spoke of her life, reminded her of mostly good things.

"They do. This is my space."

He smiled. "You should have seen my dormitory, a long, long time ago."

"Let me guess, a typical boy's room."

"Yeah. I love baseball, my friend was crazy about football. We waged war, and each available bit of room was plastered with posters, trinkets and so on."

"Tell me about your friend."

A few minutes later the coffee was ready, and she handed him a cup, then poured herself one. One good thing about her profession was that having a cup of coffee so late in the day wouldn't affect her ability to sleep. Not that she ever slept well at all.

She took a sip of the too-hot liquid, then put the cup aside. Her kitchenette was tiny on the best of days, but with the two of them in here it was crowded. Or it was her nerves. Who knew? She steeled herself. At the end of the day, she didn't want to go to bed feeling like a coward.

Chapter Twenty-Two

"Luke, we need to talk."

He registered her tone of voice at once, and put his cup onto the kitchen counter as well. "Why so serious all of sudden?"

He stepped closer, well into her personal space. She had to look up at him if she wanted to talk with him now.

"This has been a nice evening, yes?" He made sure to keep her gaze.

"It was, yes, but…"

He put one hand on her shoulder, the other coming to rest at her waist. She tensed slightly, which had him raising an eyebrow.

"I don't understand. Is this about the fact I was your boss for a few years?"

"No, it isn't. I said it earlier, it's about me."

"I like you, Sharon, and I think we could be good together. I only ask for a chance."

He leaned in, covering her lips with his. While she'd registered his move, there hadn't been time to evade it.

He wasn't forcing himself on her, yet she'd have preferred the chance to stop it before it was happening.

As if she hadn't known it before, there wasn't any sign of desire, no wish to deepen the connection.

That she didn't react to his kiss finally registered with Luke, and he stepped back at once.

"I apologize." The kind man with the warm smile, the easy attitude, was gone, replaced by the cop. It made her want to bang her head against the next wall.

"I don't want you to apologize, dammit. I told you, it's me. I started seeing a man lately. We went out a few times. Nothing's set in stone yet, then you came along and you're...nice, and I wanted to give us a chance." She stopped, took a deep breath before she continued. "I thought there could be something between us, that you'd make a better choice of partner. But it seems my heart's set. I am so, so sorry."

It wasn't easy to hurt him — quite the contrary. It hurt her too.

Luke looked away for a long moment, his body rigid. As sorry as she was, sometimes a clean break was needed. He deserved the truth, and she felt better for telling it.

"You could have told me."

"Yes, I could have and maybe should have, but I wasn't sure if that thing with this other man was a mistake, and I was kinda interested in you before all this. Still, I made a mistake. I know it. And again, I'm sorry." Maybe interested was too strong a word, but she had never ruled him out point blank either.

"So I am too late." He finally met her gaze.

"Yes, it seems you are."

"Who is this other guy?"

It was the very last thing she could tell him. "Just someone I got to know."

"There's something you're not telling me."

She held his gaze, knowing it was crucial not to give anything away now. "I'm just not comfortable discussing this with you, especially given the circumstances."

"Then why are you unsure about this relationship?"

"Because he's a quieter man. It's harder to read him than it is to read you."

Luke sighed and shook his head as if trying to shake himself out of a nightmare. There were no words about how sorry she was for him. She'd been in his situation before, had had crushes on people who weren't interested, although she'd never gotten so far as kissing someone only to find out the person had someone else in mind. Dinner churned in her stomach.

"I hope you know what you're doing," he said.

"I hope the same."

His voice was hard when he spoke next. "Listen, if this thing with this man should go awry, please don't come to me."

It stung, even knowing where he was coming from. "I won't. I promise."

"Good. Maybe we can be friends at some point, but not now, and I'll need some time. Good night, Sharon."

He turned around and left her apartment without looking back. The door fell shut with a loud clang, and Sharon looked at it for some time, unable to feel a thing. Taking up his cup, she carried it to the sink. It was still warm.

Finally, regret hit her full force. Not for calling this off—it had been the thing to do—but for hurting him. She took up her own cup, but she'd lost the taste for it. Rinsing both cups, she stood at the sink, the scene of the last few minutes replaying itself time and again.

She should go to bed, hope to fall asleep and forget about it. Too bad she doubted sleep was in the cards for a while longer. Making her way to the bathroom, she dressed in her PJs before walking back to her living room and sitting down on the couch. Her cell phone lay on the couch table, and she picked it up to see she had a text message. Simon. Telling her he was missing her, was looking forward to tomorrow.

Fantastic. He was opening his heart, his life, to her, and she had thanked him with going on a date with another man. Realizing it might be the worst mistake of the day, that she could lose it all, she reached for the phone and tried Simon's cell.

She was about to end the call when he picked up.

"Please tell me I didn't wake you," she said. "I didn't realize how late it was."

"I wasn't asleep yet, just reading. But you sound troubled. What's up?"

She'd lost her sense of what was right and wrong, wanted to talk but didn't dare to. "I…"

She could hardly start with 'I went on a date with another man', could she? "You remember you met my former boss, Luke Hastings?" she began.

"I do."

She wasn't sure if it was her imagination or if his voice had cooled down a little. It was too late now — she'd better finished what she'd started. "He was my superior for a few years, recently transferred."

As quickly and succinctly as she could, she spoke of the mostly one-sided attraction between them, the fact he had asked her out, that she thought she owed him a chance. "I know how this might sound."

It was the first time he interrupted her. "It sounds like you're attracted to him, that he seems a better choice of man than a suspect with a penchant for sadomasochistic play."

What is Simon feeling? She couldn't quite read the tone of his voice right now and wished she could look at him.

"Yeah, it does, doesn't it?" she spoke quietly. "It was what I told myself, too. Or better phrased, I told myself I should feel something for him. Only there wasn't even one spark of attraction. You might believe me or not, but I didn't enjoy this evening."

"Sharon, why are you calling and telling me this?"

She could hold back or put her heart on the sleeve. Love was always a risk. It would change her life, no matter the outcome. "Because you said you wanted a relationship with me. If there's one thing I need in my private life, it's honesty. I deal with enough lying when it comes to my job. I demand nothing less than I offer. So I offer you honesty."

"Are you offering me a relationship, too?"

"Yes, I am. If you still want it."

He was silent for so long she wondered if he'd speak at all. "I do, Sharon. But please be aware, I am who I am. My needs won't change."

She knew. "I can live with them. I might never accept blood play or a ball gag, but I can live with the rest. And as long as you're not seeing any women on the side…"

She was only halfway kidding. The thought that he could have dated other women while proposing a relationship to her didn't sit right with her.

"I'm not."

"Good. Then…" She trailed off, unable to finish the sentence.

"Then we're talking about starting a relationship, yes. But, Sharon, I thought long and hard about this too."

Was this the part where he let her know he wasn't actually all that interested any longer? Had her confession thrown him more than he let on? Her hand tightened around the receiver of her phone.

"Yes?"

"I need you to know who I am. So far our games have been mild, all things considered."

She thought she understood, hoped she was right. "You want to unleash the beast onto me to see if I can take it."

"Yes."

He didn't make any excuses, and offered honesty for honesty. It wasn't even hard to understand his point. If he held back part of himself on a constant basis, it would lead to one-sided frustration later. She'd learned the hard way that playing with fire would only leave her burned. It was the same with him.

"You said you didn't have all that many relationships," she probed.

"Yes, and I meant it."

"Has it happened before? That someone left you when you showed all of yourself?"

It was forward to just ask — he'd have every right to refuse to answer. Nothing about their relationship was particularly *normal*, though, a thing she considered to be refreshing. To be oneself in a relationship was the most precious gift of all.

"Yes. Around three years ago I dated a woman for a few months. Her name was Lisa. Her friend, a regular customer, gifted her with light bondage play at the club for her birthday. Lisa had expressed some curiosity and her friend thought it would make the perfect gift. I thought it would be best to take over the assignment. I didn't want one of my employees to go too far."

He paused. Was he thinking about the past now? The past shaped one into the person one became, but memories would always have the potential to hurt, to reopen old wounds.

"It was a good session, she fell in love with me and I liked her very much, was convinced I could fall for her, too. But over time I found out she wanted lovemaking with a little edge, not the full package. Holding back cost me too much."

Constantly holding back would put him on edge, and if the preferred way of taking care of that edge was not an option, it couldn't work, not in the long run.

"Did you end the relationship?"

"Yes, I did. Lisa wasn't happy, didn't want to accept it for quite some time, but I'm sure it was best for both of us."

"What happened to her?"

"I have no idea. For all I know she still lives in New York. I hope she found happiness, but I don't know."

It had to have been hard for Lisa to realize she couldn't be the woman he needed her to be. At the end of the day, everybody could only be who they were. A person could pretend to be someone else but sooner or later the core of them would come to the forefront again. Some synapse in her brain fired, and she let out a gasp.

"That's it. Dammit. That's why nothing fits."

"Sharon?"

"Davis. I know who killed her now."

"Who was it?"

"Let me make sure I'm right about this, and I'll tell you tomorrow."

How could she have been so blind? The answer had been right in front of her all the time.

"Should I be worried about you now?"

She laughed out loud. "I am and will always be a cop. Either you're constantly worried or you try to forget about the dangers that come with the job. Still, I don't expect a shoot-out this time."

"I see. Then I'll just say, stay safe. And see you tomorrow."

"You will." She almost ended the call, but her finger rested over the button. "Simon?"

"Yeah?"

"I can't promise to be who you are looking for, but I can promise to be myself."

"Thank you."

"Not for that. I just hope we can be good for each other. I care too much by now."

"Me too."

It was good to have said it, to have come clean. She felt so much better for braving honesty. It wouldn't work with every person—some people weren't ready to face the truth—but with him, it did.

After Sharon went to bed, sleep was a long time in coming and when it did, her dreams were a crude mixture of playing a game of hide and seek with Simon while the shadow of Marlene Davis roamed the room, always there and always out of reach.

Chapter Twenty-Three

"Thank you for coming in, Miss Davis."

The blonde woman nodded once, looking from Sharon to Detective Ramirez, who had agreed to cover for Jenn and do the interview with her. If Sharon was right about the woman, she'd react better to a male presence anyway.

They all sat down, Davis on the opposite side of them. Davis brushed a strand of hair from her face and tried a smile. Today, she was wearing a tight red dress accentuating her curves, her beauty.

"I'd do everything to make sure you find out who killed my sister."

"That's good. Would you like a cup of coffee or anything else before we start?"

"No, no. I'm good." Davis looked around the room again.

"Nervous?"

The young woman laughed out loud. "No, it's just...surreal. Makes me almost feel as if you're suspecting me of having killed my sister."

"Oh, I'm sure you didn't kill Marlene. Never mind, just let me read you your rights so we're on the safe side."

Davis' eyes narrowed, but she remained still while Sharon recited her rights.

"So, do you want a lawyer present?"

"What is this, Detective? I thought you only had some more questions."

"And it's the truth." Sharon gave her an innocent smile, and was amused when it worked.

"Then let's start. Yes, I understood my rights. No, I don't want a lawyer present. I really have to get back to work. I've got to finish a…painting."

"Now that you mention work, I'm surprised to find you and your sister chose such different careers."

Davis shrugged her shoulders. "We were different people. My sister was always more interested in succeeding in the business world."

"So she loved money?"

Anger flashed in the young woman's eyes. "Why not? There's nothing wrong with wanting to accumulate some wealth. It makes life a lot easier, you know. But why should you? Cops aren't paid big bucks, are they?"

Ramirez, a good-looking Latino man in his mid-twenties who had charm in spades, spoke out. He was a good cop, with sharp instincts, but he managed to hide the fact well until people had told him what he wanted to know. "No, we aren't. It's a pity, really. But you as an artist will surely understand."

"I…well, yes." Davis smiled at Ramirez. "It was Marlene who earned the big bucks, not me."

"Weren't you ever envious? A little?" Ramirez asked.

"No, why should I have been? We both knew what we wanted to do with our lives. You know, we always had the same grades in school. It was up to me what to do with my life. I wanted this."

"Is that why you're living in your sister's apartment now?" Sharon asked.

The woman's head whipped around to her, her eyes shooting daggers at Sharon. If the whole affair weren't so sad, it would almost be funny.

"I'm her heir. There's nothing wrong with wanting a bit more space."

Sharon took a sip of the coffee she'd brought in, uncrossing her legs before she leaned forward with her elbows on the table.

"I see. And what about dressing like your sister? Do you love her so much that you wear her dresses now? Do you want to be her?"

"This is insulting. I guess I better leave. Unless you want to charge me with something."

Ramirez coughed, directing Davis' attention to himself. "I'm sorry. We only have some questions here, really. But are these really your sister's clothes?"

Davis looked from him to Sharon and back. "They are. I miss her. I loved her so much. She'll never be with me again. We are twins. I know you can't understand this, but it feels like I have died."

Tears appeared in her eyes, but they didn't affect Sharon. "It does, doesn't it? Now let's stop this train of thought and start with the science lesson of the day."

"What is she talking about?" Davis asked Ramirez.

He just shrugged. "Don't ask me."

Sharon hid her smile, although Davis wasn't even looking at her. "It's about twins."

Davis looked at Sharon again, her eyes flashing with anger. "Could you come to the point, please?"

"I could. Yes. Do I have your attention, your full attention now?"

"There's no reason to insult me," Davis snapped at her.

"We are sorry," Ramirez said, his smile so sweet as if butter wouldn't melt in his mouth. He'd have made a nice actor.

"As you should be." Davis mellowed a little.

"Anyway," Sharon interrupted them. "Identical twins, like you and your sister, can't easily be told apart. If you want to, you look alike, and you share the same DNA."

"Old news. So what?"

"But there's one thing differentiating one twin from the other. Their fingerprints."

There was a flicker of unease in Davis' expression. "So?"

"Let's make this short, shall we? I found it curious you wanted to live in your sister's apartment, and I find it strange you started wearing her clothes. We took fingerprints from Marlene's office, from the corpse, the crime scene and from Carrie's apartment, her pictures, and even some from a picture she'd given a friend a few years ago. You know what we found out, right?"

"No." Davis got up. "I really have to get back to work now."

"I don't think so. Sit down."

For a moment it looked like Davis would just storm out of the room, but then she sat down again, her arms crossed over her chest.

"Good. Now before I'm going to charge you with the murder of your sister, let me explain. The fingerprints of the murder victim matched most of the ones found in Carrie Davis' apartment and the ones on the picture in said friend's apartment."

"You can be proud of us," Ramirez said, smiling. "We started taking more prints and comparing them only this morning and already have you in for an interview in the afternoon. That should tell people who think the NYPD can't be fast."

"Are you all crazy? What are you trying to tell me?" Panic and a deer in the headlights look, mixed with a shrill voice, raised the hairs on Sharon's arms. Davis, a siren revealing her true self.

"I'm trying to tell you what you already know. You, Marlene, killed your sister, Carrie. We think it happened like that, and please feel free to correct me. You got into hot water at work. You betrayed your clients, put some money aside and were found out. There was an investigation scheduled and soon you'd be facing the loss of your job and with it the loss of any credit in the business world. You knew you were facing prison time."

"That's bullshit," Davis screamed, not so beautiful any longer.

"I don't believe so. Anyway, we think you decided the best way to get out of this was to die."

"You are so full of shit."

Sharon chuckled. "You know, I have it on good authority that Carrie wouldn't talk this way. I talked to your parents this morning, to some friends from your past while waiting for the results of your fingerprints. They all told me basically the same story."

"People know shit."

"They told me Carrie was rather quiet, always lost in her own thoughts, interested in creating art even as a young girl. Marlene, in contrast, was wild and wanted more, always more. Whatever your parents got you, it wasn't enough. You were envious whenever your friends had something you didn't, so you went to university, deciding to become rich yourself by any means necessary. One could say you decided, as you'd surely phrase it, to shit on people."

"I didn't kill my sister."

"Marlene, it's over. Even if I let you go now, do you think your parents and close friends would believe you any longer? They all sensed Carrie was different, and felt it was more than just shock over her sister's death."

"You bitch. You spread lies. I'll sue you. I'll make you pay for the rest of your life."

Ramirez spoke next, his voice soft. "Marlene, you're not Carrie. The shoe doesn't fit. You might have looked the same, but you weren't."

Marlene faced him as if drawn by his soothing voice.

"We only want to understand. I want to understand what happened. Why did you kill your sister? If you can make me understand, you can make the jury understand."

"You think I'm stupid?"

"No, but I think you didn't mean to kill your sister."

Sharon didn't move, watching the scene unfold. There was no question Marlene had killed her sister in cold blood, and they'd prove it without a doubt. First they needed a confession, though.

"Make me understand." Ramirez reached for Marlene's hand, and she let it happen. Something gleamed in her eyes, and her voice softened, asking for pity that wouldn't be coming.

"I...well, all I wanted was for these charges to go away. They needed to. Then, suddenly, I had the perfect idea of how to get rid of this problem and still keep my money. I called Carrie. I told her to meet me at the club. She didn't even know I used to go there."

Marlene snorted. "Geez, she was always so sweet. Not perfect, no, but sweet. She wanted plain vanilla and no spice, please. How could we have been sisters? Look alike? Anyway, I was early. I let her inside the club after she called me and told me she'd arrived. I made sure no one was in the hallway."

She laughed, the hard, egocentric woman once again. "Damn, I only hoped no door would open right then. Best adrenaline kick I had in years. Carrie was shocked. She started to argue with me and wanted to leave. But I told her I had a serious problem at work, that I was facing prison time."

Davis rolled her eyes. "The poor thing couldn't believe it. Anyway, I told her I needed her to stay at the club for a while, then leave when she was sure someone was seeing her, so I would have an alibi. At the same time I'd drive to work, pretend to be her, wanting to meet Marlene only to find out Marlene wasn't there. While being in Marlene's office—well, my office—I'd steal the files incriminating me and leave after making sure people knew Marlene wasn't in. I promised I would never make such a mistake again, that I would change my ways."

"And Carrie believed you?"

"Oh, she was mad. The little kitten showed me her claws, but blood is thicker than water, so she finally agreed, put on the dress I gave her and gave me her own."

Sharon spoke for the first time in minutes. "With Carrie dead, you'd inherit your own money, could try to *rescue* the money you had put to the side and start your life from scratch."

"Yes. The thought hit me out of the blue and…I grabbed the pistol I had with me and shot her."

"So you always run around with a pistol in your purse?"

Their eyes met. Marlene realized she couldn't fool Sharon, and her eyes hardened. "It's New York. It's a dangerous city."

"Give her a break, Detective."

"No, I won't. Come on, Marlene. There are many things I am willing to believe about you, but not that you are stupid and prone to give in to impulse. Your sister was getting on your nerves anyway, always being the one people liked best. Why not get rid of her and the investigation and start over? You got yourself a pistol, went there, shot her, problem solved. It was a good plan, really. So be at least proud enough to own up to it."

Marlene looked ready to pounce on her, face red, her whole body tense. "Okay, yes, I planned it. Carrie was a fucking bitch. She deserved all she got. End of story."

"Indeed, end of story. Detective, would you accompany Ms. Marlene Davis to booking?"

"It will be my pleasure, Detective."

Sharon ended the video recording, looking over at the other woman.

Marlene was shell-shocked for a moment, but then she shot Ramirez a hopeful look, expecting to find the cop who had soothed her. He was gone, replaced by one who had no love lost for a murderer. Sharon smiled when she watched the two of them leave the room.

When she got up herself, her smile was gone, though, replaced by sadness. She'd solved a murder, but Carrie Davis remained dead. Even worse, her parents had to live with the fact that the victim was Carrie and the killer had been Carrie's own sister.

One person's greed and envy had destroyed the lives of many others in the process. Life wasn't fair.

Jenn was in the office when Sharon got in. She was packing up.

"Early night?"

"I don't know if anyone told you, but it's Sunday. We're both off rotation. I should be home and you should, too."

"I'll leave soon."

"So you got her?"

"Yes, we did."

Sharon ran a hand through her hair, exhausted.

"I know Carrie's still dead, but eventually her parents will find their peace again," Jenn said.

"Knowing their other daughter killed her twin?"

"It's better than wondering who killed their baby, right?"

Sharon wasn't sure, but she wouldn't get a definite answer either. She wouldn't go and see the family again. Those people deserved to come to terms on their own, and didn't need the reminder of Carrie's violent death when seeing her. Her job was a bit like reading a book—at the end of an investigation, she'd close it, never knowing what would happen to all the featured characters next.

"Go home, Sharon. You look like shit."

"Thanks for the compliment, Jenn."

"Always. But I mean it. Go home."

"I will. I've got a date."

Jenn stopped mid-motion, waiting for her to elaborate. "Damn, I knew I had wanted to play catch up with you. Who is the lucky guy? Carter or Hastings?"

"Curiosity will still kill the cat."

"We'll all have to die someday. So you could enlighten me before that happens."

"Carter. I...Hastings and I wouldn't be able to work out."

"Too bad, really."

"Yes, but that's how it is."

"You don't sound sad." Jenn slung her bag over her shoulder.

"Sad for making him think that I toyed with him, but no, I'm not."

She couldn't feel bad when she longed to be with Simon, when this was the man that had fear of failure and excitement mingling inside her.

"I hope you'll find your happy ending, Shar." Jenn smiled at her.

"I hope so too."

Whether she and Simon would move forward or had to realize they weren't compatible after all would be decided tonight. It was time to get home, to change into fresh clothes and hurry over to the club.

Sharon and Jenn left the precinct together, parting at the subway. The temperatures had actually dropped again, so Sharon was glad when she got out of the relentless wind.

At home, she found her mother had left a message. She considered letting it rest until the next day, but she wanted to hear if it was anything urgent. Since the day her father had died, she had dreaded the red, blinking light on her answering machine, and she'd rather deal with what life was throwing at her at once.

It was a brief message, asking her to call back. Her mother had sounded relaxed. It didn't do anything to ease the tension, so she grabbed the phone and called her back.

"Sharon, honey. You didn't have to call right back."

"I had some time, so, what's up?"

"No one died or is about to, if that's what you're asking."

"I wasn't. Well, I was, and I'm happy to hear it. So what is it?"

"Can't I call my daughter and ask how she is? Anyway, I wanted to ask how things are with Simon and you and if he'll accompany you to the wedding."

Would he? She hadn't contemplated that scenario for one second. A month ago, she'd have said she couldn't imagine him attending something as simple and pure as a wedding. Now she knew him better and would like to have him at her side.

"I'll see him later and will ask him, okay?"

"Make sure you do that. I might have told some of my friends about this handsome man my daughter's dating lately." Her mother coughed.

"You didn't."

"I didn't say that I have. I said I might have."

"Same difference. Mom, really. I'm not eighteen anymore with everyone looking at me, expecting me to announce I'm going to marry my high school sweetheart come spring."

"If you had ever announced you were going to marry that jerk, your dad and I would have hit you over the head with his baseball bat."

She snorted. "I can just see it."

"Well, you know how your dad was. He was fiercely proud of his wonderful daughter."

"I do. I miss him, Mom. Every day."

"Me too." Her mother sighed. "More often than not I wake up in the morning, wanting to turn to him, to tell him what's on my mind this very moment. Then I realize he's gone, and it hurts. I doubt that will ever stop."

"I'm sorry."

"Don't be. I'm not. I only wish for you to find a love like this one yourself one day. It was worth it, Sharon, and I would do it all over again. By the way, I think your brother might be finding himself in hot water."

It reminded Sharon she had to call her brother sometime soon. Even as adults they still got along well and spoke to each other every other week. The last time she'd spoken to him, he had called her. Damn, she'd make sure to rectify that as soon as possible.

"What's up?"

"He doesn't want to talk about it, but there are rumors Connie's got a lover."

Sharon shook her head. That bitch. She'd always known it had been a mistake for her brother to settle in Vermont, only five miles from their former home. It had been a mistake to marry the homecoming queen, too. He wasn't as happy as he liked to pretend he was, but she hadn't had any idea that matters were that bad.

With their son only four, this would cause heartache for everyone involved if it were true.

"I really hope that's just some bullshit gossip."

"Sharon...but yes, I agree. I'm about to head over tomorrow. I wanted to talk to Connie."

"Do that, and let me know what you find out."

"I will. But you just continue with your evening, darling."

She was about to say she had all the time in the world, but in fact she didn't, not when she wanted to meet Simon on time.

"Just call me tomorrow. I love you, Mom."

"Love you, too. Bye, darling."

All but running for her bedroom to get a change of clothes before she showered, Sharon mused about the nature of love. Many people had told her that her parents had been the perfect couple. They had been. Still, her mother had ended up a widow way too early. People had also said her brother and Connie made a great couple. They weren't, as they both wanted different things in life. Connie wanted an idle life, nice dresses, luxury, and her brother wanted a steady life with romance. Sharon didn't think they would work out in the long run.

What would people say if they saw Simon and her together? That they weren't compatible? At first glance they might make for an interesting couple, the millionaire and the lowly cop. But what if they learned he owned a S&M club? No one needed to know. Although why should he have to hide who he was?

God, she was glad she'd be meeting him at the club tonight. He knew how to make her thoughts stop. After her shower, she put on a black dress that almost reached her knees. She suddenly stopped her motions. He wanted to show her all of himself tonight. What if it proved to be too much?

The thought was useless. She wanted to know. Brushing her hair and pulling it back in a ponytail, she took a light jacket and entered the cab that was waiting outside. Usually she liked to save the money, but tonight she was pressed for time and didn't want to bother with the crowds of people.

Even with the bad traffic, she made it to the club in less than half an hour.

Chapter Twenty-Four

Like the last time, Sharon found Carter outside the club, smoking.

"Still not my business, but don't you think your health should be more important to you?"

It had become natural to walk toward him, to have him embrace her. She loved the feel of him, his scent. With a mind of their own, her hands followed the hard contours of his chest through the fabric of his shirt.

"Did I say you could touch me?"

She couldn't see his face, but his voice was gentle, and when she stepped back and looked up at him, his dark eyes were twinkling. It should be forbidden for any man to be so attractive and alluring.

"The game's not started yet, Sir."

"I like when you say that."

"Me too. Or would you prefer it if I called you *Master*?"

Something dark began to gleam in his eyes. It sent a shiver of pleasure down her back. "We'll see about it, kitten."

She laughed out loud. "I'm no one's kitten, Mister."

"Master. And yes, you are. I love to make you scream, and I love to make you purr."

"You actually make me want to purr right now."

"I'd like that," he said.

"Later, maybe." Their gazes met. She didn't want to look away, wishing she could stay in this moment. She sighed, and knew she still owed him the truth about Marlene. He deserved to know he wasn't an official suspect any longer.

"We found Marlene's murderer. Or rather, Marlene was the murderer." She smiled at his frown and began to tell him the story of Carrie's murder from the beginning. He didn't interrupt her, although his gaze was dark, brooding.

"Anyway, we booked her, and I've got no doubt she'll be convicted on premediated murder."

"I didn't know Marlene well, and still, I wouldn't have expected it. It only proves you can never truly know what another person is thinking. Well, shall we?"

"Yeah."

Could she be sure about what was going on in Simon's head? She thought she could read him, but could she, really?

Stubbing out his cigarette, he threw the rest into the bin. "Then let's go and play."

"Can't wait to get your hands on me, huh?" Teasing was easier than entertaining thoughts she wouldn't find an answer to.

"Yes, I can't, and you know it." They shared a small smile. *Does our banter help ease his nerves a little as it does mine?*

While they walked inside, too many thoughts flickered through her mind. She wanted to tell him of her mother's invitation, but this was not the time. She wanted to talk about Davis, her brother... She didn't. Anxious expectation made her hyperaware of her surroundings, the sounds and sights of the club.

They encountered another couple in the hallway. He was wearing leather pants, and she was wearing only underwear, her hands bound behind her back. Glancing after them, she watched them making their way down to the dungeons.

"I will take you there, too."

She stopped and looked at him, her heart missing a beat. What had she expected, to go back to the privacy of his room? This was his club—he supported any kind of BDSM play offered here. He'd been honest with her, had told her what she knew anyway, that their encounters had been mild, all things considered. The dungeons were the natural evolution to what they'd shared before.

She met Simon's gaze, knowing him well enough to see the little signs of tension, his mouth drawn into a straight line, his body rigid. He'd have to feel the same trepidation she did, only for different reasons.

He waited. He wouldn't take her to the dungeons until she gave him her final okay. Swallowing, she nodded her assent and he took her hand. The way downstairs seemed to take longer than it had the last time, which was ridiculous. It was her own fear stretching time, each exhale of breath ringing harsh in her ears.

Once inside the dungeon he'd chosen, the last one to the left, Sharon looked around, trying to see if anything had changed, if she could spot new toys, although right now it was hard to remember what had been here and what might not have been.

He didn't give her the time to process her surroundings.

"On your knees. Hands behind your back and head down. I don't want you to move or speak until I tell you that you can."

They had never started a game so abruptly. Not obeying wasn't an option, though. Kneeling down, she faced the floor, wondering what Simon's plan was.

One minute passed, then another, then many more. A few times she thought she heard him move, but he never touched her, never spoke. After a while, her knees started to hurt, her back all but killing her.

All day she'd considered the various ways this scene could play out. The idea that nothing at all could happen for the longest time hadn't crossed her mind. She came close to moving to relieve some of the pressure on her knees and back, but didn't. She thought she heard him move again, saw him pass her from the corner of her eyes, but all she could see were his shoes. He was daring her to look up, but she resisted, closing her eyes instead. He hadn't told her she couldn't— hadn't told her that she could, either—but it would lessen the distractions.

She wouldn't lie to herself or to him. If this became too much, she'd end the game, but she hoped it wouldn't come to that, that they'd prove to be compatible after all. Trying to think of anything else but the situation she was in, Sharon pondered her latest case. The not-so-grieving husband had killed his wife, but she didn't have a way to prove it yet.

Her mind struggled with staying focused, as did her body. She took a shuddering breath, then a deeper one. This was driving her crazy. She took another breath.

Finally she managed to calm down enough to be able to think again, to forget her aches, if only for a while.

"Get up. Undress."

She startled, having withdrawn into her own mind for she didn't know how long, and opened her eyes. Her knees protested when she moved forward so she could brace herself on her hands before she got up from the ground, her legs shaking slightly. She groaned, rolling her shoulders.

Simon was standing in front of her, his gaze meeting hers. She could see his want, the fire of suppressed passion in his eyes, but his face remained otherwise impassive.

Her hands shook slightly while she undressed, and she was glad when the last item of clothing had slid to the ground.

"Here's how this is going to play out now," he said. "You're walking over to this wall, turning your back to me and waiting. Understood?" He pointed at the wall the St. Andrew's cross was attached to.

"Yes, S—Master."

The corners of his mouth twitched, and she knew he was fighting a smile. Yes, she had remembered. Yes, she'd address him as "Master" and submit to him inside these walls.

She would never allow him to make up her mind for her when it came to the rest of her life. What they did in their bedrooms, in his club, were scenes out of time, which couldn't and wouldn't reflect the rest of their lives. To Simon's credit, he hadn't tried to order her around outside the bedroom even once, and she trusted him for it not to change.

Walking over to the wall he'd indicated, looking at the cross, Sharon wasn't sure what he expected her to do. Stand in front of the wall beside the cross? Stand in front of the cross? She had expected this to be on his mind as soon as he said he'd take her down here, but the reality of it had her breath catching. She stopped in front of the cross, hoping she had guessed right.

He was with her a moment later, putting his hands on her shoulders, the warmth of his fingers welcome on her skin. It was even colder down here than it was in the room upstairs, and she had goosebumps spread all over her body. Her nipples were nothing more than cold, hard pebbles.

"I will fasten you to the cross now."

The sight of the leather-padded cross in front of her was daunting. There were built-in restraints for wrists and ankles, and the idea of feeling them around her extremities had her crossing her arms in front of her chest. Could she really do this?

"One more step forward," Simon directed her. He sounded so sure of what they were doing. Didn't he fear this could be too much for her, too?

It was her decision. Taking a deep breath, she decided to trust instinct, anxiety causing her legs to shake a little when she bridged the last of the distance. She spread her legs and lifted her arms so they'd align with the cross, hoping she was doing the right thing.

Simon had to know her nerves were about to make her quit the game, and he quickly wound the restraints around her ankles and wrists, not speaking or dragging it out.

He left and came back with a cloth that he swiftly wrapped around her head. It was the right move. Her nerves settled a little. For no reason she'd be able to describe, this was easier to bear if she couldn't see.

It was hard enough to be so vulnerable, spread out, unable to move. Right now, she was totally at his mercy. She had to trust he wouldn't go too far, that he would stop if she asked him to.

The heat radiated off Simon's body, standing as close as he was to her.

"Don't forget your safe word," he said, leaning even closer so she could feel his breath on her neck and the shell of her ear. She expected him to retreat, shuddering when one of his hands came around her neck instead, squeezing lightly before moving on and travelling down the length of her spine, making her shiver, wet heat flooding her core in spite of her nervousness.

She moaned when he fully pulled away. Damn, couldn't he just take her, hard and fast? No, she wouldn't lie. She wanted more than simple sex. A male scream from one of the other dungeons almost made her jump out of her skin, adrenaline coursing through her veins. Would her own screams echo through the hallway before long?

Not having noticed what Simon was doing, she yelped when soft leather connected with the skin of her back, warming wherever it hit her.

The flogger... He'd used it once. It created a sensation unlike the others she'd gotten to know, the strands of leather connecting with her back and thighs in a softer, yet more intense way over the duration of the flogging.

She hissed when he hit exactly the same part of her back again, reminding herself to keep her breathing as calm as possible—to start her retreat into her own personal subspace, the oasis of peace within her own mind that Simon helped her find while he was overloading her system with sensual pain.

He took his time between blows, his aim exact. How much did he have to be in control of himself to never let himself get carried away? She didn't have time to wonder about it.

Another blow had her skin drawing tight and her nerve endings shouting out in pain.

Before he'd used the flogger the first time, he'd explained to her what he'd be doing, that flogging always had to be a slow, precise process, to allow the build-up of endorphins for maximum effect.

She whimpered, absorbing the sensations while enjoying the feeling of light-headedness. Another blow, only this time, he waited a few seconds before caressing her back with the faintest touch of the palm of his hand, turning pain into pleasure in a way that had her vaginal muscles clenching in search of a friction that couldn't be found.

For a hysterical second, she was glad to be tightly secured to the cross, as she feared her knees would buckle any moment.

Sharon couldn't determine how much time had passed before Simon stopped, having repeated the process of dealing out pain and desire in equal measures countless times. The tension inside her had risen to a level she found almost unbearable, the need for release overpowering all other sensation.

"Are you wet? Answer me?"

Couldn't he see? She was all but drenched in need. "Yes, Master."

"Do you want to come?"

"Yes, Master."

He put his hand on the inside of her right thigh, the contact welcome, making her moan. "Beautiful," he murmured, sliding his hand up, parting her folds with his index finger. "Beautiful and so, so wet."

She gasped when he didn't slide his finger inside her sex but circled the small, puckered opening he'd never paid attention to before instead.

"Relax. I won't take you that way tonight."

She shuddered, thoughts whirling in her mind. Would she even want it? She didn't know. His soft caress felt good, though, and she didn't protest when he applied soft pressure, sliding the tip of his slippery digit inside her. It was an intrusion into her body unlike any other she had ever felt before. Before she could make up her mind whether she liked it or not, he'd withdrawn his finger.

"Did you like that?"

"I don't know, Master."

"Have you ever tried a butt plug?"

"No."

She wasn't a prude, but just hadn't felt the inclination to get herself one before. One of her ex-boyfriends had wanted to take her anally, but she had stopped him before he could. She had liked him, not loved him and not trusted him enough to let him do that.

"Well, I'll give you a little while to think about it. Now, listen. I'll take you and you won't get to come."

"But..."

"I didn't allow you to talk."

He slapped her ass a few times in rapid succession. She groaned, trying to process the sensation.

"You do as I please. And I tell you that you won't get to come."

She didn't think she could do it. It was one thing to accept pain, to let it flow through her body until she embraced the sensation, but quite a different thing to block out pleasure.

How could she feel him move inside her, and not come? They had played similar games before and although he'd liked to make her wait, he had let her come each time.

She bit down on her lip. She couldn't fault him — he'd told her there was more to him than she'd gotten to see yet. Wrapped up in her thoughts, she hadn't heard him unfastening his pants and was surprised when she felt his cock against her backside.

"You are so beautiful with your ass all red."

She didn't reply — couldn't have as he slipped a hand around her, his slender digits parting her folds, brushing over her clit. She moaned, pressing into the hand even though she would only prolong her own misery. *If my body is already betraying me this badly now...*

He withdrew his hands and before she knew it, he'd slid inside her with one long thrust. She held her breath, releasing it when he paused to let her adjust. She loved the feeling of him inside her, the way he filled her, the way he took her.

"You don't get to come," he repeated one last time before he pulled his hard flesh almost all the way out before surging back in. Again and again his pelvis collided with hers, all but shoving her into the cross. She groaned at the sensation and sounds of their flesh colliding.

The angle was good but thankfully it wasn't intense enough to throw her over the edge. She began to think she could make it. Then his hand was back, teasing her clit, rubbing the engorged nub in tight circles.

Pleasure overloaded her nervous system, and she began to pant, sweat breaking out on her skin while she desperately tried to distract herself. She tried thinking of old crime scenes, blood and gore, but nothing truly helped. The combination of him moving inside her while he stimulated her most erogenous zone would prove to be her downfall soon.

She moaned, tugging at her restraints even knowing it was pointless. If she could only get him to remove his hands. Her safe word lay on the tip of her tongue, but if she used it, the scene would be finished.

"Fuck, you feel good," Simon ground out and it startled her, as she hadn't heard him use such coarse language before.

So he was close. Good. Only she was even closer, could feel herself edging towards her own climax. Balling her hands into fists, she tried to focus on the sting of her fingernails in the palm of her hands. It was a distraction at least.

Maybe, maybe she could do it. *Please*.

Simon's thrusts became more jerky, then he came with a loud groan. She was relieved, holding still until he pulled out of her, though then she began to cry. Her own body was humming with need, and he wouldn't do a thing about it, wouldn't allow her to finish herself off.

She heard him right his clothes. When he was fully dressed once again, he unfastened her from her bindings. Her wrists hurt, her arms felt heavier than she'd ever known and her back still burned from the flogging. Still, all these sensations paled in comparison to her unfulfilled need. She contemplated disobeying his orders after all and sliding her hands between her legs to find release. It wouldn't even take much.

Was it worse than the consequences, though?

She debated the question when he turned her around to face him, his hands on her shoulders. He pulled away the cloth taking her sight. The light in the room stung her eyes. She felt his gaze on her but refused to meet his eyes.

"Look at me."

She'd known this command was coming, yet it was almost unbearable to follow it.

"You're pissed," he stated, an amused glint in his eyes.

She wasn't so much pissed as she was frustrated, not that she wanted to argue the point. She wasn't allowed to speak anyway.

"How do you feel? Answer me."

His tone of voice might be carefully neutral, but she knew him well enough to understand he wanted the truth.

"Frustrated, keyed up. A bit angry."

He raised an eyebrow.

"Master," she added.

"Good."

Was he referring to the fact she was feeling unsettled or the fact she'd been addressing him correctly after all? She considered asking him, and decided against it.

"You've been doing good. I'm proud of you." Was he proud enough to let her come after all?

"Get on the bed, put one of the pillows under your stomach. We're going to try the butt plug."

No. She had seen such things, and didn't think they'd fit in *there*.

"You can call off the scene at any time." he assured her. "And it won't change a thing between us. I told you earlier, it's your choice," he added.

Won't it?

He sighed and shook his head for a moment. "Listen, Sharon. Yes, it's true, I want you to know who I am, but it doesn't mean I wouldn't settle for less than a hundred percent. You'll never like everything I do, and I won't like everything you do. That's natural. So let's try this out and if it doesn't work out, you give me your safe word. Is that okay for you?"

She couldn't help the small smile breaking free. "Yes, Master."

Chapter Twenty-Five

Simon's hands trembled just slightly. Sharon realized that he hadn't expected her to still be in character. He couldn't know it, but he'd given her what she needed to hear to fully trust him right here, right now.

Without waiting for further instructions, she walked towards the bed and positioned herself as he'd asked her to. Her ass was sticking into the air slightly, leaving her exposed and aroused at the same time. From the sounds behind her, she gathered he was undressing, and as he hadn't told her she could move, she stared at the sheets underneath her, trying to ignore the taut skin on her back and thighs.

Having retreated into her own mind, Sharon startled when the mattress dipped behind her. She thought he was kneeling behind her.

"This is going to feel a bit cold," he warned her and a moment later, some fluid trickled down the crack of her ass.

Lube, she realized.

Apprehension made her hold on tighter to the sheets underneath her.

"Relax."

It was easier said than done. She trusted him more than she had any other partner in the bedroom before. It didn't mean she trusted her body could handle as much as he thought it could. She was safe. She could end this at any moment. That more than anything else made her take another deep breath, trying to relax her muscles at least a bit.

His finger following the trail of the lube wasn't unpleasant—quite the contrary—the feather-light caress reminding her she hadn't gotten to come. He stopped at her small anal opening, spreading the lube, his touch light and not invasive. She had never believed this could feel good, but it did. Nerve endings she hadn't considered before signaled pleasure right to her brain. Her core throbbed.

It didn't take much of his light touches before she wanted more, preferably his cock fucking her into oblivion or his fingers stimulating her clit, letting her come. *Please, let there be more — anything, really — as long as it's more.*

"This okay?" he asked.

"Yes, Master."

"Okay, I'll slide the finger inside you now and when you're properly stretched, a second will follow."

She wasn't sure if telling her what he was about to do was easing her worries or stoking them. At least he didn't give her time to contemplate it for too long. Making good on his promise, he pressed against her anus with his finger and entered her body, showing patience as well as tenderness.

She was amazed to find the intrusion was less alien than she'd have thought. His finger slid in easily once he had worked it past her entrance. Keeping it still for a moment, he withdrew slowly, slid it back inside, only to pull out completely. He began massaging her anus with his thumb next.

It felt strangely good, and Sharon wasn't ashamed of the moan she couldn't quite suppress. He stopped the massage, his finger slipping back in, coated in more lube.

He wasn't taking any chances, which was soothing to nerves that had only slowly begun to settle. It was a thought quickly forgotten as his finger started fucking her slowly. It wasn't as arousing as a real fuck would be, but far from unpleasant either.

"Remember, you still don't get to come."

She wouldn't, not this way anyway, but his command made sense when a second finger pressed in beside the first and his free hand covered her sex, the heel causing delicious friction against her engorged nub.

God, what was he doing to her? If he kept this up, she'd be fighting a lost battle. She was sure of it. And while it wasn't the anal penetration making her feel like she was about to come at any moment, it wasn't unpleasant.

Sharon didn't want to find out what would happen if she came, so once again, she tried clearing her mind, to think of completely different things when it didn't work. When he stopped stimulating her bundle of nerves, she sobbed out her relief.

She wasn't even angry this time. He was slowly depleting all of her energy, all her conscious thinking. He pulled out his fingers next and she moaned, not sure if it was out of a relief or maybe even disappointment. Her mind was drifting when the pressure came back a moment later. The butt plug.

"Listen to me, I need you to press against it. Open up for me."

It was an order even when it was issued in a soft and gentle voice. Doing what she was told, something hard and solid pressed inside her. Her ass stretched, and she came close to ending this game. This wouldn't work. The plug was too big. Though suddenly it breached her tight ring of muscles, the rest slipping in easily.

"Good girl," he said.

She'd been holding her breath, but released it now, her heart beating almost painfully hard in her chest.

"How do you feel?" Simon asked.

"I feel okay, Master."

"It's not supposed to hurt, so if it feels that way, starts feeling that way, tell me."

"I'm not hurting. It's...strange."

"It tends to feel this way at first."

Did he know this from his other lovers, or had he tried it himself? She'd have to ask him later.

"Now, listen to me again. I'll rub your clit next and this time I want you to come, but only when I tell you that you can."

Relieved as she was at his words, turned on even, Sharon knew he wouldn't make it easy for her.

"Do you understand and agree?"

"Yes, Master."

Like that, his hand was back, this time his thumb rubbing slow circles over her clit. Involuntarily her hips began undulating in an instinctive counter-rhythm, the plug in her ass rubbing inside her in a way that was new yet nearly pleasurable.

Simon picked up his rhythm and she moaned. She was close.

"Hold it."

She didn't know if she could, and sweat was breaking out all over her back again.

"I said, hold it."

She whimpered, wishing she could curse him. No, she couldn't win this battle.

"Now, I want you to come."

It took her mind a second to register his words before her body began convulsing, as pure pleasure set her body aflame with sensation. She barely noticed one of his fingers sliding inside her sex, even when her inner walls clenched around it. It was hard to get enough air as her body continued to spasm so hard she was seeing stars behind her closed eyelids.

Sharon's knees were buckling and she wondered if she would crumble on the mattress when Simon's hand collided with her ass in a sharp smack that sent her mind reeling, the sensation overlaying the pleasure.

Another blow to her other cheek—she didn't know where the pain began and the pleasure ended. She heard loud moaning and whimpering, and realized it was herself making those animalistic noises. She had come here wanting to lose herself in the game, and she had. Her mind was floating, her thoughts scattered, and she hardly realized that Simon's cock was sliding inside her once more.

The double penetration of his hard cock in her vagina and the plug in her ass made her hiss. This was too much, made her feel too full, though as soon as Simon began to move, the slight pain transformed into pleasure again.

It was all more than she was able to comprehend, and there were tears pricking behind her closed eyelids. She didn't try keeping them in. Another climax began to build inside her and no matter what he might command her to do, she wouldn't be able to hold it back.

But he wasn't talking. He took her hard and fast, wrapping one hand around her body, squeezing a nipple between thumb and forefinger up to the point it hurt. Even so, her core clenched around his cock in reaction.

Another blow to her ass and he squeezed her nipple harder than before. She came, crying out her release, not caring who heard or not. Her legs gave up underneath her. All that was holding her up were his strong hands. He fucked her even harder now, his rhythm becoming irregular before he found release as well. She hardly noticed — the signals sent to her brain were too much to handle. Blackness engulfed her but she embraced it.

* * * *

"Psst."

Something cold on her back made her hiss and jerk but Simon rubbed her back with slow, sure strokes.

"It's only ice, relax."

She tried to keep her eyes closed, absorbing the feeling of cold colliding with overheated skin. She remembered they'd played with ice cubes before. First hot wax, followed by ice cubes trailing over her breasts, stinging and arousing.

The game was over for today, and she didn't hesitate when he offered her the rest of the ice cube, realizing how parched she was, that her lips were slightly cracked.

She let it melt in her mouth while Simon dried her back then began applying salve to it. He didn't talk. He moved without hurry. This was her lover now, not her master, and she let out a tiny sigh.

"Are you okay?"

He sounded worried, and she realized she'd blacked out.

"Yeah, I am."

Her voice was rough and her throat hurt slightly. She'd cried out during their scene, yet hadn't realized how much it had affected her.

"Good. I'd hate if I'd been too rough with you."

She didn't know why but his quiet words brought tears to her eyes, even though she refused to let them fall. Most likely it was just the beginning of the crash she felt after almost every scene when her endorphin levels began to decrease.

Although this was more to her. He cared. She had known for a while, but it only truly hit home right now. Even knowing he wasn't done with caring for her back yet, she rolled onto her side so she could look at him. His expression was slightly annoyed and worried. It made her smile.

"Hey, I'm good."

"I'm glad. So now turn back around so I can finish up here."

"I will. In a moment."

"Sharon."

"Simon. Now listen to me, will you?" She was tired but she needed to make this point.

"Yes, I will. Although I fail to see what is so important that we need to discuss it now."

She rolled her eyes at him. "I…this was intense and I felt uncomfortable for a few moments, but…it wasn't too much. You're not too much for me. And…I love you. Just as you are."

Sharon was scared. She feared rejection. She wasn't one to use "*I love you*" in vain. In fact, she hated the vulnerability of those three words. It was true, though. She had fallen in love with this man and wanted to be with him. He had a right to know.

Simon stilled, his jaw clenching. Her heart was beating way too fast in her chest while he processed her words.

"I love you too, Sharon."

He, too, didn't like to be vulnerable. She knew that much about him.

God, this was crazy. He owned a sex club and she was a cop. Their relationship would come out at some point and there'd be hell to pay…

It wasn't a bridge to cross today, though. No one could predict what was going to happen at any point in the future. They could only live in the now.

"This is me. This will always be me. Do you think you can really handle it?"

He was still giving her an out. She smiled and touched his cheek with a not quite steady hand, thanks to the intensity of their game.

"Yes, I can. So, about the butt plug?"

"You didn't like it."

"I think I did, after a while. Does that mean you'll want to fuck my ass next?"

He snorted at her coarse language. "Well, as I said, not tonight. But how about you let me finish here, then we can get some rest and leave the everything else for later or tomorrow?"

"Sounds good."

A tomorrow with Simon Carter. It didn't sound as crazy as it would have a mere few weeks ago.

Perfect Taboo: The Shame Game
Hannah Murray

Excerpt

James Douglass walked through the front door of his home and sighed with relief. "Thank Christ that's over."

Behind him, his wife let out a snorting laugh and shut the door. "You say that every year."

"I mean it every year." He turned to watch her slip out of her coat, the soft faux fur he'd given her for Christmas gleaming under the light of the foyer chandelier. "Tell me you don't feel the same."

Amanda smiled as she hung up her coat, then held out a hand for his. "I like your mother."

He dropped the bags he held and shrugged out of his overcoat. "It'd just be nice to be able to spend one New Year's somewhere else."

"Well, that's your fault for being born one minute past midnight on January first." Laughter colored her voice, deepening the Texas accent that still lingered more than a decade after she'd left the Lone Star State. "If you'd stayed put for another week like you were supposed to…"

"Oh, so now it's my fault for being born early?" He raised an eyebrow, wondering if his wife of twelve years would respond with sass or respect. He figured the odds were about seventy-thirty in favor of sass.

She took his coat with a wink. "Pretty much."

"Insolent wench," he muttered, and stifled a grin when she rolled her eyes. *Sass it is, then.*

"You could always tell your mom no when she invites us," she pointed out.

He sighed and bent to pick up the bags. "No, I can't."

"I know." She closed the closet with a snap and crossed to him, her bootheels clicking on the tile, and rose on her toes to plant a smacking kiss on his chin. "That's because you're a big old softie."

The eyebrow went up again, almost of its own volition this time. "What was that?"

"Sorry," she said, not looking sorry at all, her dimples popping out even as she lowered her eyes respectfully. "You're a big old softie, *sir.*"

"Better," he allowed, fighting a smile of his own. "But you're lucky my hands are full."

She glanced down at the bags he still held, then back up at him, her brown eyes dancing. "Oh, yes. Thank goodness for those two duffel bags, otherwise I'd be in so much trouble."

James gave a bark of laughter. Apparently, he wasn't the only one tired of being on his best behavior for the last couple of days. "If I didn't know better, I'd say you were looking for trouble."

She walked past him, her dimples still winking. "Well, then it's a good thing you know better, isn't it? Besides," she continued, her voice drifting back to him as she moved toward the curved staircase. "Even if I was, it's not like you could do anything about it."

She paused on the first stair, her hand resting lightly on the banister, and looked back at him. They'd been together fourteen years, and still she took his breath away. Soft dark hair, a little tousled from the nap she'd taken on the drive home. Sparkling dark eyes, full of mischief and promise and affection. Her dimples flashed again, pulling his attention to her soft, full lips, curved in the faintest of smiles. That mouth had given him a jolt at their first meeting all those years ago, and its impact hadn't lessened over time. If anything, it had only grown stronger, because now he knew just what those lush lips were capable of. He knew just how swollen and red they grew from his kisses, how they looked wrapped around his cock. And how she bit them when she was in pain, or in pleasure.

Then those lips spread in an impish grin, bringing him back to the present, and the game she was trying to tempt him into playing. "It's not like you could chase me up these stairs or catch me even if you did. You're fifty-one now. An old man."

He growled because he knew she wanted him to, and with a rollicking laugh, she ran up the stairs.

He stayed where he was, enjoying the view. The yoga pants she'd worn for comfort on the drive home curved over rounded hips and a rounder ass, the soft sweater in misty green—another Christmas gift—covering bouncing breasts. He'd seen her dress that morning in a pretty lacy bra, the kind built for maximum visual effect rather than physical activity, so there was a lot of bounce.

It was pretty fucking hot.

He stayed where he was until she hit the top of the stairs and turned to look down at him. Even from this distance, he could see she was surprised he hadn't taken the bait. They'd been at his parents' house for three days, unable to play or even fuck the way they liked with his mom and stepdad sleeping down the hall, and only a few thin walls between them. A flash of uncertainty crossed her face, then it was gone, replaced by smirking confidence.

"Not up for a chase, old man?" she called, the mocking and teasing in her tone calling to him so strongly that he had to force himself to stay put. "That's fine. Why don't you go ahead and take those bags of dirty clothes to the laundry? Feel free to start a load. I'll just have a little reunion with my vibrator."

That nearly got his feet moving, but he was enjoying the anticipation too much. "You know the rules, little girl," he warned.

"Rules?" She smirked, leaning over the banister so her sweater gaped, giving him a tantalizing view of soft breasts and white lace. "Rules only count if you can enforce them."

Anticipation sang in his blood. "You're taking big chances."

A flicker of unease crossed her face before she smoothed it away. "You don't worry me," she called back, and only he would've heard the nerves in it.

"Oh, yes I do." He let his grin turn feral, loving the way her body tensed even as she sneered. "Because you know if I get up there and find you touching what's mine without permission, there will be consequences."

Her laugh was full of anticipation and apprehension, a heady mix that had him going rock hard in his jeans. "By the time you manage to drag your old bones up here, I'll have had two orgasms, a shower, and will already be asleep."

She gave a little toss of her head, sending her short sweep of dark hair flying. "Don't forget to start the laundry," she said, then disappeared down the hall.

James waited until the bedroom door slammed before he started up the stairs. He took his time, going first to the second-floor laundry room to drop off the bags. He set them on top of the washing machine where she couldn't miss them, then continued on to his home office. He'd told his clients he was taking the week off for the holidays, so there was nothing pressing waiting for him. Still, he checked his voicemail, and glanced at a set of blueprints that had been delivered just before Christmas. He frowned over them for a moment, jotting down a few ideas for his meeting with the engineer next week and making a note to ask his assistant to check that the soil testing at the site had been completed.

Then he set down his pen, shut off the lights, and walked down the hall to the bedroom.

The double doors were shut, the room beyond silent. He thought about giving her a few more minutes, to make sure she'd had enough time to get started, then shrugged. If she hadn't already begun to masturbate — strictly prohibited without permission, as she well knew — then he'd punish her for the threat of it.

Though their D/s dynamic was fairly flexible, and almost everything was open to negotiation, rules were rules. She liked to push from time to time, as though testing to make sure those rules were ironclad, and he liked to remind her that they were. He didn't mind her pushing — in fact, he'd be disappointed if she didn't. Just as she'd be disappointed if he didn't hold to the line they'd agreed on and punish her appropriately for crossing it.

He did so hate to disappoint his wife.

He rolled his shoulders and stretched his neck, loosening muscles that had grown tight on the long drive. There was always a chance he'd have to wrestle her down, and Amanda was much stronger than she looked. After three days of enforced celibacy, he was almost hoping she'd run.

He pushed open the doors.

The room was brightly lit, both bedside lamps and the chandelier above the bed glowing, banishing the shadows of twilight to the far corners of the room and spotlighting the woman on the king-sized bed.

She'd propped herself up, a pile of pillows at her back so she sat almost upright. Her clothes were scattered across the foot of the bed and the floor beside it, leaving her bare against the bright blue of the duvet beneath her.

He took a moment to drink in the sight of her, his beloved. Soft breasts, their weight resting gently on her ribcage, her reclining position widening the space between them so he could clearly see the small scar over her breastbone. Her nipples were still soft, pale brown puffs that would pucker and tighten as her arousal grew, and looked their best, in his opinion, when they were pinched in a set of clamps and glowing bright red.

Her belly was a soft curve, round hips flowing to firm thighs that he loved to dig his fingers into when he fucked her. The harder the better, so she'd see the bruises left behind the next day and preen a little in the mirror.

She spread her legs, revealing the soft skin of her inner thighs with their pale stretch marks and the tuft of dark hair at the top of her sex. She would have preferred to completely wax her pubis, but he liked having something to get his fingers into, so they compromised. She left the hair on her mound alone, the dark curls a wild tangle for him to play with, but her pussy below was stripped bare of hair. The soft pink flesh glistened in the bright lights, already slick with her own arousal and probably some lube, because she likely wouldn't have been able to get the huge purple dildo wedged all the way inside her cunt so quickly without it.

He stared at the offending object for a moment, to increase both her unease and his control, then raised his gaze to hers. She was biting her lip, nibbling at it the way she did when she was unsure but was trying hard not to be, and her nipples were already hardening.

Aroused, and a little scared. Perfect.

"I thought I told you not to touch what's mine without permission."

She shrugged, a smirk on her pretty face despite the growing anxiety in her eyes. "Oops."

He had to fight to keep his lips from twitching. "Oops? You're going with oops?"

"Oopsie-daisy?"

He forced himself to frown. "Being cute won't save you."

"No?" She shrugged again, her tits bouncing enticingly with the movement. "I might as well enjoy myself, then."

She lifted her hands to her breasts, her short red fingernails gleaming against her skin. Her breasts were delightfully responsive, the nipples puckering and lengthening at her touch. She pulled them with her fingertips, her breath hitching at the contact, and he grew even harder.

"This might take a while," she said, her voice thin and tight with arousal. "I used the Velvet Swing."

His gaze darted to the bedside table, and the distinctive bottle that sat there. Velvet Swing—or the good lube, as they sometimes called it—was a cannabis-based lubricant sold by their local pot shop. Infused with both THC and CBD, it increased blood flow and intensified arousal, and often triggered Amanda into multiple orgasms. They tended to save it for those times when they wanted a long play session, as it required about forty minutes after application to reach full potency.

Apparently, Amanda wanted to play hard tonight.

"You have until the count of three to stop touching my property, Amanda," he warned her. "One."

She brought one hand to her mouth, sucking two fingers inside with a noisy *pop* that had him grinding his teeth against the surge of desire. "Two."

She pulled her fingers away from her mouth, sliding them down her throat and between her breasts, leaving a damp trail behind. She skimmed them across her belly, drifted past the thatch of pubic hair, to hover over her clit, out of its hood and clearly visible. He held his breath as she kept them there for a moment, teasing both of them, before she grabbed the wide base of the protruding dildo.

"Three," he growled, the word mingling with her reflexive moan as she shoved the dildo deeper into her pussy, and he was moving before the sound faded.

He was beside the bed in a heartbeat, and surprise lit her eyes when he lifted her into the air. She flailed in his arms, the dildo falling to the bed, and her laughing squeal was cut off abruptly when he sat on the side of the bed and pushed her face down over his lap. He planted a hand on the back of her neck to counter her instinctive attempt to right herself.

"You asked for this," he reminded her, and brought his hand down on her ass.

She squealed again, bucking against his hold, and he barely avoided a foot to the face. Fighting back a laugh, he shifted to wedge her legs between his, clenching his thighs to keep her in place, then shoved her face towards the floor. She grabbed his leg, digging her short nails in through his jeans as she pushed herself up.

He smacked her ass again, a short, sharp blow right on her sit spot. "Stay put," he ordered, and grabbed the dildo off the bed to unceremoniously shove it back into her cunt.

Her choked "Oh, shit!" was accompanied by a hard buck of her hips that would have resulted in her getting free if he hadn't had her legs trapped. He kept one hand firmly between her shoulder blades, holding her down, and worked the dildo with the other. Her pussy was tight, the way her legs were clamped together making for an even snugger fit than usual, so he took his time, pulling it out slightly, wiggling it a bit, pushing it back in. He thought about stopping for more lube, something slicker and more viscous than the cannabis cream she'd already applied, but he didn't want to let go of her long enough to dig into the nightstand drawer. Instead he slowed down the process, drawing it out so that by the time he had the dildo fully seated in her cunt, her thighs were slick, and she was panting.

"That's pretty," he observed, and gave the wide base of the toy a firm pat that made her hips jerk. He grinned at her upturned ass and did it again, her strangled moan delighting him.

"Tell me what you're getting a spanking for, Amanda."

"Because you're old?"

He tsked in mock disappointment and smacked the base of the toy again just to listen to her moan. "Try again."

"Because you have no sense of humor?"

Smack. "You're going to find out just where my sense of humor lives if you keep playing games. Last chance. Why are you getting a spanking?"

Her body tensed as she hesitated, and he knew she was weighing her options. She undoubtedly had another smart-ass remark dancing on the tip of her tongue, ready to launch, but she was also starting to realize the precariousness of her situation. They both enjoyed the punishment games that made up so much of their kink, but there were limits, and she knew it. She wanted to come, and knew that if she pushed him too far, he'd make his point by not letting her.

He waited for her to make her choice. If she chose obedience, he'd fuck her until they both came screaming. If she chose insolence, he'd put her smart mouth to good use for his own pleasure, then send her to bed, aching and wanting.

Either way would be fun for him, but he hoped she'd choose obedience. After three sexless days, he missed her, and he'd love nothing more than to give her as many orgasms as she could take before curling up to sleep with her wrapped around him, limp and satisfied.

But the choice was hers.

The seconds ticked by, and he was on the verge of reminding her there was a question on the table — via the forceful application of hand to ass — when she let out a resigned sigh. "Because I was masturbating without permission."

Relief and desire flooded him in equal measure. "And why do you need permission to masturbate?"

"Because my orgasms belong to you."

"That's right," he replied, and rewarded her by giving the base of the dildo a solid wiggle. "You put the lube on just before I came in?"

"A couple of minutes before, yes, Sir."

"Hmmm." He glanced at the clock on the fireplace mantel across the room. "Then we've got about half an hour before it really starts to kick in, don't we? Let's see if we can spend our time wisely. Count."

He lifted his hand, waited for her breathless "Yes, Sir," then let it fall on the fullest part of her upturned ass, making sure to catch the edge of the protruding dildo.

She jerked, moaned out "One," and he stroked his hand approvingly over the pink that had bloomed beneath his hand.

"Good girl," he praised, and, seeing that the dildo had begun to slip out, nudged it back into place. She was even wetter, the column of silicone sliding back in much more easily than it had even just a few moments ago.

Excellent.

He glanced at the clock, calculating how many swats she could take and still be in the right head space for what he had in mind. One smack every two minutes should do it, he figured, and, drawn out over half an hour, wouldn't be too taxing. And while he was counting down the seconds to the next spank, he could play.

Amanda had no idea how much time had passed. She knew it had been a while, because she was counting the spanks, and he'd just delivered number fourteen. James pulled her up by the hair every five smacks so some of the blood could drain out of her head. It also gave him the opportunity to play with her nipples, now clamped—he must have had the alligator clips on standby—for a few moments before he pushed her back down. But the lightheadedness wasn't so bad, and at least while her pussy was in the air, he was paying attention to it. At this point the lube was kicking in, her pussy swollen and engorged, tingling on the verge of a hard orgasm, and God, she wanted it.

Unfortunately, he didn't seem to be interested in making her come. He kept his touch light, even careless, every move seemingly geared toward reducing her to a mindless puddle of helpless lust. And it was working.

In between smacks — which *hurt*, dammit, he wasn't going easy at *all* — his fingers were busy, scraping over the heated skin of her ass, their calloused tips rough against the tenderized flesh. Gliding through the moisture that pooled between her thighs, drawing light circles around her clit and stroking over the stretched lips of her pussy, or tapping with a firmer touch on the slick pucker of her asshole. And slowly, too slowly to bring any relief whatsoever, fucking her with the dildo she'd so foolishly thought to tease him with.

If he didn't let her come soon, she was going to start drooling.

Well, she was already drooling, but since she was chewing on the leg of his jeans to muffle her moans, at least he'd be the one to have to deal with it.

She couldn't remember the last time she'd been this worked up. Her ass was raw, and little pulses of pain radiated from her clamped nipples. The chain that connected them was just heavy enough to act as a weight that pulled at them unceasingly — *thanks for nothing, gravity* — adding to both her distress and her arousal. Her pussy was on fire, pulsing and throbbing around the thick toy, and she'd swear she could feel her heartbeat in her swollen, aching clit.

The Velvet Swing might, in hindsight, have been a mistake. Sure, the orgasms she had with it were longer and stronger than the ones she achieved without it, and she could often count on having more than one, but none of that did her any good if he *won't let me come*, something she should've considered before putting her *tease James into a scene* plan into action.

She could only hope he'd be horny enough to put an end to this torture soon, but she knew from experience he was capable of denying himself for hours to draw out a scene.

She was contemplating all the ways she could grovel her way into an orgasm when his hand landed on her ass again, and sent her thoughts scattering.

"Fifteen," she managed, groaning out the count along with her frustration as need and pain burst through her. The blow was hard enough to rock her forward on his lap, making her breasts bounce and setting the chain connecting them swaying. Tension spiked, sharp and sweet, drawing another groan. Her hips rolled, a helpless, instinctive motion, her searching for relief. The dildo began to once again work its way out of her with the movement, and she flexed to help it along, needing the slick slide of the silicone against her swollen cunt. But instead of fucking her with it as he'd been doing for the last half hour, he pulled it free.

Surprised, she started to turn, and suddenly found herself being lifted up. The room spun for a moment as the blood rushed from her head, and by the time her vision cleared, she was flat on her back in the middle of the bed, almost in the same position she'd started in.

Oh, thank God, he'd decided to stop toying with her. No doubt the last half hour of play had aroused him, especially after three days at his mom's house. She sent him a smile, sure she'd find him shedding his clothes, preparing to climb on top of her and give her the solid fucking they'd both been craving. Instead, he was fully dressed and frowning at the bench that sat at the foot of their bed.

She watched, confused, when he pushed it away from the footboard. "James? What are you doing?"

"Who?" he asked, his voice hard, giving the bench a solid nudge with his knee, not even looking at her, and she felt the first real twinge of *uh-oh*.

She swallowed. "Sir, what are you doing?"

"Setting up the spectator area, of course," he replied. Apparently satisfied with its placement, he turned to face the bed and sat on the bench.

"Um." She swallowed, eyeing him cautiously. He was leaning forward slightly, silver-streaked hair tousled, his hands resting on his thighs. He seemed relaxed, at ease, until she saw his eyes. She'd been looking into those eyes for nearly fifteen years, and she didn't need the corresponding bulge in his jeans to tell her he was aroused. And she didn't need to see the slightly mocking curl to his lips to understand that she was in trouble.

She wiggled a little on the bed, wincing when her tender butt scraped against what she'd always thought was their softest duvet cover. He hadn't hit her much—fifteen was pretty light, actually—but the whacks he'd landed hadn't been gentle. "Sir?"

He jerked his chin. "Pick up the dildo."

She glanced down to see the purple dildo, still slick from her pussy, lying next to her. Heat seared her cheeks. She didn't know why, but seeing the evidence of her arousal on it brought a wash of shame that made her grateful she wasn't looking at him.

Confusingly, it also brought a flood of fresh desire.

Swallowing hard, she did as she was told, her cheeks burning hotter when she saw the damp stain left behind on the duvet. She glanced up again, forcing herself to meet her husband's gaze, and awaited further instruction.

His eyes had narrowed slightly, and she knew he hadn't missed her reaction. For a moment she thought he might question her about it, then he jerked his head. "Use it."

The quick rush of relief at not being questioned quickly burned away as she realized what he was asking. "Sir?"

"Use it," he repeated, relaxing even further on the bench, looking as though he was getting ready to watch a very boring, very predictable sporting event. "You were so eager to come that you decided to break the rules, so go ahead. Make yourself come."

She stared at him, shocked and more than a little thrown by the order. "What?"

"You heard me," he said, no softness or give in his tone at all, pinning her with those unflinching, icy eyes. "Fuck yourself with the dildo and make yourself come. Or," he continued in the same even tone, "don't come at all."

"Until when?" she blurted out, dismay making her voice squeak.

"Until you fuck yourself with the dildo and make yourself come."

About the Author

Sira Banks is a European author who is a desk jockey by day and a writer by night, always trying to appease the voices in her mind insisting their stories need to be told.

After writing short stories for almost two decades, *Breached* is her first novel.

When she's not busy with work or writing, she manages her small family, consisting of a pre-teen daughter and a cat aspiring to become the world's deadliest hunter.

Sira loves to hear from readers. You can find her contact information, website details and author profile page at https://www.totallybound.com

Home of Erotic Romance

Sign up for our newsletter and find out about all our romance book releases, eBook sales and promotions, sneak peeks and FREE romance books!